THE LAST PASSENGER

Center Point
Large Print

Also by Charles Finch and available from
Center Point Large Print:

The Last Enchantments
Home by Nightfall
The Inheritance
The Woman in the Water
The Laws of Murder
An Old Betrayal
The Vanishing Man

**This Large Print Book carries the
Seal of Approval of N.A.V.H.**

THE LAST PASSENGER

Charles Finch

CENTER POINT LARGE PRINT
THORNDIKE, MAINE

This Center Point Large Print edition
is published in the year 2020 by arrangement with
St. Martin's Publishing Group.

This is a work of fiction. All of the characters,
organizations, and events portrayed in this novel are either
products of the author's imagination or are used fictitiously.

The text of this Large Print edition is unabridged.
In other aspects, this book may vary
from the original edition.
Printed in the United States of America
on permanent paper.
Set in 16-point Times New Roman type.

ISBN: 978-1-64358-640-3

The Library of Congress has cataloged this record
under Library of Congress Control Number: 2020932903

This book is dedicated with gratitude to
Ellen Leschek and Maureen Kelly

THE LAST PASSENGER

CHAPTER ONE

On or about the first day of October 1855, the city of London, England, decided it was time once and for all that Charles Lenox be married.

Lenox himself didn't even necessarily disagree. He lived a happy life as a bachelor in the passage through Mayfair known as Hampden Lane, but for the first time had reached a stage when he could admit that a wife might settle his days into a still more contented rhythm. Nevertheless, the city's vehemence in its new convictions about his future came as a surprise.

On the second Tuesday of the month, at an evening salon at Lady Sattle's, a footman discreetly handed him a note:

Mary Elizabeth Sharples
Throw into fire

He studied this epistle for a moment. He knew the handwriting. He looked over at Mary Elizabeth Sharples, holding a tiny glass of almond brandy across the room, a violet shawl around her shoulders.

She was a handsome woman in her third London season, Kentish, immensely rich, and also a fair four or even five inches above six feet tall—and, of greater significance than any of that, was helplessly in love with the gentleman standing next to her at just this moment, Mark Blake. It seemed doubtful that Blake himself knew anything about it. Lenox had been familiar with him at Oxford. He was a virtually penniless fellow of good birth, so short in stature that there were carnival rides to which his successful admission would be an uncertain matter, and whose only subject of conversation, whose exclusive interest, was Dutch silver.

He did have a fine head of gleaming black hair, however; that had to be owned.

Lenox glanced across the room toward his friend Lady Jane. It was she who had passed the note by the footman. She was now in the midst of an animated conversation with her husband, James, and two gentlemen from his regiment in the Coldstream Guards.

He managed to catch her eye, however, and she returned his gaze queryingly.

Lady Jane and Lenox had known each other since they were children. She was perhaps a year younger than Mary Elizabeth Sharples, and a good ten inches shorter. She was a plain but pretty person, with dimpled cheeks, kind gray eyes, and hair that fell in soft dark curls. This evening she wore a wide blue crinoline.

He crossed the room toward her, an icy pewter cup of punch in hand.

When she was just loose from the group's conversation, Lenox said, "Hello, Jane."

"Ah! Hello, Charles," she said innocently.

Lenox leaned close. "Shall I really throw her into the fire?"

"Excuse me?"

"I will do it if you insist, but I feel people would notice. I am almost sure."

Lady Jane looked at him crossly. "What are you talking about?"

He consulted the note. "You write, *Mary Elizabeth Sharples,*" he said in a quiet voice, though the lady in question was some thirty feet away. *"Throw into fire."*

A look of wrath came onto Jane's face. "The note, you fool. You're to throw the note into the fire."

"Oh, the note!"

"Yes, the note, as you very well know."

"I was going to eat the note," he said.

She shook her head. "How I hate you."

He smiled. "I could ask her to marry me in front of all these people and it wouldn't make a whit of difference, Jane. She is going to marry Blake, whenever he stops talking about sterling cow creamers long enough to notice that it is possible. I imagine they will be transported to the church in a carriage of Dutch silver."

"I think her a very agreeable person," said Jane stiffly, not just yet prepared to laugh at her

11

suggestion. "And I am not at all convinced that her affections are as settled as you say. But you may suit yourself."

Lenox held up the note. "I must go to the hearth, now that I understand your meaning. Be good enough to watch my back, please. For enemy action."

"I hope you fall into the fire," she said, and turned back to her husband and his friends.

So it had been for weeks, mysteriously. Ancient, distant, respectable cousins had dropped in on Lenox after years of silence, mentioning their friends' grandnieces. Peers from his schooldays delicately proffered their sisters. Even his close friends, Lady Jane, for instance, and his brother, Edmund, seemed to think he was in desperate want of a wife.

Part of it was no doubt that the season had just begun. After the long summer, in which those who could mostly retreated from the city into the clearer air of the countryside, all had returned, and every night there was a different salon or ball. The next night these same people would be crowded into Mrs. Wilcott's immense ballroom in the guise of either "lions" or "lambs," however they chose to interpret that directive. (Lenox hadn't chosen. He dreaded it.)

Still, this was his sixth autumn in London, and the assaults upon his liberty had never been this concerted or numerous.

He was, after all, an unusual match. It was true that he had a good deal to recommend him. He was a slim, eligible young man of twenty-seven, always well dressed, with a thoughtful face, hazel eyes, a short hazel beard, and an easy smile. In his manner there was a simplicity that perhaps derived from his background in the Sussex countryside. He had been born the second son of a baronet there—sometimes a tricky position—but was fortunate enough to have means of his own. He had a good character, lively, happy friendships, and a family respected on both sides.

What's more—though perhaps he did not see this for himself, bound like all men and women in the intense, confused impressions of his own inner world—he was an appealing young fellow. It was hard to say precisely why. Perhaps primarily because he was that most fortunate creature, from whatever class one might pick: the child of two parents who loved him.

"Lenox!"

He had just tossed Lady Jane's note into the fire, and now turned. It took him an instant to place Robert Dudding, a fashionable clubman of roughly forty-five.

They only knew each other remotely. "How do you do, Dudding?" said Lenox, surprised at the enthusiastic greeting.

"Oh, fine, fine. I had a bad Goodwood, you know. After that I stayed off the turf. Dull without gambling, life. But a decent summer still. See here, though—I particularly want to introduce you to my sister's ward. Miss Louise Pierce, this is Charles Lenox."

Only then did Lenox notice a young woman standing next to Dudding. He bowed to her.

"How do you do?" she asked, curtsying.

How indeed?

Many hours later, as he rode home in his carriage alone, it occurred to Lenox that Dudding's friendliness was the best representation yet of this unexpected new element in his life.

He would have felt by no means sure of the man's handshake even three months before. Dudding was a snob, and Lenox, though he had nothing to be shy of concerning his parentage, was something of an odd figure, ever since, upon his graduation, he had come to London and taken the unexpected step of becoming a private detective.

It was a decision that had, whatever his connections, immediately disqualified him from certain parts of the best society. Bad enough that he should work in some field other than the clergy or the military, traditional realms of the younger son—but outrageous that he should become . . . well, what? Nobody seemed sure. At times, Lenox himself was least sure of all. It was a profession he was designing on the fly, like a railroad thrown down a few desperate ties at a time ahead of the train.

14

His motivations had been complex. A mingled desire to do right and to do something unique, a sense of adventure, and an unbecoming kind of inquisitiveness to be sure—all alongside, crucially, a fundamental and irresistible fascination with crime. Murder was his own version of Dutch silver. His interest in it was intense and long-lasting, galvanized when he was a boy by penny magazines and consolidated, since he had arrived in London, by a serious and comprehensive study of all the endless, multifarious crimes that occurred here.

He was convinced that it was a subject worth close attention. Most people were not. Men and women who would have eagerly solicited his good opinion had he chosen to remain utterly idle, living off his income and staring at a few hundred hands of whist a week, had cut him again and again in the past few years, some even going so far as to bar him from their doors.

Their stance wasn't universal. His friends remained staunch, and the great majority of people didn't have the energy to care much, viewing him more as eccentric than ruined. But men like Dudding, conscious at every moment of status . . .

The only thing Lenox could think was that there must be some shortfall of unmarried men this year.

As he stepped out of his carriage at home,

he sighed. At times he wondered whether this profession was even worth his time. The fact was that his progress as a detective had been halting: one or two notable successes, but also long periods of stagnation, and the derision of his class and of Scotland Yard. A less stubborn person might have given the folly up.

But if he kept at it—would it not be nice to return to a comfortable hearth, bedecked with a lady of sweet disposition and aspect, and perhaps even one or two small humans, playing blocks in that mood of intense concentration he had noticed in the visages of his friends' children?

"Graham?" he called, entering the house.

"Good evening, sir," said Graham, the house's butler, standing up from a chair in the small alcove in the front hall, which served as his version of an office. "A pleasant evening?"

Graham was, though a servant, one of Lenox's closest confidants, a compact, sandy-haired, gentlemanly person of about Lenox's own age, attired in a subtly faultless suit of clothes.

"I was married off twenty times or so. Other than that it wasn't so bad."

"I'm glad to hear it, sir," said Graham, taking Lenox's cane and hat.

Lenox looked at the grandfather clock. It was past midnight. "I know you must be tired, but what do you say to ten minutes on the Claxton case?"

This was a peculiar death in Nottingham that they had been studying.

"With pleasure, sir," Graham said. "Mrs. Huggins has left tea on the warming plate. And there are cheese-and-pickle sandwiches at your desk, sir, in case you didn't have supper."

CHAPTER TWO

Two nights later, Lenox sat in his study, playing chess with his next-door neighbor, Lord Deere.

This study was a large, high-ceilinged, rectangular room that overlooked the street from just a few feet above it. At the other end of the chamber a fire burned in the grate; books and small paintings lined the walls.

It was a rare night away from the social round, made possible by a thunderstorm—and not just any thunderstorm, but a hard one, almost moralizing in its intensity. A whipping rain was falling across the ancient gray stones of London; water flushed days of autumn grime from every narrow fissure and channel in the cobblestone streets, eddying around clots of fallen leaves until it loosened them all at once. An October storm. The last stale heaviness of summer heat being rinsed clean away.

"One of the troubles with cinnamon toast is that the edges never have much cinnamon on them," said Lord Deere.

Lenox glanced over the board, irritated. He liked Deere, and loved Deere's wife, Jane. But he was about to lose, and it had been extremely close this time, too. "*One* of the troubles? What are the others?"

"Where to begin. It doesn't dunk well."

"Doesn't dunk well."

Deere grinned. "In tea."

"Doesn't dunk well in tea."

"No, it falls to bits immediately." He gestured at the board. "Rather like the little triangle of pawns you set up around your king."

"That's a very dishonorable comment, if you ask me," Lenox replied darkly, staring at the board.

"I am detestable in victory. Everyone must have his flaws," said Lord Deere in a cheerily philosophical tone, munching a piece of the cinnamon toast with what appeared, despite his objections, like great relish. In his other hand was a cup of tea, steam drifting upward from it in a loose coil. "Listen, why don't we start over?"

Lenox was not prouder than the typical young man of good education, ample means, and a strong intelligence. Alas, even the average pride of such a specimen of person must be very high.

"That is the most cowardly offer I ever heard."

Deere was a tall, thin man with fair hair and striking blue eyes. Somehow, in whatever the circumstances, he always looked crisp and tidily arranged.

He protested. "I was only hoping we might fit in another game!"

Lenox glanced at the gold carriage clock on his

desk. After a hostile pause, he knocked over his king. "Fine," he said.

"There you are, see?"

"Hm."

They began setting up the pieces, or rather Deere did, because Lenox had started hungrily eating toast and sipping his own tea.

He had never been a soul to hold a grudge, even in childhood, and before the pieces were up the last game was forgotten, replaced in their conversation with Lenox's frank admiration for his opponent's skill. Somehow he always managed to slip through the narrowest slivers of logic when they played, Deere. He might be two important pieces down, yet invariably he found a way to recover his balance and best Lenox. Or so it seemed anyhow.

"Don't forget that I am in the army," he said, after Lenox pointed this out. "Much of our training is calculated for dire strategic situations."

"True. I wonder if chess in the military is played to a higher standard than among us civilians."

The young lord looked contemplative. "I could not promise you that. We have our share of dullards. I suppose all professions do."

"Of course."

"Indeed, I would wager many among the infantry would get the better of their officers. It's a great hobby—they all have pocket boards. Handy when you are stuck on some hillside for a week with nothing to do."

When Lenox had learned that Lady Jane had married a military man, he had been predisposed to look upon the gentleman as something of a cavalier, one of those soldiers who marry and then return home but rarely, glad as they may be when there.

But of course Jane—always the smartest person he had known—would never have married for less than true love, and Deere, as Lenox had very slowly and somewhat reluctantly learned, was a special sort of person.

He was entirely open with others, entirely generous; wanted to see only the best in them; above all, wanted to learn what they were like, what they loved, who they were. For instance, he delighted in Lenox's profession, pressing questions upon him about it in a way almost no one else did. When he did travel, he brought home innumerable local objects, which he studied and collected with careful attention. He knew the names of flowers, grasses, trees, and stars. He especially loved dogs: He knew every breed, and though an earl, and thus entitled to be extremely haughty, would stop with anybody in the street who happened to be walking one for a long chin wag.

He was commissioned as a captain in the Coldstream Guards, a demanding position. He was away from home more often than not, but hoped that he would be here for a decent stretch now. (He was still awaiting new orders.) It was commonly agreed that he had a very bright future.

Halfway through the next game that he and Lenox played, there was a sharp knock at the front door.

The young detective frowned. He wasn't expecting anybody. Lady Jane—whom he would normally have suspected—was at the bedside of a friend in South Kensington, who had just been delivered prematurely of a son.

"I wonder who could be abroad in this weather," Lenox said.

"The devil knows."

After a beat, Graham appeared at the door of the study. "Inspector Hemstock wishes to call upon you, sir."

"Hemstock!" Standing up, Lenox glanced at his friend. "You'll have to forgive me, Deere. Graham, would you ask Elliott to get the horses warmed, please?"

This was the groom. "Of course, sir."

Lenox held up a hand. "No. On second thought, don't. But please show Hemstock in."

"Very good, sir."

He didn't need to go out on a rainy night at Thomas Hemstock's whim.

Deere knew something of Lenox's business—indeed, it sometimes seemed to Lenox that all of London did. "Not in the mood for a case?" Deere asked.

"No. I have rarely been busier."

It was true. After long stretches of idleness in previous years—though he tried his best to stay busy during these, through an improvised course of self-instruction—at present Lenox had two cases, besides his conjectures from afar about the Claxton murder. Both were minor. Still, he was pleased to be occupied.

Graham returned with Hemstock, who had left his hat and his cloak in the hall but was nevertheless dripping wet.

As usual, he was in a state that you might certainly call jolly, if you wished to be polite—outright drunk, if you were blunter.

"Hullo!" he cried. "What's this? Chess? Sport of kings, chess."

That was horse racing. No matter. "How are you, Mr. Hemstock?" Lenox said, putting out his hand. He liked the inspector, taken all in all. "Much occupied this evening?"

"Yes! Thought you might want to come round with me, learn a trick or two. It's a murder."

"Whereabouts?"

"Paddington Station."

Some piece of ha'penny violence, Lenox supposed. A burglar, a gang member, a sailor. The motive probably petty vengeance or drunken ire.

"Unfortunately I don't think I can. I have a guest, as you see."

Hemstock looked surprised. It was the first time Lenox had refused such an offer.

An affable, short, solid fellow, about forty, with a squashed face and an infectious gaiety, Hemstock was the worst detective Scotland Yard had. Indeed, the job belonged to him only because his late father had been one of the original Peelers, a figure of legend and lore, revered at the Yard. The son did little harm in his sinecure—if not, unfortunately, much good either. Lately, however, he had been allowing Lenox to solve his cases, under the guise of his "helping" the young squire, showing him "a trick or two." Most men at the Yard despised the idea of Lenox's amateur involvement in their work, but Hemstock had noticed that he could be useful.

"It's a strange one," the inspector said.

"Perhaps I could come in the morning and see you about it then," said Lenox.

"Of course. Until the morning."

"The morning. And I say, I am sorry. Thank you for stopping by."

Hemstock had recovered from his surprise. "May be dry by then, eh? Or else we'll soon be boarding the animals two by two. Any time after ten o'clock."

He accepted a drink to see him on his way—a brandy, which vanished quickly—and left.

Deere, surprised, watched Lenox take his chair again. They were not quite close enough that he could ask why Lenox had declined. (If Jane were here, she would have done so without hesitation.) Instead they played out their muddled, unsatisfying third game.

The instant it was clear that Deere had won, the detective stood up.

"I'm sorry, Deere," he said.

He called for Graham. "Sir?" said the valet— somewhere between a butler and a valet, really—appearing at the door.

"I'm sorry, Graham," said Lenox, who was handing out apologies this evening at such a rate that he would soon run short of them, "but could you get the horses warmed after all? I think I must go to Paddington Station, or I won't rest."

"They are ready in front, sir."

Lenox gave a look of surprise, then a rueful smile. "Thank you, Graham," he said. "I suppose I am predictable after all this time under the same roof."

"Not at all, sir."

"Just give me my hat and my cane then, if you don't mind. I bet I can beat him there."

CHAPTER THREE

The storm only gathered strength during the short trip to Paddington. Lenox felt keenly for poor William Elliott, the raw-faced young groom, just seventeen, who sat atop the box of the carriage with the reins and whip in hand.

Inside the carriage it was tolerably dry, though water beaded at the joints of the door. Lenox's view through the small windows was impenetrably dark. As they drove northwest on Edgware Road, he could just make out the ghostly pale silhouette of Marble Arch at one point. But that was all.

The benefit of the weather was that they were virtually alone on the road; in only fifteen minutes or so they had made the journey.

"This will do," Lenox called out when they were near the front of the station.

"Shall I wait, sir?"

"Please—but look, I'll point out where."

Paddington Station was new. It had opened just the year before, the design of a gentleman, Isambard Kingdom Brunel, who was reshaping the nation building by building, one of the most celebrated men in Victoria's realm.

He had constructed Paddington as a long, slim rectangle—rather like Lenox's study, come to think of it. You entered on one of the short sides, here on Praed Street, and were immediately a few feet from the station's two tracks. (Many a tardy traveler had blessed Brunel's name for this touch.) At the far end, which lay open to the city, the trains departed.

Then there were the two long sides of the rectangle. On the left was a series of rooms and offices. On the right, partially open to the air, was an ingenious carriage route that allowed taxis and wagons to pull up directly to the trains.

This lane was where Lenox directed Elliott. It would offer him and the horses at least a bit of warmth and dryness, he hoped.

Lenox alighted from the carriage and into the shelter of the awning in front of the Great Western Hotel, a new establishment, catering mostly to travelers, with a splendid and blindingly bright façade, as dramatic as a Scottish castle on this stormy night. A bellman glanced at him inquiringly, but Lenox declined his assistance with a wave that he hoped implied his thanks.

He studied the train station from the short distance across the street. It was desolate, no light stirring behind its doors. Lenox had checked his Bradshaw's, the book of timetables every Londoner kept a copy of. The last train that evening had been expected at 10:14, and now it was past 11:00, which must mean the last travelers had long departed, most of them drying themselves by cozy fires, coats dripping in front halls humble and grand across the city.

He pulled out his pocket watch: 11:12, to be exact. He placed the watch—his late father's, a battered and dented gold object—back in his waistcoat pocket and strode across the street.

Murder. He might act as if he had grown too grand for Hemstock's patronage, but he had still only ever been involved with two murders of any note—that is, which had taken longer than ten minutes to solve. Though it was doubtful this would be the third, his pulse nevertheless quickened as he entered the station.

His eyes took a moment to adapt. He made out the great curved roof that swept overhead, making the hall at once grand and intimate. All around were shuttered stalls, which during the day did a roaring trade in newspapers, tobacco, and various foodstuffs to be eaten on the hoof.

Soon he grew accustomed to the dark. Receding up the left interior side of the building was a long row of signs projecting out from the wall every ten feet or so.

Cloakroom
Gentlemen's Lavatory
Telegraph Office
Parcels
Dining Room
Booking

For discretion's sake, perhaps—certainly not for convenience's—the last was WOMEN'S LAVATORY. It was near this distant spot, which Lenox took to be the scene of the crime, that he saw a small group of people, the only ones visible in the station, glowing by the light of at least two lanterns. They stood next to the only train left in the station. Lenox set out to see who they were.

Despite his footsteps, which he thought would have alerted them, they started when he said, approaching, "Good evening, gentlemen."

A craggy old man in a huge sealskin cloak took a step forward. "Who're you?"

There were three men. One was a police constable with a cherubic look, but Hemstock wasn't among them. This was no surprise; the inspector was likely at a bar, taking his leisure. He was on duty until six the next morning and rarely rushed himself.

Lenox bowed his head slightly. "Charles Lenox, gentlemen. I am an associate of Inspector Hemstock's."

"Hemstock? Is he from the Yard?"

"He is, sir."

Lenox always avoided saying that he himself was from the Yard—when he could. "We sent the constable for him over ninety minutes ago," the older man said.

"I have just seen Mr. Hemstock. He will be here

29

shortly. In the meanwhile, may I ask the pleasure of knowing your name?"

"I'm Joseph Beauregard Stanley," the old man in the sealskin coat said. "Late of Her Majesty's Navy. Presently the stationmaster on duty."

"There's been a death, Mr. Hemstock says? Possibly a murder?"

One of the other two men snorted. Not the constable. "If it was anything else, I'd like to know what."

"A violent death, then."

"Violent, yes," the man replied, as if the word could scarcely describe what he had seen. He wore a black frock coat and no hat. Anticipating Lenox's next question, he went on, nodding at the train, "I'm the conductor of the 449."

"This train."

"Yes. From Manchester."

"So you found the body?" asked Lenox.

"I did. By chance, mind you."

Lenox was curious about that statement, but said, following the conversation's momentum, "Perhaps we had better have a look." When there was a pause, he turned to the constable, a very young man, he saw now, who held the other lantern. "Good evening. Charles Lenox."

"Rossum, sir," said the lad in an accent conspicuously of the East End. Lenox would have laid a shilling coin that the boy had been born within hearing of Bow Bells: the traditional definition of a cockney.

"You were on your beat?"

"No, sir. I was round the Nimble Peacock on Chapel Street, sir, just by. Day finished. Enjoying a pint of beer. I only came at the whistle, sir."

He looked a bit proud as he said this—not without reason. It had technically been his duty to answer the call of his fellow officer, but few of London's constables would have taken the trouble on a dark and rainy night. The whistle usually blew to ask for nothing more than assistance with a drunken brawl.

"Well done, Mr. Rossum," said Lenox. "I shall inform Sir Richard in the morning of how responsible you were in performance of your duties."

Rossum's eyes widened in his lantern's light. Sir Richard Mayne was the head of Scotland Yard. "I thank you friendly o' that, sir."

Lenox nodded. Then he said again, trying to sound unrushed, "Shall we go and look at the body?"

"Hadn't we better wait for the inspector?" replied the old stationmaster.

"The sooner the body is gone, the sooner your station is yours again, Mr. Stanley," Lenox said. "I'm happy to wait if you wish, however."

Stanley sighed. "No, I suppose you'd better go aboard." He didn't like the idea though. "I'll let these chaps take you. It's not a sight I care to see a third time. And someone must be here when the inspector comes. If he ever does."

They boarded the train single file, led by the conductor.

The 449 from Manchester had four passenger cars, it appeared. The conductor, whose name Lenox still hadn't caught, took them to the first of them, the third-class carriage. This would have been the cheapest seat to reserve, its hard benches usually populated exclusively by men of the working classes. They traveled closest to the clamor and powerful, if not unpleasant, coal smell of the engine room.

The first-class carriage—quieter, much more expensive, and outfitted to a high standard of comfort—would be at the rear. It was in the first-class carriage that Lenox traveled, generally; Hemstock, by contrast, was a classic man of the second-class carriages, which occupied the middle two cars.

A funny place sometimes, England.

Both the conductor and Constable Rossum had lanterns, and it was by their light that Lenox saw the victim.

He was slumped on the last bench at the rear of the car. He looked young, his light brown hair combed back. His head leaned against the window next to him, as if he were asleep. He had, Lenox thought, a handsome face, clean and strong.

The other two made way for Lenox to go first. The fire from the lanterns danced in the glass windows. Moving forward he tried not to betray his nervousness—concealing it behind an intent gaze that took in the details of the carriage. But this was pointless. There was nothing to see, all the luggage gone, every seat emptied, the carriage cleaned even of the usual refuse.

At last he drew close to the body. He saw that the man was young, perhaps the same age as Lenox himself. He was extremely pale in the light of the lanterns.

Then Lenox looked down and saw why. It was no wonder the stationmaster hadn't wished to come aboard again. The victim had lost a tremendous amount of blood, and even now remained in a desperate pose, as if trying and failing to hold in his entrails. His stomach had been slashed open.

A butchery of a murder. There was a sour, metallic smell in the air. Lenox turned back to the conductor and the constable, trying his best to be professional. "I take it nobody saw anything."

"Only me," said the conductor. "I had collected all the tickets from the seats before London, but I was missing my own return bus ticket, to get home. I came through to see if I had dropped it. 'Twas then I found him."

"Did you clean the carriage? It appears spotless."

"No—that would have been one of the station's men. Probably tidied up my bus ticket along with everything else. But there is occasionally a drunken man asleep aboard the train. Whoever cleaned the car would have assumed that had happened here. Ignored him."

"Despite the blood?"

The conductor shrugged. "It was dark and it's the third-class carriage. A quick tidy."

"I see."

Lenox thought for a moment. There was a great deal to take in, and, beginning with an inspection of the body, he noted it all with a pencil in the small leather-bound notebook he kept in his front pocket, each small detail.

Still, when he stepped down onto the platform again, some fifteen minutes later, it was not the inhumane manner of the murder that filled him with consternation. It was that for the first time in his young career, he had encountered a case without a single clue.

CHAPTER FOUR

Hemstock arrived about half an hour after Lenox. Only the young amateur detective and the grizzled stationmaster remained on the platform. The conductor had been raring to get home, his lost omnibus ticket nothing to the price of a hansom if he could merely get some sleep, he'd said, and while Rossum, the young constable, had played his role admirably, he had asked after they got off the train if his presence was still necessary. Lenox had let him go.

Hemstock strolled in without a care in the world. You had to hand him that much: He had insouciance.

"Lenox!" he cried upon approaching. "Dashed glad to see you joined the hullaballoo after all."

Stanley, the stationmaster, took in Hemstock's approaching figure charily.

"Is someone coming along to fetch the body?" he asked. "I must write my report. And this train must be cleared and empty by morning. It goes to the south coast at 7:33."

"Oh, yes," said Hemstock. "A medical examiner will arrive before long."

"What time is the first train of the morning?" Lenox asked the stationmaster.

At 5:49, came the answer. Did they have

anything further? If not, Stanley said, he would return to his office. They could find him there, the large brick-and-glass stand lofted a few feet above ground level near the front doors of the station.

When Hemstock and Lenox were alone, Hemstock sighed. He would have preferred to be somewhere else, the noise suggested—perhaps a tavern scene by Frans Hals.

"Well?" he said. "What do we have?"

"Perhaps you'd better come and look."

"Must I?"

"I think so."

Thus they boarded the third-class carriage again, and Lenox described how he had passed his time here. Hemstock, after staring with a furrowed brow at the dead man for a moment, sat down heavily on the bench opposite and looked up at the young amateur, listening.

Lenox had begun with the body. The general cause of death was obvious: The victim had been slashed and stabbed repeatedly in the stomach and ribs. Whether it was loss of blood or a specific wound that had in fact killed him was for the medical examiner to say.

"But the more interesting bit came next," said Lenox. "When I looked for identification."

"Why? Who is he?"

"I don't have the slightest clue."

Hemstock looked sincerely surprised. "How's that?"

Lenox demonstrated what he meant. He turned out all of the man's pockets, showing that there was nothing inside them. "I lifted the body up after I found his pockets empty and looked to see if a billfold or valise was underneath him. Nothing."

"Hm." Hemstock looked still more curious. "No identification on the body, then. Stolen?"

"I don't think so, because of what I saw next."

"What?"

Carefully, Lenox opened the dead man's jacket. It was a charcoal-black sack coat, a casual fashion imported in the last few years from Manhattan. Lenox had recently been talked into having one made for himself. "Look."

Cut raggedly from the inner pocket of the man's coat was a rectangle where its tailor's label would have been sewn. There was blood around the area—mostly dry, but certainly fresh.

He proceeded to show Hemstock the jacket inside and out—it was a ginger business to remove it—and then the shirt. The victim's pants, which were of a light gray, unmatched to the jacket, had had *their* label removed, too, from the inner right leg.

"What about behind his neck?"

"Another label torn out."

"Very, very strange."

Last of all, Lenox observed, the man's boots were gone entirely. "And even his socks—they are cut at the top."

Hemstock was indifferent to his work, not stupid. "Where a monogram might have been. This is odd indeed." He blinked his eyes a few times quickly. "What do I—what shall I make of it?"

Lenox shook his head. "That I still do not know, unfortunately."

"Hm."

Hemstock looked disappointed. It was a more complex case than he had been hoping would fall to him.

But Lenox felt a kind of pure, racing thrill, somber to be sure but not without a tincture of joy. This was a real and serious crime, with a horrible mixture of violence and methodical cunning to the way the murderer had slashed the man to death and then carefully cut away the labels of his clothes. It had to be solved—he had rarely felt anything so strongly. Either violence or wit could make a criminal dangerous. Lenox had learned this in his painstaking study of the history of crime. But together they could make the same criminal truly diabolical.

"You no doubt observe what else is missing, too, of course," said Lenox.

"Eh? Oh?" said Hemstock, as if in fact he did reserve the right to doubt that he had noticed it.

"No hat," said Lenox.

That was indeed uncommon for any man, of any class. "No hat."

"To go with no money. No watch. No overcoat. Nor even a handkerchief. I checked all of his pockets twice."

He had checked the rest of the carriage, too, every inch of it. Empty.

"Those are all items of value," Hemstock said. "They might have been taken more easily than the boots."

"*All* of them?" Lenox asked.

"No," Hemstock said. "I suppose not."

It took Lenox an instant to realize what Hemstock was really feeling: fear. This crime lay beyond his regular abilities. He was like a schoolboy sitting to an exam for which he was unprepared.

"It will be all right, you know," Lenox said. "It is just a case to be solved, not more, not less."

"Perhaps a bit more," muttered Hemstock.

"We shall manage it."

Just then there were voices outside the carriage. Lenox glanced at his watch. It was nearly one o'clock in the morning. In another version of this evening, where it had never rained, he was at a ball attaining its last raucous crescendo.

Instead, he and Hemstock descended the train's stairs. On the platform were two men, one Lenox recognized, one he didn't.

"Good evening, Inspector," said the one Lenox did.

"Good evening, Dunn."

This was Hemstock's superior, a fellow named Ephraim Dunn, short, handsome, and officious. He had jet-black hair, which he pomaded into a brilliant slickness, so that despite his height you could see the glint of him from a London block away—as the constables would joke. He was clean shaven, the better to show the expression of a man who looked for ill in the world each day and never went to sleep disappointed.

"And Mr. Charles Lenox," he said. "How exceedingly benevolent of you to come to our assistance!"

"Mr. Dunn," said Lenox, nodding his head.

"Still, I think you may leave. Winstanley—the body. Hemstock, go and fetch the two men with the stretcher, please. They're in Praed Street. They'll have to drive round."

Hemstock jumped to it, glad to be a soldier rather than a commander. Meanwhile Dunn and Winstanley boarded the train. Winstanley, a thin, wistful person who looked as if he needed a solid meal, was apparently the medical examiner.

Lenox stood on the platform, gazing down at the gravel between the wooden railroad ties.

He had learned to use moments like this to think. Of course, he reasoned, the lack of clues in this case *was* the clue. It would have taken the murderer precious time to cut the labels from each garment, to remove each boot. To gather the hat, handkerchief, boots, and watch, all the small

40

outward gestures of acquisition that defined a person by a glance.

Then to leave Paddington with all of it, unnoticed . . . he must have had a large piece of luggage, Lenox thought. If it was well after the station had emptied, perhaps he had been seen.

Winstanley and Dunn descended from the 449 to the platform about ten minutes later, just as Hemstock returned with two burly constables, there to carry the body to Winstanley's wagon.

Winstanley, peering carefully at the group above his round spectacles, said, "The victim appears to have been stabbed to death."

"I thought so, too," Hemstock said.

"It is hard to conceive of anyone disagreeing," Dunn said shortly. "Was there anything else?"

"No. It is all perfectly straightforward."

That, in fact, was a statement with which one could conceive some disagreement. But at that moment Lenox realized something.

"I saw no wounds on his hands," he said. "Only blood."

Winstanley's turtlelike scrutiny shifted to him. "Sir?"

"Perhaps he didn't see the attack coming," Lenox said. "Perhaps he was asleep. Or perhaps he knew his murderer."

"It is high time you left speculation to the professionals," Dunn said. "Good evening, Mr. Lenox. No doubt there is some champagne breakfast or horse racing event at which you are required early tomorrow."

"None at all," said Lenox, anger rising in him.

"Nevertheless," said Dunn, "I'm sure you will welcome your rest. Good evening."

And so Lenox had no choice but to leave. It was useless to point out that he had helped Scotland Yard; still more useless to point out that he knew already he wouldn't sleep much that night. He nodded goodbye and made his way back to his carriage, the rain thrumming relentlessly on the station's glass roof.

CHAPTER FIVE

The next day dawned chilly, innocent, and clear, with a soft white sky. Lenox, after studying his notes from the scene, stirred the banked coals in the hearth. He had already put on a morning coat with a heavy wool collar since coming down twenty minutes before. A first October taste of winter.

There was a quiet knock at the door. "Yes?" Lenox called.

Graham entered. He had brought a pot of tea. "Good morning, sir."

Lenox checked his watch. "It's not even six o'clock," he said. "How did you know I was awake?"

"I must have heard you, sir."

Lenox doubted it. But Graham had an infallible sympathetic understanding of this house—who was moving within it, who was awake, asleep, eating, coming, going, skiving off work. The latter category occasionally included Lenox himself.

But not now.

"Thank you," he said, as he accepted a cup of tea "A hot drink's very welcome. Sit, please, if you wish."

"Of course, sir."

Lenox laid down his pen and reclined in his desk chair, holding the delicate cup in both hands. His careful notes were complete. He looked out through the windows at pretty, peaceful Hampden Lane, with its booksellers and bakers, its slumbering houses, its maids coming to the doors to fetch the milk. Weak sunlight filtered through the wet trees, which shook drops onto the pavement at each gust of wind.

"The papers are in, sir. Only one has the story. The *Morning Illustrated*."

Lenox turned. "Them! Do you have it?"

"Right here, sir."

"Thank you."

He read the article.

MYSTERIOUS DEATH ON THE 449 TO PADDINGTON

Stabbing wounds thought to be gang-related
Information sought by Hemstock, Dunn

A body was discovered late last night on the 449 from Store Street, Manchester—that of a man slain in most gruesome fashion. The police have not yet identified him but believe he was a victim of the deadly gang conflict currently taking place in that city.

"His guts were spilling out," Inspector Dunn informed the *Morning Illustrated* exclusively and vividly. "It had the mark of their vicious kind. It's not the England I know and love, but Manchester has troubles it can't get in hand. Now they're coming to the capital."

Sharp-eyed readers of this journal may recall that the 449 was also the site of the unsolved death of Gabriel Taylor, 17, of Salford, in May. Taylor was thrown from the train near Wilmslow and suffered a broken neck.

Inspector Dunn would neither confirm nor deny that the deaths are related.

Check later editions for further information.

Lenox looked at Graham. "Dunn would have had to go straight to the offices of the *Morning Illustrated* to squeeze this into the early edition. I wonder that he bothered. Though perhaps it is in his interest to be on friendly terms with the paper." He looked at the article again, then murmured, mostly to himself, *"The England I know and love."*

He recalled the death of Gabriel Taylor clearly. It had been by no means decided whether Taylor—a promising boxer, well known in Manchester's sporting circles—had been thrown from the train, jumped, or fallen by accident, inebriated. Lenox remembered having been inclined to the third explanation. It was the lad's first trip to London.

"Did you read the article?" Lenox asked Graham.

"I did, sir."

Lenox took a sip of his tea, which had cooled, and picked up a custard cream from the silver dish next to it. "And what did you make of it?"

"I was curious how it matched up to your visit to the scene, sir."

Lenox nodded, thinking. He soaked the biscuit in his tea until it was just on the very edge of breaking, a skill that he had spent arduous years at school mastering, ruining many a cup of tea in the process.

He took a bite and found it mostly softened to mush yet still just firm. Perfect. Ah—he had been hungry, thirsty. He was tired. This was better.

Taking another, he told Graham about his visit to Paddington. Graham was a careful listener and asked several questions.

"And what did he look like, sir?"

Lenox frowned. "Fairly handsome, I think. It's always difficult to tell, after death. But he was young and had good bones. Light brown hair, a bit longer than mine."

"Was there any damage to his face or hands, sir?"

"No, there wasn't—no evidence of defense."

"I see, sir," said Graham, nodding. Then added, in his customarily courteous way, "I had wondered whether he was a boxer. But self-defense is the more pertinent question, sir."

Lenox hit his forehead. "No—like Gabriel Taylor. I should have thought of it. Anyhow our man was young, like Taylor, but not a boxer. No nicks, no scars I could see, hands as soft as or softer than the average man in a third-class carriage's would be. Neither a boxer nor a gang member, at least that I would have guessed."

"Did you look through the other carriages, sir?"

Lenox shook his head. "Dunn had arrived to see me off by the time I could have. As I was leaving, though, Hemstock and the constables were setting about the job. Presumably even they would have found a hidden murderer."

"Yes, sir."

Something was bothering Lenox. Was it from the article? After a moment he wandered over to the mantel. It was here that he left the debris of his comings and goings, with strict instructions to Graham, Mrs. Huggins, and the rest of the staff not to touch it. (Mrs. Huggins was Lenox's housekeeper—something he would not have said he needed, though in fact her management of the household had taken a great deal off of Graham's shoulders, and the minor details of her care all made the house gleam, freshly polished by her attention in a way it never had been before.)

Among the coins and calling cards, he found a worn ticket from the same line as the 449. It was from a trip he had recently taken to Birmingham for a case.

The ticket's letters had been smudged and faded by the friction of his pocket; he rubbed the smooth cardstock with his thumb, thoughtful.

No genie emerged. Worse luck.

Then he had a thought. "Graham," he said. "Is Ellie awake?"

This was the house's cook, who made a wonderful, delicate potato soup and swore as if she had been raised in the navy. Graham glanced at the carriage clock on the desk. "I'm quite sure she is, sir."

"Would you fetch her, please?"

"Did you want breakfast, sir?" asked Graham.

"No, no," said Lenox. "In fact, better yet, I will go down to the kitchen."

Graham looked alarmed. "If you wish, sir."

Lenox was already crossing the hall, and after an instant took the thin stairwell down to the kitchen two steps at a time. "Ellie!" he called.

"What?" a voice replied irritably. He came into her view and saw that she was rolling out crescents. She looked in no way abashed to discover that her curtness had been directed at the master of the house. She merely stared at him. "Well?"

"Your brother is a train conductor, isn't he? Do I have that correct?"

"Yes," she said. Her face softened. "Our Sam. The youngest of us. He works for the London and North Western."

This was the largest of the rail lines. It ran the 449, as well as the train Lenox had taken to Birmingham and whose ticket he was still holding. "What's his route?"

"His route, sir? He doesn't have one as such. It varies, see. Sometimes he'll come out of Glasgow a week—then Lancaster—then Rutland. They always get him home to Chester in the end. Might be a night in an inn somewhere between, but the line pays for his board in that case."

Ellie was herself from Chester, in Cheshire, a lovely city on the River Dee. "But he doesn't have a regular route?" asked Lenox.

"No, he's only thirty-one. Them as get the regular clockwork routes are quite senior. He might be directed any old place. He doesn't mind it that way, Sam. Chance to see the whole of the—"

"Thank you!" Lenox cried, turning and flying.

"All sorts barging about," he heard Ellie mutter as he left, but he paid her no heed.

Graham, who kept up with him pretty well, was

asking what it was, but Lenox was already in the front hall putting on his topcoat.

He realized he still had his morning coat on—"Your tie, sir!" cried Graham, as Lenox began to open the door—but didn't care. He had to get to the Yard as soon as he could.

CHAPTER SIX

Sir Richard Mayne looked down at the small rectangular rail ticket that Lenox had placed on his desk.

2	**L.A.N.W.**
	*
0	**Birmingham to Fenchurch St.**
	*
6	**First Class**

Sir Richard was a formidable man. He wore full side-whiskers, and was sober in his dress. The son of an important judge, he had been born in Dublin, then educated first at Trinity College in that city and subsequently at Cambridge, before becoming a celebrated barrister. Finally he had risen to the position of Commissioner of the Police of the Metropolis. He was so strict in this capacity that the year before he had ordered his police force to crack down on children who were making snowballs.

By virtue of any single one of those facts—even the whiskers—he would have been intimidating. For Lenox there was the additional fact that he was Lenox's only, uneasy ally in official police work. Like Dunn, Mayne resented the interference of an amateur; unlike Dunn, he appreciated Lenox's thoughtful investigations and attention to detail.

And after all, he was still only a man. Lenox had not personally noticed any decline in the incidence of snowball fights among children the previous winter—thank goodness.

Mayne looked up from the ticket to Lenox. "You are proposing that I deploy ten of my men along the rail line on the strength of this ticket."

"If that's all you can spare," said Lenox.

"Ha!"

Mayne looked down at the ticket again with the bitter expression particular to an administrator of whom everyone expects five times what he can afford and twenty times what he can achieve.

The ticket was unusual in no way. The initials L.A.N.W. at the top stood for London and North Western, the rail line that also operated the 449. 206 was the number of the train.

The only consequential fact about the ticket was that Lenox *still had it*.

It was this that led him to believe he had stared into the eyes of the murderer the night before: the man who had presented himself as the conductor of the 449.

There had been just this one reason at first, the ticket. What had the man said about finding the body? Something roughly like: *I had collected all the tickets from the seats before London, but I was missing my own bus ticket to go home.*

It was an understandable slip. There were numerous smaller train lines that did, in fact, collect the tickets wedged between seats before their journeys ended. They were then reused. But as Lenox's possession of the ticket from Birmingham to Fenchurch Street showed, the big rails—and specifically the London and North Western—did not.

There it was, then: a lie.

After Lenox realized that the conductor had lied, he replayed their encounter in his memory, and the exercise produced several other puzzling details in his mind.

Arriving at Paddington, for instance, Lenox had assumed that the conductor and the stationmaster were acquainted. But then (as he had explained just now to Sir Richard Mayne, who was still staring at the ticket, sipping from a cup of black tea with lemon), he had gone downstairs and spoken to Ellie. In fact, as the cook had confirmed, it was just as possible that they had never met. No doubt many conductors and stationmasters were friendly, but it was not a hard and fast rule.

After that, as Lenox told Mayne, there were small things, odd little skips in the tune. The man had never given his name. Meaningless or meaningful? Was it actually possible that a custodian had mistaken a dead man for a sleeping one and cleaned around him? And then—the conductor had mentioned losing his omnibus ticket. But wasn't it the widely known rule that conductors lived as close to their home stations as possible?

Finally, there had been his dress. The conductor had worn a black frock coat and no hat. Lenox had not remarked on this at the time, but as all Londoners and most other Britons knew, conductors and train guards generally wore a single style of uniform: a long blue coat with two rows of vertical buttons, usually buttoned only at the very top so that the conductor had easy access to his pocket watch—the time being very important to this line of work, of course—and a flat-brimmed hat, generally with the number of the train fixed to it on a detachable medallion by two small brass chains.

The conductor Lenox had met might have changed out of this uniform. But would he have, if he were going straight home from the station? And more damningly, if he had changed, where had been his luggage?

Having heard all these questions, Sir Richard looked up at Lenox now with an appraising eye for a long moment. It was all circumstantial, Lenox would grant that—and thus, he felt a surge of gratitude for Mayne's faith in him when the commissioner began to write out a note.

"I can let you have four men from the Bays-water station."

This was a police branch close by Paddington. "Thank you, Sir Richard."

"For five hours. Not twelve."

"Ah. Thank you."

"I don't have the time to fall out with Inspector Dunn today, either. So steer clear of him."

"Happily, sir."

Mayne looked away through the window to the Thames. It was busy—small ships crossing each other's wakes, a few large ones turning fat into the tide, bound for the ocean after weeks in dry dock.

"What do you think it's about, this murder? Is it really a problem for Manchester?" he asked. "The thing bothers me."

Lenox shook his head. "I cannot say, sir. It's too soon."

"Hm." Mayne tore the sheet off and handed it to Lenox. "Very well. On you go."

Lenox crossed town to the Bayswater police station. He didn't know anyone there, but they were friendly, and complied immediately with Mayne's note. Lenox sent one of the five men they gave him straightaway to find the home of Joseph Beauregard Stanley—the stationmaster—and ask him whether he had known the conductor before the previous night.

The remaining four he took to Paddington.

There he was able to discover, from the logs, the name of the gentleman who was scheduled to have been the conductor of the 449 the evening before: Mr. Norman Haase.

This accomplished, he set about hiring horses. There was no horse path along the railroad, but Lenox didn't need one—for a very specific reason.

Though the number seemed arbitrary, it was not accidental that the width between railroad tracks all across England was exactly four feet eight and a half inches, measured from the inside of each track. It was because that was the width of a horse-drawn wagon.

At the turn of the century, it had been horses that carried coal out of the mines by the ton. This job was easier if there were metal tracks laid down upon which the wagons could roll.

Ever enterprising, it was coal barons who, forty or more years before, had understood the potential use of locomotion in their line of work. Indeed, many of the first, tiny rail lines to exist had traveled between coal mines and nearby depots.

What this meant for Lenox was that he could hire four horses from a stable near Paddington, divide them into pairs pulling small dog carts, and move with ease along the train tracks that ran on either side of the line upon which the 449 had traveled into London.

Lenox explained all of this, with some small pride, to the two constables with whom he rode.

To his surprise, one of them, a tall, graying fellow called Simonson, said, "Not only that, sir—they were the same width exact for the war chariots of ancient Rome."

They had been trotting at a good pace for ten minutes and were now perhaps half a mile away from Paddington. The additional tracks would split off in different directions after about a mile. Then they would have to ride on horseback, he figured.

"Is that so?" he said, curious.

"My father said as much, at least," Simonson replied.

"How very interesting to know," said Lenox. "They were marvelous, the Romans. Did you know—"

But just at that moment there was a cry from the pair of Bayswater constables on the other side of the track.

There, lying face up in the ditch between tracks, was the body of a man.

Simonson and Lenox crossed the tracks and came down from their horses, forming a small circle around the corpse.

"Well spotted, gentlemen," said Lenox soberly.

It would have been easy to miss the body—so covered was all his skin and clothing in coal dust and dirt.

But he wore the unmistakable double-breasted cloak of a conductor. It must be Norman Haase. He lay there, pale in the few places where his skin was visible, eyes open but unseeing. His throat was cut.

CHAPTER SEVEN

That evening, after a brief stop at home to rinse his hands and face and change his shirt, Lenox, so tired that he felt he could barely make the twenty-step trip next door, dined with Lord Deere and Lady Jane.

Finding Haase's body had completed their crime. If affirmation were necessary, the old stationmaster of the night before had indignantly told the young constable from Bayswater that no, he had never met the conductor before: "That's railway business," he'd said. "I'm a stationmaster. I attend to Paddington."

(This was maddening old England, Lenox thought—its ability to divide into half-sealed compartments the fluid systems that interconnected to make up the world. The army office couldn't possibly have the army documents, you would hear; those were of course at the documents office; and when you went to the documents office, they said that all army documents were kept at their military branch in Edgeworth; which was closed for reconstruction; and so on, until you ended up at a small post office in John O'Groats, begging for the Queen's certificate of birth from a surly northerner who was drinking straight whisky and didn't trust anyone who had set foot south of Hull city limits.)

Inspector Dunn had been just on the verge of leaving for Manchester when Lenox had hastened back to Scotland Yard with the news of the body by the tracks. The inspector had been furious with injured pride, so that it seemed whatever gains Lenox had made in Mayne's estimation had been lost in Dunn's. Fortunately, it was Mayne's opinion that mattered, and he had granted Lenox the right to his own line of inquiry. The next day both would attend an early meeting at Scotland Yard.

He recounted all this in a drained, jumbled way to his hosts over a glass of preprandial sherry, which he found was most welcome—pleasantly softening the yellow candlelight flicker of the room, taking the hard edge off of his sensations. Arriving not much later to make up the rest of the quiet party were Lenox's older brother, Sir Edmund Lenox, the 15th Baronet of Markethouse, and his wife, Molly.

The pair had been married about seven years and had two sons. Molly was a pretty, plump, countryish woman; not an intellectual, but more intelligent and intuitive than most of those who were better lettered than she, a superb judge of character with a quick laugh and an endearing manner.

They sat down and Charles resumed his tale. Among them, only Deere was not of very old

60

childhood acquaintance—and he was such a decent fellow that you barely noticed.

"What a horrifying day," said Lady Jane, after Charles had finished his story.

"Oh, no, I found it rather thrilling."

They were in the drawing room. It was a blend of the couple's tastes, full of portraits of Deere's childhood beagles and his wife's many books.

"What stop was closest to the body?" asked Edmund.

Edmund was abundantly occupied by the stewardship of Lenox House and its lands along with his duties in Parliament. But from the start he had been his younger brother's staunchest supporter—and keenest auditor—in this choice of career.

"The body was thrown from the train long after Nuneaton," Charles replied. He took a seed cracker with a morsel of Stilton; Lady Jane put cheese out before supper, one of her eccentricities as a hostess. "The last stop between Manchester and Paddington."

"Have you spoken with any passengers from the train?" asked Jane.

"Not yet," said Charles. "We must locate them first."

"And you still have no idea who the young man was, the victim from last night," said Molly, looking unhappy. "These poor fellows. You never hear of it happening in the country."

61

"There I can contradict you, Lady Molly, if you won't take offense," said Deere. "For I will never forget what Thurtell answered when the Crown asked whether his and his fellow criminals' supper was postponed after they murdered William Weare."

"What did he answer?" said Molly.

"He said, 'No, it was mutton.' "

They all laughed except Molly, who colored and said she hoped they weren't having mutton for dinner. It was enough to remind Lady Jane (who assured her they weren't) that they ought to sit—for which Charles was grateful, as he wanted, just now, nothing more than a good meal.

Perhaps out of deference to Molly's dislike of the subject of Lenox's case, the chief topic of conversation during the meal's first course, a clear autumn vegetable soup, was Sir Edmund's stockings.

"Do you not like them?" he asked Charles, astonished, when his younger brother raised the subject.

Charles frowned. "I don't know if that's putting it quite strongly enough."

Edmund gazed at him, wounded, and stuck a leg out from beneath the table. "They are from that town in Scotland with all the weavers—Paisley."

"They should have stayed there."

"Charles!" said Molly, then added, to Edmund, "I think they're handsome, dear."

Edmund looked as if he suspected a wife's compliments might be less sincere than a brother's insults, but thanked her. "My tailor particularly recommended them to me, you know, Charles. Your tailor, too, for that matter."

Lady Jane said, "I am in accord with you, Molly. Charles has no sense of dress, Edmund. He never had."

"To be truly elegant, one should not be noticed," Deere observed. "It was Beau Brummel said that."

Charles was still examining the stockings, which stood out so markedly, in turquoise and blue, from Edmund's restrained black suit and shoes. "Well, I don't see there being any risk of Edmund's not being noticed, alas."

"Oh, leave off," responded Edmund moodily. "You never had any sense of dress."

"We all still speak of Beau Brummel," said Lady Jane, "so I suppose by his own definition he was a failure."

"He died penniless, insane, and alone, as I recall," Lord Deere replied.

"Unnoticed, then," said Lady Jane. "Elegant at last."

Deere laughed, and said it was true. After the soup, a chaudfroid of salmon with hot buttered potatoes came out, and proved delicious with their chilled white wine. It was followed by a dish of roasted turkey covered with a gravy of nutmeg, brandy, and onion. Lenox barely spoke—merely sighed and tucked in more deeply as each course arrived.

"This is really very nice," Edmund remarked. "I don't think I've had it here before, Jane."

"It is a new recipe, given me by Lady Laura Gentry."

Here she looked pointedly in any direction but Charles's, and Edmund said innocently, "I only know her by name, but I am certainly impressed with her cookery."

Which confirmed to Lenox (who was a detective, after all) that they had contrived a plan together for him to marry her—whoever she might be, Lady Laura Gentry.

"She was presented at court just two weeks ago. Beautiful—a cousin of Duch's. She dances and paints."

"At the same time?" said Charles. "Now I must see that."

Lady Jane threw him a dark look. "Everything must be a joke to you."

"You have my word that if Lady Laura dances and paints at once, I will attend the performance with the most solemn gravity."

And at this even Jane was forced to smile.

As they ate and conversed, a happy party, much of Lenox's train of thought nevertheless remained with the case, tracing and retracing his plans for the following day. But some time around the second glass of burgundy he drank, a deep ruby liquid, he was able to let the case go and join in the conversation, hearing about Molly's works in the town of Markethouse and who conveyed their greetings to him from there, what the cricket team had been doing, and Sir Edmund's hours in Parliament (he was a dependable vote on the liberal side, as their father had been, though he hadn't any special interest in politics—preferring, as he said, horses).

Dessert arrived, a gooseberry fool with whipped cream. Here, before the sexes separated, Lord Deere stood up.

He held aloft a small leaded flint glass, clear, achingly thin—specifically designed, indeed, to make the purest of chimes during a toast—and traced in gold with his family's crest. "A brief announcement, though it is Charles's day."

"Mine?" Lenox said. "I reject the notion."

"I have just had my orders. We are to perform field exercises in Buckinghamshire for the next twelvemonth, which means that I shall be able to spend a great deal of my time here in London, for the first time as a married man."

There were loud congratulations and clinking of the glasses all around—and indeed it was welcome news, for Deere had been traveling almost from the moment of his betrothal to Jane.

"Ask him why he is so happy," she said in a derisive voice, though her face shone with unusual joy, her eyes brilliant and happy. "It is because two puppies are on their way here from his family's stables as we speak."

"It's true that I did not want a dog until I knew I could train it properly myself—and that a handsome litter has just been whelped, according to my father's groom—but of course the reason for my happiness is that I get to remain with my dear wife and"—here he graciously turned to each of them in turn, in his bearing that faultless squared-off uprightness of the military man— "her splendid friends. May I ask you to toast to Lady Jane?"

"To Lady Jane!" the company called in unison, Lenox included—happy, truly, for his friends.

Nevertheless, he was glad that he could soon make his excuses and drag himself home, more beast than man after thirty-six hours virtually without sleep, upstairs, and into bed, where within twenty minutes of the toast and twenty seconds of lying down he had fallen into a fast and dark and deep-fathomed slumber.

CHAPTER EIGHT

At eight o'clock the next morning, five people gathered in the office of Sir Richard Mayne. Besides Lenox and Sir Richard, there were Hemstock, who looked forlorn to be up at such an hour; Dunn, with his shining black hair and wretched angry look; and an official from the railway, whom Mayne did not introduce by name. This gentleman sat off to the side of the room, a heavy, silent presence. He carried himself as became a man of influence. He was well dressed, and gold glinted from his watch chain and his cuffs.

"Good morning," Sir Richard said when his efficient young secretary, Wilkinson, had ushered the last of them in. "Thank you for coming. No doubt you have seen this morning's papers. What we supposed to have been a matter between two villains from Manchester becomes more grave in the light of Lenox's discovery."

Lenox inclined his head.

Mayne went on. "The second body has indeed been identified as that of Norman Haase. I am informed that Mr. Haase was a loyal servant to the rail line, a deacon at St. Mary's Church in Epping, a widower, and the father of four children, adult now. We must exert ourselves doubly on his behalf and theirs."

All present nodded—Lenox alone doubting, perhaps, whether the second murder was any additional incentive to pursue the murderer, but remaining silent about this particular reservation.

"We'll get him, sir," said Hemstock.

"Yes, no doubt," said Mayne. "Now, I have two questions. The first is how we are to discover the identity of the man in the carriage."

"We are circulating his description in London and in Manchester," Dunn said.

"Good. The second is why on earth this fellow murdered Haase."

"Sir?"

"The motive for the murder in the third-class carriage could be anything under the sun: money, a woman, drink. We all know the disputes that arise in that class. But why Haase?" said Mayne. He was no fool, Sir Richard. It was the question Lenox had been carefully pondering that morning as he shaved. "Did the conductor recognize him? A picture from the illustrated papers perhaps? Is he a known criminal?"

Dunn replied, "We are also circulating a description of the man who passed himself off as a conductor, based on the descriptions of the men who met him. Including Lenox. We know that he was about five foot and nine or ten inches, with dark hair, large eyes, a strong chin, and no visible scars. He carried himself respectably."

"Though perhaps that is what we were all

prepared to see," added Lenox. "Though I know I could pick him from a group, my memory of his particular features grows dimmer the harder I try to remember them."

"Sir Richard," said Dunn, "I must again question why Mr. Lenox's presence is necessary here."

That seemed rude.

"He identified the murderer and found the dead conductor, Dunn. Any progress we have made belongs in his credits column—not the Yard's," Mayne said, with a pointed smack of his desk.

"Someone would have found the body," Dunn muttered.

The representative from the railway moved forward in his chair. "That is not necessarily the case. It is a section of the line close to no village, and as Mr. Lenox observed, gravel and dust covered the body quickly, and might have concealed it further as time passed."

"Mm," said Dunn.

"Moreover, Mr. Haase lived alone," the man said. "Of course, he would have been missed after three days at a minimum. He was assigned to be the conductor of the 858 overnight train to Edinburgh on Friday."

Dunn looked murderous. "I was not informed that every man in London capable of scheduling a train to Bournemouth or gambling on cards at Cambridge had suddenly become a detective," he said, glancing between the railway's man and Lenox.

"Watch your tongue," said Sir Richard. "I mean it, Dunn."

Dunn, apparently realizing that he had shaded beyond complaint into insult, begged their pardons—with what some keener observers of nature, Lenox thought, might have called less than complete sincerity. But the words would have to suffice. It didn't seem the moment to mention that he had been not at Cambridge but at Oxford.

"I have one observation, Sir Richard," said Lenox.

"Go on."

"The clothes must be our most important clue."

"The victim's clothes?"

"Yes."

"Why?"

"Because at a time when the false conductor had just committed murder, and every fiber of his being must have yearned to put as much distance between himself and the body as possible—"

Dunn interrupted. "Not if he was one of these brutes from Manchester. As good as a cow carcass to them, a human body."

"Please continue, Lenox," said Mayne.

"At a moment when every instinct he had was most probably to run, our criminal took the time to remove all traces of the origins of the victim's clothing. Down to his boots and his hat."

Mayne considered this. "I assume he didn't want us tracing them back to some specific tailor. Was our victim very—what's the word—stylish?"

Lenox shook his head. "He wore the average attire of a man in second or third class, Sir Richard. And the murderer removed every single label, not just one. It leads me to believe that all the clothes pointed to a specific *location,* wherever that might be."

"London," said Sir Richard.

"Manchester," said Dunn.

Lenox didn't think so. "But he was on a train between those two cities. Why bother to conceal that he was from one of them? There are only two possible answers that I can see: One, his identity is absolutely crucial; two, his clothes come from a place that would reveal who he was.

"In fact," Lenox went on, "I suspect this may be the reason for the murder of Haase. So that the killer could be assured of the time alone to perform this very task after the second murder without the conductor entering the carriage and interrupting him."

"Or the reverse," Hemstock said. "Perhaps Haase was the intended victim, and the poor chap in the carriage saw it happen."

"It's possible," Lenox replied, "but I do not think likely. It is the second victim's clothes that were disfigured. And what would the motive be for killing an aging train conductor leading a quiet life in Epping?"

"What do you propose to do with all this theorizing, Lenox?" asked Dunn.

"I don't know," Lenox admitted. "But it cannot be bad to think through the murderer's motivations."

"I agree," said Hemstock, encouragement from an unexpected source.

Lenox nodded to him, grateful.

For the rest of the meeting, he was silent as they discussed Scotland Yard's normal procedures. There would be questioning of witnesses here and in Manchester, and the railway representative said that they would post notices offering a reward for information in all trains running between the two cities.

Mayne asked them to report to him each day. Dunn and Hemstock were to work together. Lenox was free to pursue his inquiries, provided they did not interfere with the official investigation.

"Or reveal additional information to the press," said Dunn severely.

Lenox thought that a bit rich, given that Dunn himself had spoken to the *Morning Illustrated.* But he only assented. "Certainly not."

"It would be good to know what you plan to do," the Yard's commissioner said to Lenox, tapping his pencil on his desk.

"There we agree," Charles responded regretfully. "I am not quite sure. It is close—I know that something is lurking in my mind."

"What cause for optimism," Dunn said.

"That is enough, Dunn," said Mayne. "As for you, Lenox—less lurking, if you wish to remain involved. This is no game."

"No, Sir Richard."

The meeting ended at 8:35. Lenox left the pale, imposing building that housed the Metropolitan Police and walked east. He was due to meet Graham at nine. He might be slightly late, for it was halfway across town in the Strand that their rendezvous was planned, but he needed the walk to think.

Though it was sunny, it was cool enough that the streets were still damp, orange leaves pasted stubbornly to the pavement, a smoky scent in the air. Lenox passed the usual fellows: men hawking newspapers, children selling cigars and tobacco, ladies and gentlemen shopping in the quiet midweek morning.

He had hoped that he might solve the case—ambition never hurt!—on this walk. Instead he found that his thoughts kept returning to Deere.

Lenox had once imagined himself, briefly, to be in love with Lady Jane. It had made things uncomfortable, until Jane, with her characteristic sensitivity, had contrived to put her husband and her old childhood friend in each other's way

73

more and more frequently over the course of a few months while Deere was at home.

Lenox had rejected the military as a career—and this had perhaps, unconsciously, created in him some prejudice against Lord Deere.

But he had been wrong. This realization had been slow, but in the end unambiguous. In its aftermath it came to seem obvious—for of course Lenox ought to have known from the start that Lady Jane would never marry anyone unworthy of herself.

He was glad they were friends now, very glad. Still, it left Lenox with a residue of sorrow. For he had proved, in a way, his own unworthiness of Lady Jane; and in truth, some dormant part of his heart still did, perhaps, just flash with love for her.

Was this life? This lack of resolution, and unease? To begin seeking a marriage while old memories still lingered?

It had not seemed as if affairs of the heart would be quite so involved when he was younger. Love, proposal, marriage, happiness: Such was the progression he had expected.

But he was twenty-seven now—rather old, he thought wisely, as he walked up Carting Lane, his cane thumping lightly alongside him—and knew something of life. He resolved (as so many do, and so few do) to leave the past behind. With that settled, closed in his mind, he walked into the Saltire Inn to meet Graham.

CHAPTER NINE

Graham had placed an advertisement in half a dozen newspapers the evening before. It had been intentionally bland.

Information requested
Any person who traveled on the 449 between Manchester and London Paddington three nights ago, Tuesday 8 October, will find it to their benefit to appear at the Saltire Inn, the Strand, between the hours of 9 and 11 tomorrow morning. Particular consideration granted those able to prove they were aboard the train.

The Saltire was a discreet hotel of about two dozen rooms. It must have been a comfortable secret among a certain class of middle class English gentlemen; it tended to attract owlish, solitary travelers who did not belong to any of London's clubs but did not mind paying rather high rates in order to ensure themselves prompt, hearty meals, large rooms with comfortable beds, all the latest journals and newspapers in a lounge of absolute silence, a central location within the city, and a general air of quiet, competent privacy.

A cousin of Graham's managed the hotel, and

once or twice had permitted them to hire a small side room off the entryway—which had its own door—to conduct this kind of meeting.

The advertisement brought, as such placements always would, at least fifteen or so variably cunning swindlers, who had clearly never heard of the 449, much less ridden it. But all of them were prepared to swear in a court of law to whatever Graham and Lenox wished. After brief conversations, Lenox and Graham discharged these fellows with half a shilling, a sum at which Graham frowned but which Lenox viewed as a tax, justly to be paid, for the imposition he had made upon the world by being born into a sphere of affluence he had himself done nothing to achieve.

There were another four or five men who were simply nosy about the murder, having connected the ad to the train number; they were turned away curtly.

Amazingly, however, two of the visitors actually seemed to be of some use.

The first was there before Lenox. Graham said he had been waiting at the door at ten till the hour, and when the detective arrived he was seated at a small table in the interview room, eating a plate of eggs doused in red onion and tomato ketchup. He was a lean, hollow-faced, ashen fellow.

"Good morning," said Lenox. "What is your name?"

"Walter Swain, sir. My ticket, sir. I'm glad I

kept it, sir—didn't think I had, don't know why I did, but there you are, I'm glad I did."

Lenox examined this ticket, which showed that Swain had traveled third class between Tamworth and Nuneaton. Lenox asked him what his reason for doing so had been. He'd been in search of work, was the reply. He had heard there were field jobs there. In October? Yes, apple picking. He did hops in the spring, whatever paid best in summer, and managed as he could in winter. Lenox inquired what had resulted from the journey. Swain said he had returned the next morning, disappointed—walking much of the way between Nuneaton and London, though he had been able to ride partways on the outside box of a carriage with a kind owner.

Though he had been on the train but briefly, Swain swore that he had seen the victim, whom Graham had described to him.

"It makes no difference to the reward if you did not," Lenox said gently.

"I did though," Swain said, soft cap in his sooty hands.

"Was he with anyone?"

"Alone."

They showed him the sketch of the man they believed to be the murderer. He hadn't seen this person, and to his credit was quick to say so.

"Was the carriage fairly empty, then?" asked Lenox.

"Only four or five of us, sir—uncommon empty."

"Did you speak to the man you saw, the victim?"

"No, sir. I didn't speak to anyone."

"Can you remember anyone else who was in the carriage?"

"Their faces, sir, but nought else."

"I've taken descriptions of them, sir," said Graham.

"Thank you. Did you see anyone at all speak to the victim, Mr. Swain? What was he doing?"

"I did not, sir. As I recall he was asleep some of the ways. When I fetched off at Nuneaton I had to pass him, and he said, 'Excuse me,' uncommon polite."

"Did he have an accent?"

"An accent, sir? Of what sort?"

"Any sort at all—northern, southern?"

The man frowned. He looked so painfully desirous of being helpful that Lenox was again concerned he might dissemble, but in the end he said apologetically, "No, sir, no accent. It was just the two words, sir."

Lenox asked Swain a few more questions. At the end of the exchange he asked where Swain was from. From? Nowhere, Swain said; or rather, nowhere at the moment. He had heard there was work in some of the port cities.

Lenox gave him two pounds. It was a large

sum, as good as a month of apple picking. Swain was grateful, but for some reason he didn't appear inclined to leave, despite there being a line at the door.

"His breakfast, sir," Graham said quietly.

Lenox glanced at it, half-eaten. "Oh! How inconsiderate of me. Swain, please remain and eat—you may take it into the next room—and they will pack you up some sandwiches for your midday meal, too, if you don't object."

"Ah! Thank you, sir! It does make a difference to a chap."

So they knew their victim had been traveling alone. That told them something about the murderer.

The other person who had actually ridden the 449 was in almost every respect the opposite of Walter Swain. He looked to be somewhere between forty-five and fifty-five, with a substantial light gray overcoat, fine leather gloves, a gleaming black top hat, and a fresh haircut and shave. Indeed, he might have been one of the out-of-towners staying at the Saltire on city business. He arrived on the stroke of eleven o'clock.

Lenox and Graham had planned to remain here until eleven thirty—someone always arrived late—but the gentleman, in a bit of haste, said he was glad he had made it on time. They stood up and introduced themselves, and he said he was called Alfred Baxendale.

"Thank you very much for coming, Mr. Baxendale," said Lenox, sitting. "Please have a seat. You were on the 449?"

"I was, sir. I only saw your advertisement twenty minutes ago, and I wouldn't have come if I hadn't also seen in the papers that there was a death aboard the very train I rode. Remarkable thing. Are you from the police?"

"We are," said Lenox. He was not quite lying, though he was bending the truth.

"Then I am glad I came," Baxendale replied. "Here is my ticket. I am prepared to be of whatever use I can."

The gentleman presented them with a second-class ticket for what was indeed the correct train. He had traveled the whole route, he said, from Manchester to Paddington.

"May I ask what brought you to London?" said Lenox.

"I work for a shipping agency in Manchester. I come here every six weeks as part of my duties and stay for three or four days. I am at the Mancunian Club. You may inquire about me there if you wish. They know me."

"You are native to Manchester, then."

"Since Roman times, or at least my grandmother always said, sir."

"Did you notice anything strange on this trip?" asked Lenox.

"No, sir."

"Did you recognize the conductor? Did you speak with him?"

"I didn't recognize him, no. They vary. Nor did I speak with him, except to show my ticket. He thanked me when he took it and put it in his pouch. That is all I recall."

"He was a young man with dark hair?"

Baxendale looked surprised. "No, an older one, with spectacles—perhaps ten or so years older than myself. I am forty-eight."

Norman Haase. "And the other passengers? No peculiarities? Nobody noticeable?"

Baxendale had been fiddling with his pipe, and now he looked up, face screwed tight in thought; but he had to conclude that alas, nothing of note had taken place aboard the train that *he* had seen.

Lenox read the two descriptions they had. "Do either of these men sound familiar?"

"Not in particular. They are generic descriptions."

Lenox was just beginning to despair of this very useful-seeming person being any use when Graham said, "Did you notice the conductor when you left the train, sir? Or anything at all that you would not have seen on your normal travels?"

Then Baxendale brightened. "Ah! Since you mention it, I did."

"What was that, sir?"

"There is generally a newsboy on the platform

upon the train's arrival, with papers and his other wares all laid out. He's got a good way about him. Never pushing, seems to work hard. I cannot recall his name, if indeed I ever heard it—but I always did buy an evening paper from him. To read with my supper. There's a tavern I like just down Praed Street, the Bull."

"Close to the station?"

"Yes, exactly. On Tuesday, I looked for the lad, but he wasn't there. It was no great matter. I read an afternoon edition." The London papers appeared three or sometimes as often as four times a day, depending on the importance of the news. "But I did remark his absence."

"And can you recall anything else about the trip, sir?" said Lenox.

Baxendale shook his head. "I'm sorry to say that I cannot. It was an average journey by train."

"Of course. Thank you so much for taking the trouble to come. May we offer you remuneration?" asked Lenox.

"I would feel wrong to take it in exchange for so little help," said Baxendale. He produced a card. "But if you are ever in a way to put custom in my direction, I would, of course, be grateful."

Baxendale nodded politely to them as he left, pipe between his teeth. Lenox noticed that he had on stockings not unlike Edmund's of the evening before, this Manchester burgher. He supposed it was a vogue.

Graham and Lenox sat for some time, discussing the case and waiting for any last respondents to the advertisement.

Only as they were packing up did something strike Lenox.

He stopped in place, the papers he had been sorting forgotten in his hands. "Graham!" he said.

"Sir?" said the valet, cautiously.

"Did you notice Baxendale's stockings?"

"Stockings, sir?"

Lenox shuffled the papers together hastily and put them in his valise. "Come, we must go to Savile Row—come on this instant. He was *American,* Graham. The murder victim, he was American."

CHAPTER TEN

"To Hawkes's, please," Lenox called up to the cab driver as he and Graham clambered inside. "As quickly as possible."

They were bound for a shop of particular distinction. In 1771, a young tailor's journeyman named Thomas Hawkes started a tiny business as a capmaker in Brewer Street. His specialty was velvet hats. They were good; he quickly earned a reputation for quality among military officers. After he had been in business for around fifteen years, that reputation was so high that King George III, a steadfast friend of the army, had made a special trip to the shop to order a cap.

Hawkes made it and sent it to the King—who, true to his reputation for being slightly mad (later more than slightly), accepted the cap, said no more of it, and then, one day, wandered in off the streets and ordered something on the order of five thousand scarlet military uniforms.

That made Hawkes's career. By the time the century turned, his small hat business had become the foremost tailor's in Great Britain. He received a Royal Warrant, and though he had begun to make suits and coats of all variety, he had also gone on making hats. Indeed, it had been he who designed the shako—a hardened leather hat that could withstand saber cuts, to the relief of many a chap who, like Deere, encountered the occasional saber.

Hawkes himself had been Charles and Edmund Lenox's own first tailor. At the age of five, each had stood solemnly before his mirrors as the diminutive, watery-eyed old man walked carefully around them, a bit of soapstone in hand to mark the cloth, a tape measure over his shoulder. He never spoke a word. Still, in due course, each received his first complete suit of clothes: jackets down to the knee, top hats up to the sky.

Hawkes was gone now (his nephews ran the business), but Lenox had never had a suit from anywhere but his shop. He went twice a year, and Graham was often in and out of their storefront on Piccadilly—Hawkes's was part of Savile Row only in the notional, not literal, sense—to have something mended or replaced.

"American, sir?" said Graham as they settled into the hansom.

"If I'm right," said Lenox, "that is why it would have been essential to remove all evidence of the origin of his clothing. He is probably from, oh, Boston, say, or New Haven, or—what are the other ones?"

"I believe Portland, Maine, is rather prominent, sir."

"Portland, Maine? Are you sure?"

Graham frowned. "There was a riot there because they banned alcohol, sir. The Portland Rum Riot, it was called in the newspapers."

"Hm."

"Philadelphia is also very famous, I believe."

Lenox waved a hand. "Wherever it was, listen. He was wearing a sack coat, do you remember me telling you that?"

"No, sir."

"Perhaps I didn't, then. But it's surprising, is it not? A fellow in third class?"

Men's fashions in England were achingly slow to change. Among the upper and middle classes, the frock coat—which tapered from broad in the shoulder to narrow at the knee—was universal. In the lower classes, men usually wore only a vest, clothing being very expensive; a vest was what Swain had been wearing.

"I have only seen a few people wearing these sack coats in London, you know, and only in the last few months. But it came from America— from New York, Washington Square, they say. It has been prominent there for a decade or so. Does that not strike you, Graham?"

"I suppose so, sir?"

That meant no. Lenox put up a finger. "That is the second bit. He was wearing socks. I certainly told you that. Not stockings—socks. I would lay you ten shillings—no, ten *dollars,* that he is American. It is warmer there. Their trousers are looser, and they wear socks rather than stockings."

They arrived at Hawkes's. They entered the impressive brick building, and Lenox felt the familiar hush of the front room, with its deep red carpeting, its subdued rows of material hanging from brass hooks, its elegant line of hats. This room would always call his father to mind. There had never been a more conservative dresser than he, loyal to the end to the high standing collars of his youth in the 1790s.

"Mr. Lenox, sir," said a young man whom Lenox did not know; every tailor at Hawkes's had an eerie ability to identify all their clients by name, even after an absence of years or in some cases decades. "I'm afraid Mr. White is presently with His Grace, the Duke of Dorset."

White was Lenox's current tailor. "Does he have a moment to spare? You may tell Dorset it would be a favor to me."

It was rare to have a duke in your pocket—but in the course of a previous case, Lenox had earned Dorset's good opinion, and also his begrudging obligation.

"I shall inquire, sir," said the young man, bowing gracefully and leaving.

He returned a moment later with White, a small, cherubic fellow, always in motion. "Mr. Lenox!" he cried, as if he had never been more delighted. Indeed, perhaps his secret was that he truly did feel such delight in each of his customers. "We just had you in!"

"I know! I only had a question—a very quick question. It is this: If you saw a man in a sack coat in the third-class compartment of a train from Manchester to London, what would you think?"

White frowned. After a moment, he said, "Either that he was in the wrong carriage, or that he came from America."

"Ha!" Lenox said, turning to Graham. "And if he were wearing socks?"

"Oh, certainly American. Do you agree, March?"

He had turned to the young man. "Unquestionably, Mr. White," said March with spotless deference.

Lenox slapped his hat against his hand excitedly. "Perfect. Thank you, Mr. White. Thank you, Mr. March."

"Careful banging that hat!" called White, as Lenox departed.

"Apologies! Thank Dorset for me!"

He and Graham hailed a cab. A handsome old bay mare was pulling it, and Lenox absentmindedly massaged the animal's neck with his hand as he directed the driver to Hampden Lane. They got in and were soon on their way.

Why would a young American have been traveling from Manchester to London? The reason might be anything at all, obviously—family, business, pleasure. Still, it was just a bit odd. Most Americans who went anywhere in northern England went to Liverpool, since Liverpool was a port city. Manchester lay about forty-five miles inland of it. Not an inconsiderable journey.

Lenox looked out through the window of the cab, searching his memories of the scene of the crime for anything else he had missed, anything else on the body that told a story. He wished now that he had taken more time.

"A productive morning, sir," Graham said.

Lenox shook his head. "Yes, but I should have seen it sooner. It was there right in front of me— the coat, the missing labels. Now I'm sure I must have missed other clues. But the scene of the crime is gone. The train is probably in—who knows, Bristol, Plymouth."

"Could you inquire, sir?"

"No. It will have been in use these three days fully. The body was removed that night and the train thoroughly cleaned."

He reflected that it was a lesson to take more time at the initial scene of a crime, however thorough he thought he might have been. Ah, well—no mistake was wasted if one learned from it.

His career thus far—could he call it a career?— had been a balance of triumphs and failures. He was proud of the assistance he had lent Scotland

Yard in the case of the Thames Ophelia. And the two small cases he had now, one a burglary in Wisden, the other a missing husband in Covent Garden, neither very difficult to parse, were a good sign, steady work.

But he longed for more. What, exactly? He searched his feelings as the cab rolled across the cobblestones of the city, smoke rising in untidy columns from the rooftops upon this cool midday.

For this kind of case, perhaps. He had been too proud to join the Yard even when invited to do so. His courage went so far as to pursue this eccentricity, but not so far as to do it professionally, which would have damned him conclusively in the eyes of his class. Pure cowardice, really.

But he wished as well that he were *better* at this thing, whatever it was. He had seen the sack coat on the murder victim, it had passed through his mind that this was the fashion he knew of from Manhattan, yet he had allowed the fact to work itself off of his line and swim away, disappearing for the last seventy-two hours . . .

On the other hand, he now had a few new facts to work with. The victim was American. For most of the train ride, if Swain was correct, he had not been in company with his murderer— if indeed the false conductor was his murderer, which seemed overwhelmingly likely, at least to

Lenox. That meant that this had been a plotted crime, full of care and deliberation.

A boy who usually sold papers had not been on the platform. He might have been sick, or out of papers. Still, it was a small wrinkle in the story of the evening. Anything that stood out like that might matter.

By and large, life had come easily to Lenox. He had always been a fair student, excellent in the areas that prompted his interest. He had friends who loved him, family, a comfortable life.

But it was inadequate to congratulate himself on that fact—indeed, dangerous. He had been raised to the idea of serving his fellow human beings. This arena might be an unusual one in which to do it, but nonetheless, he must do it better, become more detailed and more diligent than he had ever been before. Even as they neared Hampden Lane, the man with the longish dark hair might be preparing, for reasons Lenox was no closer to knowing than he had been before he first went to Paddington, to commit murder again.

CHAPTER ELEVEN

It was early afternoon when they returned home. Armed with their new information, Graham and Lenox composed another advertisement for the papers:

> ### *Information sought*
> Any person who knows the identity of a missing American male aged between 18 and 35, fair-haired, dressed in dark sack coat and gray trousers, expected in London, possibly having recently been in Liverpool or Manchester, is asked to respond by mail to this newspaper, c/o Mr. C. Edmundson. Information leading to correct identification rewarded with £5 sterling.

Five pounds was enough to catch the eye. The ad would appear among the requests about "the young lady, with a most comely brow, espied upon the omnibus near Shoreditch yesterday morning at 8:12" and the "business opportunity for an enterprising young man willing to live in Stowe" that filled the pages of every paper, every day, and which all Londoners seemed to read through top to bottom, regardless of whether they had comely brows or were willing to live in Stowe.

As for the newspapers, they would forward all mail for C. Edmundson to Lenox's house; in such a broad search for information, it was not practical to sit at the Saltire all day. The pool of people who could have been on the 449 from Manchester had been much smaller.

Graham went to place the ad. Lenox ate lunch in his study, a roll of bread with cheddar and a cup of hot, sweet tea, which he refilled liberally. When he was finished, he called for his carriage and directed Elliott to drive to Paddington Station.

It looked radically different in the middle of the day than it had at night. At the Great Western, streams of men were going in and out upon business, attired in the invincible invisibility of the city suit, canes and newspapers and valises under their arms. Each no doubt with a mind full of important plans.

As for the station: Every stripe of society moved beneath its sturdy brick face. There were fine carriages, vagrants, stockbrokers, businessmen. Young women who looked like parsons' daughters and young women who looked like parsons' nightmares.

Lenox put his head down and ventured into this crowd. He stopped just inside, at the small structure with STATIONMASTER upon the frosted glass of its window. There were train schedules in chalk on a blackboard next to it.

"Sir?" said a portly chap sitting behind the window, in the same red hard-brimmed hat that Joseph Beauregard Stanley had been wearing on the night of the murder.

"Good afternoon," Lenox said. "I am part of the team investigating the 449."

"A journalist? Gone with yourself."

"No—Scotland Yard." Lenox produced the note Sir Richard had written out for him on his commissioner's stationery. "I was here on the evening of the murder. I met Mr. Stanley."

The stationmaster took the note, studied it, and then, pushing his lips out in a look of surprise, nodded his assent. "I see. I'm Smythe. How may I help you?"

At that moment a nervous elderly voice cried, from behind Lenox, "How in heavens is one meant to find the Newcastle train!"

Lenox turned and saw a man shaking a walking stick at the stationmaster. There were signs in virtually every direction that said NEWCASTLE, PLATFORM 1, but the stationmaster patiently repeated the information for the old man. He showed no appreciation, unless you counted leaving; which Lenox did.

"There is a lad who sells newspapers to the passengers of the 449," Lenox said when they were again alone.

"Willikens," said the stationmaster.

Lenox was surprised. "You know him quite well."

"Yes, Willikens is here every day. For all I know Brunel installed the boy himself."

"Where might I find him?"

"From twelve noon until ten each evening, here. Otherwise, I have no idea."

Lenox glanced at his watch. "It is just two."

"Then I would check Platform 1—a busy hour there. Follow the gentleman going to Newcastle."

Lenox smiled. "Thank you, Mr. Smythe."

"You'll spot Willikens easily enough. He only has one coat, and it's a horror."

Lenox followed the signs to Platform 1, wondering how bad a coat could be. When he arrived, he saw. A small boy with a handcart went among the customers, offering copies of the *Times* and the *Noon Caller*. He also had a small row of pouches of tobacco for sale, though there were plenty of stands near the stationmaster that sold every variety of tobacco, pipe, cigar, and so forth. In case of last-second emergencies, perhaps. Regardless, he was unmissable: He wore a mustard-colored wool coat, out at the elbows, with a broad green windowpane pattern. It was a dozen sizes too large. He had rolled the sleeves up but they ballooned around his arms.

"Willikens?" said Lenox.

The boy turned quickly—very quick, London

quick—and looked at the detective suspiciously. "What?"

"I was hoping to have a word with you about train 449. I am with Scotland Yard."

"I'm allowed to sell papers here," said the boy.

"Oh, yes—no question of that. Here." Lenox gave him sixpence. "I'll take one, in fact, to show you."

"Which?"

Lenox had read them all, so he chose the least expensive and said to keep the change. It was the wrong move; the boy pocketed the coin and gave Lenox his paper, but his suspicion seemed to have intensified. Well, hopefully such wariness kept him alive and unharmed. He was terribly skinny.

"I only want two minutes," Lenox said. "Is it a good time?"

"This is the *worst* time."

Willikens gestured up and down the platform, and Lenox saw what he meant. He glanced at the station's clock. "Will you be free when the Newcastle train leaves?"

"For a bit."

So Lenox waited, rereading the paper, until they could reconnoiter about fifteen minutes later, just outside the cloakroom.

"How did you fare?" Lenox asked the boy, whom he had watched selling papers. He was quite good, ubiquitous but not pressing or impertinent.

"Average," said the boy, who then, to Lenox's surprise, took out a packet of shag tobacco, tore off a bit of an interior page of the *Daily Telegraph*, and rolled himself a cigarette. He couldn't have been more than ten. "Do you have a match?"

Lenox had a box of them and handed it over. "I understand from speaking to a Mr. Baxendale you were not on the platform when the 449 came in from Manchester Tuesday night. But you usually are."

The boy nodded. "That's right. I know Baxendale."

"Why weren't you there?"

"Out of papers."

Lenox felt a quick disappointment. "I see. So you went home." The boy just looked at him, and Lenox realized that he might not have a home—at least, not as the word was commonly understood. "Are your parents in the business, too?"

The boy picked a piece of tobacco off of his sleeve with expert care. "Never knew 'em, never cared to."

"Who looked after you when you were younger?" Lenox asked—he couldn't help himself.

"Not a gent you'd care to know," said Willikens. "But that was in Winchester."

Everywhere he went were stories, Lenox thought, each of them individual, complex, and every last one of them worthy of a careful and caring listener. Because of this a certain hopelessness sometimes overcame him; he wondered now, as he occasionally did, if he had been misguided, if he ought to be in politics, for instance. It was a path he'd considered.

"You simply ran out of papers?" was all he said, however.

"Oh, no."

"What do you mean?" asked Lenox.

The boy eyed him levelly. "What's it to you?"

"As I said, I'm with Scotland Yard."

"No, you're not."

"Excuse me?"

"I said, no, you're not. I see a fair few types of gentlemen on the platform. You ain't from Scotland Yard."

"Well, no, I work with them," Lenox replied, impressed. "Listen, I mean you no harm."

"Would you care for another paper?"

Lenox dug into his pocket and found all the coins there—a few shillings, a farthing, two halfpennies, a few pennies, and a shining crown, a very great deal of money. He deposited all of it on top of Willikens's handcart as the boy looked on, only briefly wide-eyed before the coins vanished into the pocket of the green jacket.

"What happened as to the 449 was, a fellow came and bought all the papers," he said.

"A fellow?"

"Tall chap, older, gray hair and gray mustache, bowler hat, dressed middling."

This was interesting. "A bowler hat. So a working type?"

"I suppose so."

"And he just bought all the papers without explanation? How soon before the train arrived?"

"Thirty minutes."

"How many papers?"

"Twenty-five. All my tobacco, too."

This was very definitely interesting. It hinted at an accomplice: someone clearing the way of witnesses for the murderer. "Is there any other description you could offer of him?"

Willikens frowned and took a pull from his hand-rolled cigar. "It was dark. I didn't see much of him." Lenox waited. "Nice teeth. Didn't smell."

"I see."

"Oh," the boy said, "and he talked odd. Not like us. He tried to talk normal, but he was shamming it."

"Shamming it?"

"Yes. You could tell he was American, this gent."

CHAPTER TWELVE

The men handling the Murder at Paddington Station—as the papers had decided, in a rare piece of unanimity, to call the case—regrouped at Scotland Yard at five o'clock.

Lenox was looking forward to sharing his information, but as it happened the canvass of local witnesses that Dunn had supervised had actually produced a scrap of evidence. A porter at the Great Western hotel had seen a man with longish dark hair depart the station at around midnight on a bright white mare. He had worn a frock coat, just as the faux conductor of the 449 had—though, to be fair, hundreds of thousands of men in London also did.

The porter had noticed the rider for two reasons, according to Dunn's interview: first, because it had still been pelting rain; second, because it was rarer and rarer these days to see a man on horseback within London town, and he had ridden well and fast. The porter was from Shropshire and had particularly noted the man's comfort in the saddle.

"What does it tell us?" asked Sir Richard.

He looked exhausted. There had been a string of knifepoint robberies in Pall Mall over the past few days, and most of his attention—and the journalists'—was set upon that.

"Perhaps that the murderer is from the country," Dunn ventured. "Not many Londoners ride well. Also that he didn't want to take a cab—be remembered by a cabman."

Dunn was sharp, Lenox realized. He was also arrogant. He had taken the seat exactly opposite Mayne, implying, with his body language, that it was a meeting between the two of them, merely to be audited by his subordinate at the Yard and the upstart crow of an amateur.

"More than anything," said Lenox firmly, "it means that he was *prepared*. He had made plans earlier in the day to escape from Paddington. A horse would have given him good maneuverability and speed. What's more, he must have had an accomplice, since the horse was waiting for him."

"He might have stabled it at Paddington and then gone north to find his victim," said Dunn.

"But that would have involved far more witnesses than hiring a hansom cab," said Lenox. "I also have a bit of new information to add on this point."

He then told the men present—including the railway official, still nameless to them—what he had deduced from the sack coat and socks, and what he had learned from Willikens about the man with the white hair and the American accent.

A satisfying silence came over the room.

"You've been busy," said Mayne.

"These Americans," said Hemstock. His voice was surprisingly bitter. "What are they messing about in London for? They should stick over to their side. They wanted it certain enough to bloody our noses for it twice."

Lenox remembered—from a dropped word at the pub, early in their acquaintance—that Hemstock's older brother had died in the War of 1812, near the city of New Orleans.

"With respect to that, it struck me as curious that our victim was coming from Manchester rather than Liverpool," Lenox said. "I should imagine ten thousand Americans see Liverpool every year, and not a tenth of that number Manchester."

"Then what could he have been doing there?"

"Anything you care to imagine," said Dunn. "It doesn't matter a whit where he was if we don't know who he was. Perhaps he was doing a Navajo dance in the middle of Cheetham Hill Road. Perhaps he was handing out flyers for Franklin Pierce. Perhaps—"

"Who is Franklin Pierce?" asked Hemstock.

Dunn looked at Hemstock as if he were too stupid to be ambulatory. "The president of the country across that big watery bit to our west right now."

"Oh."

"My point," Dunn said, "is that we have no idea why an American was in Manchester, so it's a fact of minimal use to us at the moment."

There was some truth to this, but Lenox said that he had nevertheless ordered the last week's papers from Manchester—just in case. They ought to be waiting for him at home.

"You've done well," said Mayne. "But still I cannot see that we are very close to solving the murder. What do you propose to do next?"

"I am going to visit the American consulate in the morning." Even to Lenox's own ears this sounded rather uninspired, so he added, "I am hoping they have been expecting a visitor to London who has not arrived. Many Americans write ahead to inform their government that they shall be in the city."

"Not ones who ride in the third-class carriage and come in from the blasted bloody north," said Dunn.

He was right, unfortunately.

"I suppose it's worth a try," said Mayne.

Lenox hadn't wanted to tell them about the advertisement asking about missing Americans in London, in case it proved fruitless.

But he told them now. Mayne responded with more enthusiasm than he had expected—the Yard was apparently loath to place ads, but Mayne thought they were often effective. He added that of course Lenox would have to sort the wheat from the chaff.

"Of course, sir. I have the time," Lenox said.

Sir Richard nodded. "Very well. All speed

please, gentlemen. Haase's family is in great distress. Two of his daughters visited me themselves—fine girls, graceful and elegant manners—both engaged—I felt obliged to see 'em, but it was damned awkward not to be able to give them any hope." He shook his head. "A white horse. There can only be a million or so in the country."

Lenox walked back home through St. James's Park in a contemplative mood. The rains had left it a lovely emerald-green color that was rare to see so late in the year, the limbs of the trees just whispering in the cool early evening wind.

At home, Lady Jane was waiting in his study. She sat in a white dress covered in small purple flowers, flipping through a handsomely illustrated catalogue from Tattersall's, the horse auctioneer.

"Are you planning to buy a horse?" she asked as Lenox came in, tossing his hat toward his desk and missing.

"No. I would buy the name of an American if you're selling one."

"George Washington. That will be one shilling."

"He was British."

She frowned. "I imagine he would take issue with that, but as you like—Samuel F. B. Morse. He sent the first telegram."

"Yes, I know he did, damn him. It's the name of a specific American I'm after."

She closed the catalogue and looked at him. "Paddington, is it?"

He had gone to the small mirror-topped liquor cart near the window and poured a bit of brandy into a glass. For Lady Jane's part, she had been sumptuously provided with toasted teacakes and jam by Mrs. Huggins. He sat down.

"Paddington," he said, nodding. "By the way, I'm awfully happy that Deere will be here for a spell."

"So am I. And I have exactly the thing to cheer you up, Charles."

"Jane, I cannot get married tonight."

"It wouldn't be tonight."

"It's an extremely inconvenient time."

"Even you must eat supper! And she's different, Charles. I spoke with her at length this afternoon, and she's lovely."

"Like Mary Elizabeth Sharples?"

This was the giantess from Lady Sattle's, who was so in love with old Blake, bless her. "She is not like Mary Sharples."

"No? What a relief."

"I'm not too proud to admit that I may have erred regarding Miss Sharples. There. Now will you come?"

He slumped down a little lower in his armchair. It had been getting quite cold outside as six passed, and the warmth of the fire and the brandy had brought a stinging into his cheeks. "Answer me sincerely—please. Is there some reason for this concerted effort to get me a wife?"

Lady Jane just looked at him. He had a strong affection for the frank, level gaze she cast upon him in moments like this, as if she cared too much for him to be honest.

"There is, actually. Your mother is anxious," she said. "She passed the word to me. Perhaps to one or two of her friends as well. Subtly, I promise—at least in my case."

Lenox was astonished. "My mother! Can she really be the cause of such a stir? Why is it even on her mind?"

"You're twenty-seven."

"Yes, I know, right on death's door. But what does it matter to her if I'm married now or at twenty-nine? I shall still have a full year of life left then."

Jane shook her head. "Perhaps it's your career, Charles."

"My career?"

Jane looked upset, as if it were hard to be as delicate as she would like. "I don't know. Yes. Either concern that it has precluded you from the right match, or . . . or hope that a marriage would stop you from risking your life." She hesitated. "To be perfectly honest, Charles, I think she hopes that a wife will make you give it up."

Despite thinking he was immune to this

criticism, Lenox found himself going bright red—he could feel it.

"Does she?" he said, in a voice trying too hard to be indifferent.

"She has already lost your father. If—"

"I understand, Jane," he said, sharply.

She paused. "I would like to see you happy, too," she said.

"I am happy enough, I think. My life is very full." He thought of *Pride and Prejudice* and said, "I dine with four-and-twenty families—at least, at least."

She smiled at that. "But it would be infinitely easier on me to plan dinner parties if you were paired."

"Ah!" He took a sip of his tea. "That is a sensible argument. The first one I've yet heard."

"She really is different, Charles—Kitty Ashbrook."

Lenox tried to remember if he'd heard the name. "Ashbrook?"

"She is the Marquess of Doulton's great-niece. Her father was in the navy, I believe. She has ten thousand pounds, and very pretty eyes, and she dresses better than nearly anyone I know. You know I do not say that lightly."

"I'm only offended that you're holding back from me the women who dress themselves better still than Kitty Ashbrook."

"They're married. Or perhaps they don't

exist. She really does, I mean it—as if she were Parisian." This was the highest compliment one woman in London could pay another's sense of dress, during this particular moment of the city's history. "Listen, there's supper and dancing at Martha Quentin's tonight. Will you come? It is quite open to you, I know—I saw her earlier. James and I would be so happy of your company."

Lenox looked at his watch. "What was her name?"

"Catherine Ashbrook. Kitty."

He could feel his notes in his breast pocket. The thought of sitting here with them in the gloaming seemed suddenly a little hard to bear, however.

"Very well, " he said. "Give me a moment to change."

"Oh, good! We'll go shares on a ride over—let me go tell James. You'll like her, I promise."

"My hope is that I will love the woman I marry."

Lady Jane laughed. "You'll love her, then—just come, and you'll fall in love."

"There's no chance I fall in love with Miss Catherine Ashbrook, Jane. I pledge that to you here and now. Make a note of it somewhere."

CHAPTER THIRTEEN

The English language possessed a small but substantial group of words, descended from medieval days, which had, in the course of being rubbed with use over the centuries—like a silver coin changing hands for the thousandth time—gained or added an *N.* The select few people who called Charles Lenox *Charlie,* for example, would have been, to a medieval person, employing his little, or *eke,* name—but time had transformed the words *an eke name* into *a nickname.* Conversely, the word that was a synonym for a snake had once been *a nadder* and was now *an adder; a napron* had become *an apron;* and as late as Shakespeare's time, *an uncle* had been *a nuncle.*

That last word still just floated in the language of the city, and Sir Crispin Quentin was (in Lenox's mind anyhow), by virtue of his gentle, old-fashioned manner and ever-present smile, the truest example of that breed—a nuncle. And his wife, Lady Martha, thereby a naunt.

They had met later in life, Sir Crispin and Lady Martha Quentin, each well past the age of fifty. They were almost identical to look at: thin, red, and, but for the fact that they were always beaming, not especially attractive. They had in all other ways besides appearance been hopelessly mismatched. He was a successful merchant, born to a butcher, while she was a spinster who happened to be the daughter of one of the most powerful men in the land—the Duke of Northumberland.

It had been a pairing made by love. As a consequence, perhaps, they were always at the greatest pains to encourage in others the happiness that they had found, against every odd, in each other—for by class they should never even have met, and once they had, her father might still have forbidden her the match. The very "Sir" in his name was an embarrassment to her bloodlines: a knighthood won from the Queen for selling hemp in industrial quantities and then funding a scholarship for orphans to attend one of the city schools, Westminster, and later, if they passed the entrance exams, a university of their choice. Next to the Dukedom of Northumberland itself, not large potatoes.

But the Quentins were beloved; for who could not love two people so full of love themselves, humble before its mysterious and surprising grandeur. Their house was (by baronial standards) relatively modest, yet all of London met there, including members of the royal family—and including, at least that evening, Lady Jane, Lord Deere, and Charles Lenox.

The Quentins decorated in the new style. It

was Victoria and her admirers who had spread it—a sort of prodigious clutter, walls and tables crowded past elegance, every piece of cloth in the room double- or triple-embroidered, little remnants of statuary, wretchedly heavy silver platters and ewers, big dark clocks, etchings of colossal ruins. The spare black-and-ivory elegance of Lenox's childhood was gone now—submerged beneath a rockslide of things, objects.

Sir Crispin and Lady Martha themselves might have been decorated by the same hand. He wore broadcloth trousers with a soft velvet coat of bottle green, she a gown with a wide crinoline and a recession of ruffles from waist to high neck that must have required ten times more material than the average dress.

"Edmund's stockings would look very subdued here," Charles murmured to Lady Jane, as Deere greeted their jolly hosts.

"You're so old-fashioned, Charles," replied Lady Jane.

"That's a slander, and I'll tell you why—I ordered a sack coat at my tailor's last month."

"Did you!"

"I didn't want to," he admitted, "but I did."

"That will look very handsome at the races next spring. Very American."

Lenox threw up his hands—everyone else on the face of the earth would have spotted the victim on the 449 as an American before he, apparently—but Jane, busy taking her shawl from her shoulders, didn't notice.

"Charles Lenox!" said Sir Crispin, striding forward with his hand out. "How pleased the young ladies will be that another dancing partner has arrived!"

Lenox smiled. He loved Sir Crispin—he had no starch in him, the old chap, would reminisce at the drop of a hat about childhood days in the butcher's shop. "How pleased I am to be here, sir. I thank you for having me."

The party was an admirable one. In all, there must have been forty people there, but one never felt jostled or hemmed in. A small room had been cleared for dancing, with a string trio in one corner. There was a different small room for socialization and food and drink—a division of which Lady Jane (who knew about these things) voiced her approval.

By ten o'clock, Lenox was sure that he had won a small victory over his friend, because the woman he was meant to meet, Kitty Ashbrook, had not appeared.

Then, though, just after the hour, she arrived, in the company of her mother, and Lady Jane led her over to Lenox—casually, to her credit, with every semblance of the introduction coming as an accident.

He did like the way she looked—that much he admitted to himself immediately. She was small, with chestnut hair and skin slightly more tanned than fashionable, even white teeth, and a sweet, dimpled smile.

Nevertheless, he was prepared to be merely polite with her—and would have been, had he not, before he quite knew how it had happened, offered to dance with her.

How did Jane engineer these things so effortlessly? He couldn't even remember posing the question—but not five minutes after they'd met, Lenox and Kitty Ashbrook were moving onto the parquet floor together.

This floor was made in a lovely geometric pattern of blond wood, which picked up the click of every shoe. When they had clicked across the room and reached the end of the line of dancers, he held out a hand and she accepted it. They bowed to each other, the music struck up, and they danced.

Such dancing was always filled with small conversation. Miss Ashbrook began it. "You are a detective, Lady Deere said, Mr. Lenox?" she said as they made a turn.

"Ah! Yes. An amateur—like a rock collector, if you will. Or a curate who practices astronomy on Mondays."

She smiled. "So inept as that?"

"I hope not, but I fear so."

It was a rather antiquated dance—pleasantly antiquated, however, and they went through their paces, matching hands, twisting away from each other and back.

He had half forgotten the pleasure of dancing with a lovely woman, not because he hadn't done so, but because his pleasure in the act itself had vanished some time before. He hadn't even quite noticed its absence until now, to his surprise, it returned.

When they passed, she said, "I warn you that I cannot marry you, Mr. Lenox."

He burst into laughter, gently taking her hand as they spun toward each other. "It is the first preemptive rejection I have received, and I offer you my warm admiration for that. Very original. And why should you marry me, after all!"

She gave him a smile of appreciation and apology. "I must seem abrupt," she said.

"Oh, no—not at all." They circled another couple and then met face-to-face. "In fact, I suspect we are in the same position, Miss Ashbrook."

"Which one is that?"

He waited until they were close once more and said, "We are both the projects of well-meaning friends."

She laughed. They finished the dance in what Lenox thought was at least respectable—and on her part, indeed, graceful—fashion. Without speaking, they stood before each other, awaiting the recommencement of the music, and he felt a little thrill at this unexpressed agreement that they would dance again. It was by no means a given. Only the knowledge that his friends would be triumphant over the fact subdued the gratification of the feeling; and not all that much, if he were honest.

They danced a *varsouvienne*, and in their third song as a pair, a waltz, they took each other into a swift embrace, swift but to Lenox heady indeed. All the while they kept up a lively conversation. He discovered that Miss Ashbrook was uncommonly intelligent—she had read books and periodicals he didn't know existed, in French and Russian as well as English—but showed it without the laborious pride one found in so many widely read men and women.

She was most fond of the novel, she disclosed. Her favorite writers at the present moment were Mr. Fenimore Cooper and Monsieur Balzac, she said, but neither of them could touch Thackeray. She adored Sir Walter Scott. She had lately been in Cornwall, and thought it the most beautiful countryside she had ever seen—but wished, in her innermost heart, to see the distant islands of northern Scotland.

Lenox knew more about travel than fiction, and replied with some knowledge of both Cornwall and the Orkneys. He said that he, too, had longed to go there—one more delicate filament of connection between them.

Before Miss Ashbrook's arrival, Lenox had drunk two glasses of chilled champagne, and as he danced he knew he had a light head. The young lady smelled of lavender, and her hair as it swung near his face had the rich indescribable scent of—well, a woman who has been dancing. He might not marry her, he thought, but he was very happy to be dancing with her.

It might have gone on, but for an interruption. One of Sir Crispin's footmen came to say that a Mr. Graham was waiting on Lenox in the front hallway if it was convenient for him to step away.

Not particularly—but of course Lenox went, leaving Miss Ashbrook among friends, curious to see what news Graham had.

"Hello, Graham," he said when they met.

"I apologize for the intrusion, sir."

"Not at all. What is it? Nothing bad, I hope?"

"No, sir—no. But there is a gentleman who may have some information in response to our advertisement."

Lenox raised his eyebrows. "About the American? More than a guess?"

Graham nodded. "I believe it is, sir."

That was as good as a guarantee. "Give me a moment to get my coat."

CHAPTER FOURTEEN

Toward the back of the first story of Lenox's house, at the end of the front hall but before the dining room, was a small chamber that everyone called the smoking room. It was rarely used. It held an armchair, a card table, a *chaise longue*, and a smattering of books Lenox didn't need. To his knowledge nobody had once smoked in this room since his tenancy had begun. Still, a household thrives on regularity, so its name was its name, and it was dusted each day, and Mrs. Huggins, supervising Alice and Joanna, made sure there was coal in the grate, though it might go unlit for a year, and that the rug was beaten in spring and fall.

Now the coals were lit after all. Sitting by their warmth was a small, neat, handsome man of middle age, drinking tea and eating toast with salmon. It had been a wise decision on Graham's part to store him here; Lenox's study was too private a place for a stranger to wander freely in.

The man wore a knit sweater with a high collar. A farmer, Lenox would have said.

Wrongly. "This is Mr. Joseph Hazlitt, sir," Graham said. "He is a typesetter at the *Telegraph*. Mr. Hazlitt, this is my employer, Mr. Edmundson."

Lenox extended a hand. "How do you do, Mr. Hazlitt?"

"Oh, fine, thank you, sir," said the typesetter in a squeaky voice.

"You came about the ad?"

"Yes, sir." Hazlitt removed and carefully unfolded a small square of newsprint, like a mouse taking out its handkerchief. "I did have one question: Are employees of the newspaper where you placed this ad, sir, ineligible for the reward mentioned—mentioned therein, sir?"

"Not at all."

"Ah! Good. Excellent."

"Please, sit," Lenox said, doing so himself. "What information do you have, pray tell?"

Hazlitt hesitated, but then put his hand in the outer pocket of his sweater. "The job of a typesetter at a newspaper, as you know, sir, is to compose each page of the paper in metal sorts, by line, paragraph, and word, and place them in rows, which go into a large wooden case matching the size of a page of a newspaper."

"Is it! Actually I have never quite known how they managed that."

"Oh, yes, it's quite an art, sir. Some of the typesetters at the down-market papers—well, one line barely matches up to the next, you know. You've seen." He smiled shyly. "And if you see a *d* where a *p* should be, you can be sure a typesetter has been shouted down for putting the letter in wrong—for they look almost the same, you see, to us. That's why we tell each other—mind your *p*'s and *q*'s, sir. For a *q* could quite easily be a *b*."

"Did the *Telegraph* have an error?" said Lenox, trying to gently redirect his visitor. It was late. "Perhaps in the section you're holding?"

Hazlitt looked down, as if surprised to find the scrap. "Oh! This! No, no sir, Mr. Edmundson. It's only that it will appear in the paper tomorrow morning. I made a one-off, sir—for of course, it was I who set the ad *looking* for an American, and offering a reward, and—well, see for yourself."

Lenox took the treasured little scrap of paper from Hazlitt at last and read it to himself.

Information eagerly sought

As to the whereabouts of Mr. Eli Gilman, of Massachusetts, USA, but lately traveling in Liverpool, Manchester, Leeds. Mr. Gilman was due in London Tuesday evening but did not appear. He is 27, with light hair, casually attired. Anyone having seen or heard of him will receive a warm welcome at the Salted Herring, Three Colt St., between the hours of 5 and 7:30 tonight.

A chill ran through Lenox. Unless there was a sad fluke of fate at play, he now had possession of the name of the man who had been murdered aboard the 449 from Manchester. Eli Gilman. It was a significant step forward.

"This is extremely useful, Mr. Hazlitt. Do you know who submitted it?"

"I do not, sir."

"Would someone else at the paper?"

"No, it is all anonymous, sir—so that people feel free to put whatever sort they like, you see. No defamation, of course, or foul language, or oaths. Otherwise you may pay by the line and say whatever you wish, so long as your money is good."

"Of course," Lenox murmured. Then he asked, "May I keep this?"

Hazlitt looked anxiously at Graham, who said, "I'm sure Mr. Hazlitt would feel happy to leave it with you if he were to receive his reward."

"Oh! Of course. Graham, you know where my billfold is." Lenox stood up and flourished the small piece of paper. "This is going to be extremely useful in righting an injustice, Mr. Hazlitt. I will bid you good evening, since there is work I must do. Thank you."

Hazlitt stood up. "Pleasure, sir."

Lenox, on his way out of the room, stopped at the door. "May I ask something to satisfy my own curiosity, Mr. Hazlitt—was your father also a typesetter?"

"A farmer, sir."

120

"Ah! A very different occupation."

"I always had a way with machines, sir, so he sent me down to live with my cousin in Fleet Street."

Lenox smiled. "My father was from the country as well. Yet here we both are in London. Good evening, Mr. Hazlitt."

He went to his study and sat in his chair, listening to the dim creaks and cracks the house made as Graham paid Hazlitt his reward and saw him back into the late evening.

The piece of paper was on the table. He memorized it, then reclined, legs crossed, staring into the dusky gaslit emptiness of Hampden Lane. Chaffanbrass, the still relatively new bookseller across the lane, had forgotten to close his shutters again; he often did. He would pay for it with a broken glass storefront and a theft one of these days. But it hadn't happened tonight.

Eli Gilman of Massachusetts.

There was a malevolence in the world that Lenox brushed against in his job. From time to time he worried that it might brush him back. His thoughts went to the swing of Kitty Ashbrook's dark hair, her secretive smile. He could have been having a last dance with her at this moment; instead he sat alone, pondering murder.

In truth it had crushed him to hear that his mother hoped he would leave off being a detective. He'd thought she understood.

But enough, enough. He jumped up and took down several volumes he had of notable people. He didn't put much hope in them, since they included few Americans, and while it had been worth checking, after half an hour of perusal his initial pessimism was justified: The volumes contained nobody by the name of Eli Gilman, though he did discover in a biography of a Yorkshire bishop of the same name that there had been numerous settlers of that surname in the colony of New Hampshire during the 1600s and 1700s.

Graham knocked and, upon Lenox's call beckoning him inward, entered the study. "Good evening, sir."

"Hallo, Graham. Thank you for coming to fetch me at the party. Very well done. The only question is whether we can contrive to see the man who placed the ad sooner than five o'clock tomorrow evening. Do you know the Salted Herring?"

"No, sir."

"It's not far from Ropemaker's Lane. Tricky area. And the days are growing shorter. Not much sunlight left to protect us at five o'clock. It could be dangerous. They mostly serve a seafaring clientele there, as I recall. They do quite a decent fish pie."

"Indeed, sir."

Lenox smiled. "I can never seem to interest

you in the menus of our destinations. Do you *eat,* Graham?"

"We must have eaten together above a hundred times, sir, I should have said."

"Yet I always get the sense that you are doing so out of politeness. Tell me, what is your favorite meal?"

Graham had one hand on the chair across the desk from Lenox—it was late, an informal conversation—and he considered the question, taking his time. At last, he said, "My mother was half-Scottish, sir. She occasionally made what we called stovies. I remember them with great fondness."

"What are those?"

"Stovies? Sliced potatoes, sir, softened up, roasted with cracklings. That was a dish I looked forward to all week."

"We shall have to put Ellie on the job."

"I once asked her if she made them, sir—she said that every Scot was a miser and a drunk."

"Good Lord! I've known many who were only one or the other."

Graham laughed. "Have you, sir," he said mildly.

"Only joking, of course. I shall order it for my own supper from her tomorrow, and she may go looking for another job if she refuses me."

"You needn't go to the trouble on my behalf, sir, though I thank you. And bear in mind that you—perhaps we—shall be in East London."

"Ah!" said Lenox melancholically. "True. Eli Gilman. The following evening, then, it will be stovies or a new cook. Don't let me forget. Someone must take this household in hand."

CHAPTER FIFTEEN

Lenox spent the next morning gathering, assembling, and updating his notes. Meanwhile Graham was out in the city, searching for information on Eli Gilman. They had agreed to meet at the Salted Herring at four o'clock.

About an hour beforehand, Lenox set across town in an omnibus toward the wharves of the East End. He liked to ride the bus from time to time; enjoyed observing the people, on this afternoon including several women out for their shopping, a young clerk on some errand, and a pair of young Germans venturing out to see St. Paul's Church and, if Lenox's German was right, sketch it.

After about thirty minutes he got out at a stop along the river. He paused for a moment, lighting his pipe, then leaned on a stone rail above the Thames. How very full the world seemed, if you ever stayed still for a moment. The dull gray wash of the river lapped up onto the hulls of ships. The dockyards were busy with loading and unloading, resupplying, painting, everyone absorbed in his own work, bar the occasional whistle or chat.

There were innumerable disadvantages to such labor as theirs, but Lenox did think that it might be nice, once in a while, simply to fall without conscious thought into a routine of work. Mostly on days like this, when his thoughts spun round and round without anywhere to land.

For who had placed the advertisement? It hung on who Gilman had been—criminal, victim, or both. Was the ad designed to draw out Eli Gilman's accomplices? His friends? Or was it the sincere request of an acquaintance that had been expecting Gilman and taken recourse to the papers to find him when he hadn't arrived?

The more Lenox mulled it over, the less sure he felt. Eventually he turned and walked into the dim, low-slung alleyways of the city's poorest precincts, hoping that they would hold a satisfactory answer.

Three Colt Street was among the largest streets in the East End, a loud, crowded, dirty, jolly, winding boulevard. It didn't look or feel markedly different than it must have in Ben Jonson's time, when tavernkeepers kept the peace and knights brought their retinues here to carouse.

Lenox walked with his eyes up, constantly scanning the crowds. Most strangers here were similarly careful, he noticed. An air of imminent violence permeated the otherwise pleasant atmosphere, despite the good humor of the boys selling jellied eels and the woman sitting placidly beside a jar of cinnamon balls, *for,* as she cried, *a-sweet'nin' the breath.*

The Salted Herring stood upon a crowded street corner, occupying two floors of a large, attractive gray-and-white-striped building, with sheaves of grain on either side of its door to mark the season. Its sign showed a great whale leaping from the sea, a ship in the distance visible beneath the curl of its immense body.

Lenox went in. The bar faced the door, and in between were a dozen or so tables. There was a space cleared to the left-hand side of the bar to play darts, a popular pub game on this side of town, and Lenox's mind flashed to one of the indelible images of his boyhood nursery education: Henry the Eighth playing the same game with the delicately decorated set of darts that the whole court knew Anne Boleyn had made him—one of the first tangible signs that Queen Catherine's time as Henry's wife was drawing short.

A few people were dotted around the pub. Almost all of them appeared to be in some state of medical distress. Two sailors played cards, tired-eyed, as if they had been out late the night before, one with a badly bruised cheek and the other with an arm in a sling. An African, dressed nattily except for the blood-darkened bandage encircling his head, was at least well enough to sit in the corner sipping ale and reading a newspaper. (For acceptance of the races, the nautical world was unexcelled—their work would have been impossible without the mingling of nationalities.) At the end of the room, a man in a cloth hat looked merely hungover.

He had eyed the door nervously when it opened, and Lenox—dressed as inconspicuously as could be, in a tweed overcoat—gave him a single hard look to make sure he wasn't the conductor.

No, unfortunately.

Lenox went to the bar and ordered a whisky with ginger ale. The barkeeper, a retired sailor, pushed it across and gave Lenox a ha'penny back out of a penny.

Lenox sat down. He watched the gray-bearded but strong old man behind the bar wash glasses in a sudsy bucket. He had tattoos all over his skin. The previous summer Lenox had made a study of scars, burns, tattoos, and other markings, with the idea that they might be useful in a case someday. They hadn't been yet, but he was patient. This fellow had crossed cannons on one wiry forearm, which meant that he had served in the Queen's navy. A single anchor beneath it indicated that he had crossed the Pacific Ocean. And on the other forearm, six swallows, Lenox knew, each representing five thousand nautical miles of travel over the seas.

Across his knuckles, eight letters, an exhortation to anyone bearing a rope in a storm: H-O-L-D F-A-S-T.

Lenox glanced at his pocket watch: 4:45. He

stood up and went to the end of the bar. "Are you American?" he asked the dark-haired man with the hangover.

"Who in the hell are you?" said the man.

He was much drunker than Lenox had realized—and, judging by his accent, from somewhere in Berkshire. "Eli Gilman?"

The man slurred back a version of the name, uncomprehending, in a loud, angry voice, and the old sailor behind the bar looked over with a scowl. "Oy," he said. "Finish your drink and be on your way if you mean to cause trouble."

Lenox put up his hands. "Mistaken about seeing an acquaintance," he said shortly. "Apologies."

He sat with his whisky-ginger. He would have to wait. After a few moments he risked asking the bartender if they had any fish pies, but he had apparently been placed on some sort of probation, because he was told no, maybe at five. Despite the fact that the two card-playing men had just been served food.

Then there was a tap on his shoulder.

Lenox—nerves already on edge—whirled in his seat. It was the African who had been sitting in the corner of the room. His newspaper was under one arm.

"May I help you?" asked Lenox.

"I thought I heard you mention Eli Gilman," the man said in a broad American accent. He was quite tall, with close-cropped hair, very dark.

129

"You are here about an advertisement I placed, I believe."

"You?" said Lenox.

"I will be around the southwest corner at Mr. Thompson's," the man said. "I hope to hear news of my friend. I'm armed, just so you know."

And with that, he left the Salted Herring so abruptly that Lenox barely had time to stand up.

Graham was still not here. He had to choose whether to risk walking into danger; he had no idea at all who had just approached him. After a moment of indecision, he dashed off a quick note to Graham, which he left in the care of the bartender, along with tuppence and a description of the butler, who would be arriving at the Salted Herring soon. With a quick pang of guilt as he remembered his mother's anxiety for him, Lenox buttoned his coat and left.

Outside, he went to the corner and peered down the narrow reaches of Newell Street. It wasn't a tenth as active as Three Colt Street. A long, dense line of houses towered ominously over either side of a road wide enough for just a single carriage to pass along it. It was close and smoky, dark.

He took a few tentative steps forward, looking carefully at each number and nameplate as he went.

After about fifty yards, he reached a door that said THOMPSON. He stopped in front of it, looking up and down the street. Graham mightn't arrive at the pub for some little while if he were held up. This was a risk. With his heart beating hard, Lenox stepped forward and knocked on the door.

A good-looking older woman answered. "Yes?"

"A gentleman asked me to meet him here just a moment ago."

"Who?"

Lenox opened his mouth, then closed it, at a loss. "I'm not sure of his name. He was—he was African."

She frowned. "No Africans here."

"I was answering an ad," said Lenox.

"There are no ads here either."

"About Eli Gilman."

That worked. The woman stepped back and guided him to a small sitting room at the front of the house. Very small—it wouldn't have fit more than five people. It was ornamented with a large wooden cross, a picture of a sailboat, and an ink portrait of a family of seven, the mother in it the woman who had answered the door.

She left without saying anything, but a moment later the African from the Salted Herring appeared.

"Good evening, sir," he said, standing in the doorway. "You came about the advertisement?"

"Yes," Lenox said, rising. "I hoped to inquire about Mr. Eli Gilman. I am a private detective. Charles Lenox is my name."

"What is your business with Gilman?"

Lenox paused. He wasn't sure what to say. Luckily, there was a knock at the door. Both men looked over expectantly; after a moment, the woman from the ink drawing reappeared with Graham.

"Ah. This is my colleague," Lenox said. "He and I have been looking for a missing American—and I came to check if it might be your friend Mr. Gilman."

The black man frowned. "You've been looking for a missing American?"

Graham reached into his leather folder and produced a picture. "Is this him, sir?" he said to Lenox.

It was an illustration taken from a newspaper. But it was finely drawn, a detailed ink drawing with *Gilman* written beneath it, above an article.

There could be no mistaking that this was the man Lenox had seen slumped and dead in the third-class carriage of the 449 from Manchester.

"Yes. That's him."

Graham looked back and forth between Lenox and the African—the American—Lenox was still not quite sure how to think of him. Simpler just to think of him in physical terms: the man with the bandage round his head and the unreadable look on his face.

"That is a portrait of Mr. Eleazer Gilman, sir," the man said. "What do you know of him?"

"Almost nothing—but I'm very sorry to have to tell you that he is dead," said Lenox.

"Dead!"

Lenox nodded. "He was stabbed aboard a train from Manchester to London. We are endeavoring to learn why."

"Dead!" The man reflected on this, looking into the distance, for an instant caught in his own universe. "Then a great man is gone from the earth. Please excuse me. I must tell Mr. and Mrs. Thompson this news."

He left. "Who was he?" Lenox whispered urgently.

Graham handed over a fat pile of newspaper clippings. "A congressman from Massachusetts, sir. And—"

"A congressman!"

"Yes, sir. A congressman. And also an ardent advocate of the abolition of slavery in the United States."

They exchanged a look as Lenox absorbed this information. "Well," he said. "Could I see the article?"

CHAPTER SIXTEEN

Lenox's first thought was that he must go see Edmund. An anonymous death on a train had become, in the course of just a few of Lenox's deductions and a day's research by Graham, an incident with international political implications.

A great number of oddities had now been explained. Chief among these was the murderer's care in removing the labels from Gilman's clothing. But there was also his desire to have the body sit in Paddington Station overnight, when the passengers and crew of the 449 had scattered as widely as possible. The longer this particular death went unremarked, the less likely that anyone would associate it with the nonappearance in London of Eli Gilman. And the safer the perpetrators would be.

Lenox remained in the small sitting room with Graham and rapidly read the clippings that the latter had brought from the Manchester newspapers.

There was news of Gilman's arrival among other dignitaries and notables aboard the *Clarissa* and a small item from the *Manchester-Guardian* recording that Gilman had spent two days meeting with business leaders in Manchester and Leeds, soliciting their support—financial, moral, political—for the abolitionist groups whose interests he represented.

But his most important meetings, it was obvious, reading between the lines, were to have been in London. So was a march, which was to have taken place the very next day. The *Manchester Guardian* reported that important members of the liberal and conservative parties had both agreed to meet with Gilman, as well as several connections at court. It was expected to be the best-attended abolitionist march in London in more than a decade.

In other words, Gilman had come to England with more than a naïve hope of finding an audience for his anti-slavery views. The question was whether this was the cause of his death.

Lenox glanced at the door; he was suddenly very curious about the bloodied bandage around the head of Gilman's friend.

"Slavery," Lenox said.

Graham nodded gravely. "Yes, sir."

Whatever America had recently achieved, there was a point upon which all Britons could count themselves proud: The transport of slaves had been illegal within the empire for nearly fifty years now, since 1807.

It was a near-miracle. Almost never in the history of human events had a people forced its government to stand against such monumental economic interests. Indeed, some might have

called it a true miracle—for the leaders of aboli-
tionism in the country had been largely either
Quaker or devoutly Anglican.

The instigators of the movement had both been
deeply religious, Thomas Clarkson and William
Wilberforce. They had performed complementary
functions: Clarkson the organizer, Wilberforce
the politician.

The first bill Wilberforce introduced to abolish
slavery had been in 1791. It was defeated roundly,
163 to 88. Between that vote and the passage of
the Slave Trade Act in 1807, sixteen years later,
British ships had transported about half a million
African slaves, to the immense profit of a few
hundred men. Some of those arguing against
Wilberforce said it was in fact the nation's single
most profitable business. This was their argument
for allowing it—perhaps, they would concede,
under heavier regulation—to continue.

But for once the moral argument had triumphed
over the commercial argument. All across
England, in part thanks to Clarkson and the
Quakers, leagues had sprung up from nowhere to
assist former slaves and to campaign against the
creation of future ones.

Josiah Wedgwood, one of the country's most
famous and important men, designed a medallion:
a black man in chains, speaking the words *Am I
not a man and a brother?* The image had become
so popular that women of the upper and middle

classes pinned it to their dresses and wore it upon necklaces and bracelets. Gentlemen kept it in their lapels.

Meanwhile, Wilberforce worked tirelessly. Vote after vote, speech after speech, year after year, never yielding an inch. At long last, on February 23, 1807, he brought the bill of 1791 to the floor a final time. This time the vote was a rout, 283 to 16—in favor of abolition.

In quick succession, France, the Netherlands, and Spain agreed to adopt some variation of its contents. The bitterest irony was the nation that adopted the act only weeks after Wilberforce: the United States of America. This seemingly admirable action came with one enormous and tragic ambiguity; it did nothing whatsoever to address the nation's *internal* slave trade.

Lenox had been just four or five years old when Wilberforce died. By the time the young Charles had reached school age, Wilberforce's name was already a legend, particularly among the boys who knew themselves to be headed into lives of religion. A weak student at Cambridge, given to socializing and flirtation, Wilberforce had found, suddenly and to his great surprise, a cause to which he had been willing to commit his life. Was this not evidence that divinity could enter any soul? Rarely had a moral crusade so perfectly matched the spirit of Christ.

Now, not half a century later, there were

already statues of Wilberforce across the country, plaques and busts. Many men and women kept his penny portrait on their walls. He was buried in Westminster Abbey. Meanwhile his equally devout and energetic partner, Clarkson, had lived the years until his own later death, in 1846, campaigning against chattel slavery in America. He had found followers there—though never the same success that he and Wilberforce had in Britain.

There was a footstep in the hall, which proved to belong to the lady of the house. She was carrying a tea tray.

"Mrs. Thompson?" Lenox ventured.

"Yes?" the woman said.

She set down the plain wooden tray, which had a chipped white porcelain pot and four mismatched cups on it, along with fragrant toasted teacakes piled on a plate.

"Is your—lodger, I suppose—is he returning?"

"Mr. Hollis. Yes. He went to send a telegram; may the Lord preserve him."

They heard the door at just that moment, and Hollis, as he was apparently called, reentered the sitting room.

Lenox had an additional moment now to examine him, and noticed a brass watch-chain, a sturdy gray cravat, and shoes that were creased here and there but well preserved. Good, functional attire.

Lenox stood. "Mr. Hollis, this is my associate, Mr. Graham," he said. "As I told you, my name is Charles Lenox. We've been assisting Scotland Yard in the investigation of a murder on train 449 from Manchester to London. I came to the Salted Herring in response to your advertisement, and now, unfortunately, it appears that we have answered your question about your missing friend—though I have just learned of his name and position.

"Given all of that, may I inquire who you are?"

The black gentleman gestured to the tea. "Please, sit, if Mrs. Thompson doesn't mind."

She nodded, and they sat, she taking her own place, Lenox noticed, very freely. As she did, he saw a wooden cross swing from her neck, and realized that she must be a Quaker. Theirs was a religion that gave women an equal hearing, he had heard—as far as that went. This perhaps explained Hollis's deference to her.

"Thank you," said Lenox, and took a sip of the very strong, almost muddy tea. At this evening hour it was welcome. "That's a bracer."

"Mr. Lenox, my name is Josiah Hollis. I hail originally from Atlanta, in the state of Georgia. For the first twenty-seven years of my life I was held in bondage not far from there, on the plantation of the Hollis family."

He spoke with a marked formality. Perhaps a

fortification against people who would judge his intelligence by his race.

"Some months ago," Hollis continued, "Congressman Gilman and I, along with a secretary to the Congressman, Mr. Abram Tiptree, formed a party to come here. We accepted donations to fund the trip and were happily surprised to receive far more in donations than we had expected.

"Our aims were twofold: to solicit support from high-ranking members of British society, first financial, second political, for the abolitionist movement in America. We were not the first such party, nor will we be the last. Yet we had great hopes. Our letters of introduction, thanks to Mr. Gilman and his friends, reached the highest levels of your society."

"And your wound?" said Lenox, motioning toward his head.

Hollis set down his tea. "Ah. Yes. As I was saying, we are not a unique party—except in this, that two of the three of us are dead, and I myself—this is the reason for my telling you I was armed—was nearly killed yesterday."

CHAPTER SEVENTEEN

T*wo* of the three?" Lenox said.

"It appears so, sir," said Hollis. "Mr. Tiptree died in Liverpool."

"Good God," Lenox said. Then suddenly he said to Graham, "What time is it?"

Graham checked his watch. "Ten past five."

Lenox thought for a moment. "Would you mind going to the Salted Herring and making a note of who comes in? Particularly anyone who seems to be looking for Mr. Hollis, obviously."

Graham nodded, stood up, picked up a guttered candle, and said to Mrs. Thompson, "May I?"

"May you what?"

Taking this as assent, Graham disheveled his hair and rubbed a few just faintly perceptible streaks of black tallow into his cheeks, mucking up his face imperceptibly but tellingly.

He removed his jacket. Lenox took it for him. Despite the subtlety of the changes, he was transformed. Lenox knew that an accent—a growling Oxfordshire intonation that he could adopt at will—would prove no trouble. Graham could blend in anywhere. He bowed toward the room and left.

"Quick work," Hollis said.

Lenox turned toward him angrily. "Did you

not consider that one of your attackers might see your ad?"

"Excuse me?"

"Now it is Graham who must do the dangerous work of identifying whatever species of villain comes through that public house."

Hollis looked surprised, and then his face darkened. "You're both free to leave."

"In fact we are not."

"I cannot see anyone detaining you."

"Our remit keeps us here. But my apologies," said Lenox tersely. He was furious on behalf of his friend, but cognizant that he must coax what information he could out of Hollis. "You were saying—did you say that Gilman's secretary is dead?"

"Yes. He fell between the gangway and the dock at our disembarkation in Liverpool. He was accompanying Congressman Gilman's luggage. Neither of us was with him. We were traveling in three different classes and had agreed to meet at the hotel. They fished Mr. Tiptree out of the water with a gaff, but his head was badly wounded, and after several days of fever he died in the hospital. Gilman wrote to his wife from Liverpool to inform her of the news."

"His name was Abram Tiptree?" Lenox said, writing it down in a small notebook he had pulled from his pocket. A present from his mother.

"Yes."

Lenox looked up. "Why did you and Gilman separate on your way to London?"

Hollis frowned and thought.

The pause gave Lenox a chance to study him. He had a strong jawline and a good profile. He was missing a tooth near the back of the left side of his mouth. The shade of his skin was closer to tan than to ebony. The bandage around his head looked passably fresh but inadequate.

Lenox had never met a black American before. There were few people of African descent in Great Britain; those there were had a difficult time. Every second talk at the scientific academies seemed to Lenox to be an attempt to prove their intellectual *inferiority*—this was the word that had gained currency in London—and outside of places with a heavy naval population, such as the port cities of Liverpool and Cardiff, they were extremely noticeable, drawing stares, jeers, impertinences.

There was, however, a small but healthy black population in Canning Town, not from where they sat. A minor case had taken Lenox there two years before, and in the course of it he had met a man named Richard Bartlett, of such clear and remarkable intelligence that those scientific proofs had sat uneasily in Lenox's mind since. (The world was a mysterious place, and nearly everyone in it knew rather less than they thought. Such were Lenox's feelings.) Bartlett had been of no use, as it happened, in that particular case—but Lenox had kept his name and address, in the event that he ever found himself in Canning Town again.

The only eccentricity he had been able to discern in Bartlett was that he drank between forty and fifty cups of tea a day. But you could say the same of the Earl of Ascot, if you substituted sherry for tea.

All of these reflections passed very quickly, in the moment or two that Hollis pondered how to tell his tale.

"Would you like the full story, or the abbreviated one?" he asked the detective.

"It would be best if I could return to Scotland Yard quickly."

Hollis nodded. "Very well. Then suffice it to say that Mr. Gilman was an evangelist for the cause of abolition, while I am the willing exhibit and witness of slavery's evils. I was once enslaved, and there are enough otherwise well-meaning people who are amazed that I can dress in a suit of clothes and speak in complete sentences that sometimes it entices them to support our work.

"Gilman—I still cannot believe he is dead!—stayed in the north of England after Tiptree's death in order to meet with textile factory owners there. It is they who demand the cotton that keeps slavery alive. Having heard that northern attitudes in England were less enlightened than in the south, Gilman and I decided that I should come here in advance to meet with the anti-slavery societies and help organize our march."

"Where are you staying?"

"At a hotel close to Embassy Row. The Greensleeves. It is expensive, but has no policies of discrimination. Mr. Gilman had a room reserved next to mine."

"Mr. Gilman was due to arrive Tuesday?"

That was the night of the body on the 449. "Yes. I went to sleep Tuesday expecting to see him in the morning. When I didn't, I assumed he had been held back by either work or a missed train in the north. By the afternoon, however, when the fourth train from Manchester had arrived, and I met it on the platform to find that again he was not aboard it, I wired there. His hosts there assured me that he had left on time. It was then that I started to worry. I did not imagine for a moment that he was dead."

"Did you see news of the murder?" Lenox asked.

"No. I would have with my supper yesterday evening, perhaps, for I usually read a paper in the evening. But as I was returning to my hotel, walking down an alleyway, a man came toward me from the other direction, his face and appearance in all respects ordinary. Gray hair, a gray mustache, of average height and build. When we were close to each other, he dealt a tremendous clout to the side of my head. His hand must have held some sort of blackjack— so I think in retrospect, at least. It gave me the wound you see bandaged over on my head."

"And he what, ran off after that?"

"No. At that moment—by pure chance—a group of young men turned the corner. It was fortunate timing. The man who had attacked me was preparing to strike again, and it was not a busy alley. The young men didn't rush to my help, but one of them did call out. My assaulter turned, saw them, and fled."

"Did you go to the police?"

"I did not. I assumed it was a racial attack."

"Even given Gilman's absence and Tiptree's death."

"It hadn't occurred to me until I met you that Gilman might be dead, or Tiptree's death part of any larger plot."

"No, of course not."

"Now I am ready to take the first ship back to Boston."

Lenox glanced at his notebook. "After the attack you came to Mrs. Thompson's."

"Yes. Mrs. Thompson, whose mother and father worked hand-in-glove with William Wilberforce himself, was kind enough to take me in." Lenox nodded politely toward Mrs. Thompson. "I needed a doctor. I also wanted to consult with her about Gilman. We decided to place the ad against which you appear so dead set—and yet which brought you here."

He had Lenox on that score. "I see."

Mrs. Thompson added, "Dr. Harrison said he wasn't to be left alone following a head wound. I insisted he stay here."

"Mrs. Thompson placed the ad for me and tended me all day," said Josiah Hollis. "At four o'clock, I went to the public house. There, you and I met. Fifteen minutes later, I learned that Eli Gilman was dead. And now you are apprised of my present circumstances, which are as great a puzzle to me as they are to you."

Lenox contemplated this tale in silence for an instant. What he really wished to know was if Hollis's attacker was the same person who had cleared the papers and tobacco out of Master Willikens's cart. From the description it might well be.

He glanced at his watch. Half past five. With any luck, Mayne would still be in the office.

But he didn't like the look of Hollis's wound.

"Will you come to Scotland Yard with me, after we see a friend of mine who is a physician? There is nowhere you would be safer."

"It's as good a plan as any, I suppose."

Lenox produced a card. "Mrs. Thompson, here is my information."

Outside, Lenox whistled down a cab, which turned sharply off Three Colt Street. He asked

Mrs. Thompson if she would find Graham at the Salted Herring and tell him—surreptitiously—that they could meet at home. She said she would, and the Briton and the American rode off west together under the sinking sun.

CHAPTER EIGHTEEN

Lenox was eager to share his discoveries at the Yard, but he had heard too many stories of men and women sustaining blows to the head and dozing off comfortably, only to remain in that slumber forever after.

"St. Bart's," Lenox told the cab driver. "King Henry Gate."

"What is that?" Hollis asked.

Lenox was already looking at his notes. "Hospital," he said, not looking up.

It was more than just a hospital to many. St. Bartholomew's had stood in the same spot since the early 1100s; Harvey had discovered and delineated the circulatory system there, perhaps the greatest accomplishment a British scientist had ever made.

But to Lenox it was first and foremost the place where he had an acquaintance who would be awake and helpful. Lemuel Dominic was a surgeon Lenox had consulted professionally. He kept eccentric hours, luckily, working and seeing patients between four in the afternoon and four in the morning.

As the cab picked up speed, Hollis packed a pipe and smoked it in thoughtful silence. No doubt Gilman was on his mind.

After some time, Lenox addressed him. "Can you think of a reason anyone would want to kill the three of you?"

"Yes," said Hollis briefly, an answer that plainly showed how naïve he thought the question.

"Do you have any person in mind? Or group?"

"I have never given a speech in my home country without receiving a death threat beforehand."

That stopped Lenox short, and he contemplated the dimensions of the problem before him with growing dismay.

They arrived at St. Bart's. The porter at the Henry Gate—above which stood London's last remaining statue of Henry the Eighth—knew Lenox, and he and Hollis were seen straight to the North Ward. Lenox led Hollis to Dominic's door, halfway down a hushed wooden corridor.

"Lenox," said Dominic when he answered the knock, taciturn as ever, with keen hooded eyes. "Good evening."

"Good evening, Dominic. Are you busy?"

"Unoccupied."

He was a short, fat person, an expert in tumors. "This man has a head wound," said Lenox. "He is an American. I would take it kindly if you looked at him."

Dominic glanced at Hollis, then back at Lenox.

"A quick word first, if you would."

"Of course."

Lenox went into the bright chamber and closed the door behind him—and there heard, to his astonishment, Dominic say that he would not treat a Negro. Lenox expressed his surprise. Dominic said that he was not expert in their kind, to which Lenox replied that it was no doubt like treating any other adult male, upon which Dominic said that Lenox should know better than to be so coarse in his distinctions. Coarse! Lenox answered that he had heard of an oath that doctors took whose contents eluded him now—could Dominic remind him—named for Hippocrates he thought—and the conversation ended soon thereafter, without any great amiability on either side.

Lenox came back into the hallway. "He is in the midst of a dissection," he told Hollis. He looked up and down the corridor. "We will have to find someone else."

Hollis looked as if he knew full well the meaning of the word "dissection" and merely nodded. He did wince, though. The blood on his bandage had reddened.

The detective, increasingly alarmed, asked Hollis to wait upon a bench. He walked quickly back to the stairwell, his footsteps making a loud cracking racket through the empty building. There, he consulted a list on a wooden board of every doctor by his office number.

He scanned it carefully, until he stopped at

a name he recognized. It was a very slender acquaintance. Still, it might work.

They found office 119 after two left turns, and Lenox knocked on it tentatively. After a moment it opened, and a tall, extremely handsome fellow, with large dark brown eyes and hair fashionably windswept, stood before them in a white coat.

"Good evening," he said.

"Dr. Thomas McConnell?" Lenox asked.

"That is I."

"You will not recall me, I think, but we met twice—perhaps two years ago, or just a bit more. You were kind enough to come to the country to see my father, and then we encountered each other at Lady Hamilton's ball. Charles Lenox."

"Charles Lenox! Yes, I remember, of course." He was too delicate—or perhaps too callous, with a doctor it could be difficult to tell—to ask about Lenox's father, who had died of the illness that had caused them to enlist McConnell as a specialist, though through no fault whatsoever of McConnell's own. "In fact, I saw Lady Lucia Chatham the other day."

"Engaged, I hear," said Lenox, with a smile. "Listen—I know it is very awkward, my showing up on your doorstep, but Mr. Hollis here has a head wound. We called upon Dr. Dominic, but—"

There was no need to continue, however. Before a few words of this short speech had emerged from Lenox's mouth, McConnell had already nodded, shaken Hollis's hand, and begun ushering them into the small round chamber that evidently served as his consulting room. He seated them in a pair of dark chairs and sat down opposite, leaning forward on the edge of his chair so that only the balls of his feet touched the floor.

"Have you seen a doctor, sir?" he asked Hollis.

"A Quaker doctor, sir."

Lenox had observed that there were scientific journals and a cup of tea upon McConnell's desk. "You are sure we are not interrupting you?"

"Only in the most welcome way—interrupting the sheer boredom of maintaining one's professional competence. That is, I should add, welcome, if we can alleviate Mr. Hollis's suffering."

McConnell moved Hollis to a taller chair. Lenox offered to leave, but both men said he could stay. With long, subtle fingers, the doctor unfurled the bandage, sponging some clear liquid from a white basin nearby onto the wrapping where it stuck.

The wound looked considerably worse than Lenox had expected.

"Goodness," he said under his breath.

"These Quaker doctors mean very well," the surgeon said, carefully gazing at the wound. "But sometimes their good intentions outpace their medical ability. Still, between the two, good intentions and good medicine, there is often nearly an equal need."

Dominic had proved this true, certainly. "I really do thank you, McConnell," Lenox said.

The surgeon studied the wound for what seemed a very long time. At last, he said, "This wound will do very well, Mr. Hollis. The bone is unfractured. You have not lost a worrying quantity of blood—or rather, you have lost a worrying quantity for yourself, of course, but not for your medical outlook."

"You will patch it up?" asked Lenox.

"I will. First he shall have this laudanum." The Scot brought forth a small bottle of tincture. Hollis took two drops on his tongue. In the pain of the unwrapping of the wound he had closed his eyes and barely opened them since; he was sweating heavily. "Then I shall ask him to rest somewhere. This sofa is free."

"But ought he not to stay awake?"

"On the contrary, nothing would do better than for him to sleep twelve or fifteen hours. There is no hemorrhage within the cerebellum."

Lenox looked at McConnell carefully. "And you are sure that he can sleep here? I would not dream of imposing upon you. Yet I fear it is not safe for him to return to his hotel."

"Ah, your profession!" McConnell nodded his head firmly. He was already rewrapping the wound, quickly and expertly. "Yes. He is your friend—he shall stay here. Does that suit you, Mr. Hollis?"

The American muttered something that sounded like a yes. The laudanum had taken hold even in this short stretch of time, combining no doubt with fatigue, shock, and vigilance to render him stupefied. He allowed himself to be guided to a long and comfortable blue sofa in the corner of McConnell's office. There he lay down. McConnell found a loosely woven military blanket in his cabinet and placed it over Hollis.

Within what seemed like thirty seconds, perhaps less, he was asleep. "I am deeply in your debt," Lenox said, voice low.

McConnell grinned. "Yes, to the tune of nine shillings. However, since we are not in Harley Street, where I have my clinical practice, but at the hospital, we shall waive it."

"I insist upon paying," said Lenox, reaching for his pocket.

McConnell put a hand out. "Go further and you shall insult me."

Lenox stopped. "Then you must accept my gratitude. But can you really leave him here?"

"Yes. I shall be here another hour or two. When I go I shall write a note for the nurse on the wards. You may leave one for Hollis if you wish, too. They will see that he gets it."

This was just what they did. Then Lenox, thanking McConnell with quiet but fervent gratitude once more—Hollis was in a deep sleep—said it might be vitally important to him to go to Scotland Yard, that time was of the utmost importance, and McConnell urged him away, with his good wishes and his assurances that the next day when Hollis woke up they would find him a bed on the ward.

CHAPTER NINETEEN

Y ou were due a stroke of luck."
That was what Sir Edmund Lenox said
to his younger brother over breakfast the next
morning. They were discussing a large steamer
trunk—the stroke of luck in question.

Charles tipped a spoonful of brown sugar over his
bowl of porridge and shrugged, face philosophical,
as if to say that the people due strokes of luck
didn't always receive them. He watched the sugar
slowly turn liquid and then took a bite.

"It was still luck," he said, chewing. "We shall
see what we can make of it."

Just then, Molly passed through the sunny
breakfast room. In the corner, the couple's two
young sons, Charles's nephews, dressed in
matching white sailor's pants and blue jersey
shirts, were deeply absorbed in some saga of
their invention involving a toy sloop.

"Make of what?" she asked.

It was Edmund who replied. "Charles's murder
victim, the one from the train, sent his things
ahead of him from Manchester to London. A
whole steamer trunk."

Charles frowned. "I don't know that it sounds
quite right to call him my murder victim,
Edmund."

"No, true. I meant the murder victim Charles didn't murder, Molly."

"That still makes it sound as if there's one I *did* murder."

Molly suggested that they might go so far as to suspend all discussion of murder until the boys' nanny had fetched them—a request the older pair of brothers both acknowledged was reasonable.

Leaving again, though, Molly congratulated Charles on his steamer trunk.

"Thank you," he said.

"Not to mention Kitty Ashbrook!" she called gleefully over her shoulder.

"There is absolutely nothing—" began Lenox.

But the door to the servants' pantry between the morning room and the dining room had already swung closed behind her.

"She's having friends to tea this morning," Edmund said, by way of explanation for her hurry.

Usually she ate with them—a part of their tradition that every Friday, when they were both in the city, the two brothers had breakfast together. It was a ritual that dated to their childhood. Back then they had gathered in the great hall at Lenox House at seven thirty to breakfast with their father, who always commuted back from his seat in Parliament late Thursday nights, long after their bedtime. It was his first meal of the weekend—which was his favorite time of the week, and the boys', too, for they had him, then, until early Sunday afternoon.

"I heard as much, before you came down," Lenox said.

"They're from when she was quite young, but they have kept up a correspondence over the years. One lives in Bath, the other in Northhampton. She hasn't seen them in ages—has been excited for so long." He glanced at the pantry wistfully. "I only hope it goes as well as she would like."

"It will." Though life could take odd turns, Lenox couldn't imagine Molly ever having friends who had grown angry or spiteful; not ever. "What about you, this morning? The House of Commons?"

"Yes. Unending meetings."

"At least you can give me a lift."

At that moment one of the boys came over with the toy ship, and the conversation turned toward its significance. Lenox loved his brother's house, partly for moments like this. It was a short, homey dwelling with a curved window in front, always full of noises, good smells, calling to and fro, busyness. It felt full, with little reminders everywhere, forgotten toys, hastily flung-up jackets, that the whole whirl of life was transpiring here, mother, father, children, their growth and happiness an ongoing and complex matter.

The house sat on a wide, leafy street in Belgravia called Cadogan Lane. This was slightly farther from the heart of Mayfair—and from Parliament—than Charles's own residence. Edmund often commented, however, that the half-hour walk into the relative quiet here salvaged his spirit after a long day.

Lenox had walked here this morning in high spirits himself. He had woken to word from McConnell—most kindly phrased—that Josiah Hollis was asleep in the North Ward and already recovering. A good constitution, McConnell said. Then, news nearly as welcome, an overnight hunch had paid off: Graham had returned from the Greensleeves with the news that Lenox's suspicion had been right, and Gilman's trunk from Manchester was sitting in the hotel's luggage office, waiting to be claimed.

He had already been in good standing at Scotland Yard the night before, for finding out Gilman's name and unearthing Hollis. Now he knew the solution was within his fingertips' reach. He felt it with all the urgency of his young blood.

"I notice you're still dressing these boys like sailors in a costume contest," Charles said to his brother when his nephews had turned back to their game.

Edmund sighed. "Yes." He had a piece of crispy bacon, and took a ruminative bite of it. "Molly's sister swears by it."

"Better than the pinafore they made you wear for our portrait."

"It was not a pinafore!"

Charles looked at his older brother skeptically. "If you pin it afore the dress, I think it must be a pinafore."

"It wasn't a dress. As you know full well!"

This portrait (whose composition predated Charles's own memories of life) was a source of great shame to Edmund, who did indeed at least appear to be wearing a navy pinafore in it. The picture was one of their mother's most treasured possessions.

Now Charles repeated her favorite comment on it, always said with the same nostalgic passion. "You were such a beautiful child, Ed."

"Shut up."

Unfortunately Molly came through the door at just that moment and shot her husband a deadly look at this display of rudeness in front of the boys. Edmund immediately transferred the look to his brother, who acknowledged it with an apologetic smile. A maid brought in two cups of black coffee. Another habit of their father's—a cup of tea with breakfast, a cup of coffee afterward, and one could work all the night through, he was fond of saying.

The boys soon departed, shuffled off to the morning's amusement (the zoo), and Molly was busy in the larger drawing room across the hall.

The sun slanted in onto every surface, broken here and there into accidental geometries.

"Sir Richard was pleased then," Edmund said.

"Yes, I think he was," Charles replied. "I was glad he was still at the office when I left McConnell. He set out straight for the American consulate. How they shall handle it I cannot say."

"Interesting. It's a tricky moment between us and the Americans."

"Is it?" Charles asked curiously.

Edmund was a backbencher, but he picked up a great deal. He was friendly and discreet, intelligent, and well connected, and as a result had become a confidant to many men who yearned for someone who possessed those qualities without the ruthless ambition that usually attended them in politicians.

"This fellow Pierce is no good. So much depends on the president there, you know. The last chap, Fillmore, brought together a very awkward sort of compromise between the slave states and the free states, but it was at least a compromise. Pierce is from the North himself, but he's only thought well of in the South. Meanwhile they're conducting a dry run for a civil war once you go past the states—Kansas Territory."

Lenox was only obscurely aware of the Kansas Territory. He had become just about accustomed to California as a state, but everything that lay between it and Wisconsin was a mystery of reported images to him: buffalo, vast plains, red rocks, flocks of birds so dense and vast that the sky could go black for a full hour on a clear day at noon.

"But they won't really have a war."

That was the prevailing wisdom. "No," said Edmund. "Of course not. The idea is ruinous. If they did, half of our Parliament would support the South."

"Right."

"The trouble is that slavery will have to be brokered some way or another. And this new party they have is—well, it is a young country, and young countries will founder sometimes. That is what people whisper. Then it will be up to what's left of them, and to us and France and the rest, to fight over how it's parceled up. And the United States of America will be a memory."

"What new party?"

"You must read the papers for more than crime," Edmund chided him. "You haven't heard of them? The Know Nothings?"

"The what?"

"Clever bunch, unfortunately. United around a common loathing for the Germans and Irish immigrating to America at the moment. Call them dirty, lazy. Fewer jobs to go around. And people—there—seem to agree. If they win the next election it will be a disaster."

"For us?" said Charles. "It seems hard to imagine that Britain shall be put off by anything they can do."

Edmund shook his head. "The wisest men I know have their eyes on America. It is such a great deal of land and material—so much empty space into which to build. If it falls nativist, and there is a war after all, who knows what evil might come of it?"

Lenox nodded thoughtfully. "This is the background from which Gilman emerges, I suppose."

"Perhaps. I know nothing of him. But I have been, even myself, the recipient of petitions from the anti-slavery movement, and speaking generally they couldn't give a fig for anything except the plight of the black Americans."

"One sees their point."

"Of course. And yet I can never offer them hope." Edmund took a sip of his coffee, and in that moment, calm and thoughtful, he reminded Lenox very much of their father. "It's all so convoluted—I know nothing of what the Utah Territory thinks of slavery, or who's to venture down to South Carolina and dispossess them of what they consider as much their property as I consider this table my own. How could I?"

"Then what do you tell them?"

"I tell them that I will sign anything they wish protesting slavery," said Edmund. "And I always do, though people in Parliament get cross with me."

This was one benefit of having a seat in one's pocket, of course, and also of not caring about advancement; Edmund could vote and act his conscience. Markethouse would sooner return a pig to Parliament than turn a Lenox out of it.

"But you cannot do anything practical."

"No. Precisely. That is what I tell them."

"Who could?"

Edmund shrugged. "Half a dozen men in either party, I suppose." He smiled. "The Queen. All of them could help. One hears the idea that there should be no new slaves—that black men and women should be *born* free."

"It is a compromise," said Charles.

"A hard one on a young slave," said Edmund, shaking his head. "And even in that case the Southerners dislike it furiously."

"There is the idea of a colony in Africa."

"The Southerners dislike that further still."

"But how can they defend the idea in their minds!" said Lenox with sudden anger. "Slavery! And they come here and insist upon every refinement—I have met them—pure gentlemen, raised to the highest codes you would have thought, as noble aboard a horse as Cincinnatus."

"Men will square anything in their heads that keeps them rich," said Edmund, glancing at his watch. "But I must go. Do you still want a ride?"

Lenox was still pondering the imponderables of America, of Eleazer Gilman, but looked up, distracted. "Yes," he said. "Thanks. And thank you for breakfast. And for not wearing your new stockings."

CHAPTER TWENTY

The Greensleeves was an old-fashioned coaching inn that had been tossed into modernity like a drunk bundled into a country prison cell—that is, awaking to find himself at least modestly warm and comfortable, when he might have slept in a ditch. Not a bad result.

It was a small wooden building with a rickety interior arcade. It must have served every stripe of society in its earlier days—especially travelers, since it had a stable. But if Lenox had to guess, he would have said that courtesans once lived in the rooms here. The reason was the name. There was a time several centuries past when no respectable lady in England wore green: It was the most suggestive color, supposedly because of the way grass stained a maiden's white dress once she had lain down in it. It was this that had prompted the mythical figure of Lady Green Sleeves, and the song of the same name.

But now the hotel's trade seemed to be mostly in foreign visitors. Lying so close to Embassy Row, it housed an immense variety of people who had arrived at the center of the British Empire to try to pluck some bargain from or offer some entreaty to her ruling class. Lounging around the entranceway of the hotel were men who looked to be from the Continent, from Asia, from Africa. Perhaps even the Utah Territory. Certainly one couldn't wish to see a greater diversity of clothing anywhere in the city—neither east nor west.

To the surprise of precisely one of their party (which consisted of Dunn, Mayne, Hemstock, Lenox, and a bright-eyed American youth from the consul's office named Mallori Pearce), Hemstock suggested they get a drink in the bar, which even at the breakfast hour was loud and busy.

"Absolutely not," said Sir Richard Mayne.

"Not a quick one?" Hemstock said.

"A quick drink!" said Pearce, blushing, a skinny tadpole a year out of William and Mary College. He was the son of a member of Virginia's House of Burgesses.

"Mr. Hemstock must have been joking, I believe," said Lenox.

"Ah!" said Pearce, turning to him, greatly obliged for this innocent explanation. "I see. Of course. The dry British wit. Of course. I must sharpen my parrying sword if I remain in this—this wonderful country."

"Or you could go home," said Dunn.

"I think Mr. Pearce will find that people here are fairly open and kind in the end," said Lenox.

They were met by the hotel's owner. He was a stout Liverpudlian named Johnson with slick hair and a broad belly, waistcoat stretched taut over it. Evidently aware of the benefits of a friendly police force, he led them with every courtesy of manner to a room he had set aside just for the inspection of Gilman's trunk. Hemstock, who not been joking at all, nevertheless grumbled along behind the rest of them through the hotel's restaurant.

After his breakfast that morning, Lenox had gone home and found a wire from Sir Richard in response to his own. It had offered praise for his discovery of the trunk (*Very well done*) along with an invitation to meet at the Yard at ten.

In the small private room, which lay behind the restaurant and away from the noise of the street, they saw a blue steamer trunk with brass fittings, E. GILMAN in large lettering on its side, sitting on a plain brown table.

The room was otherwise empty. "I shall leave you here, gentlemen," said the hotelier.

Mayne thanked him. "It's got a lock," he said when they were alone. "Dunn?"

Dunn frowned. "Should have thought of it." He popped his head out of the door. "Do you have a pair of heavy cutters?" he asked the hotel's retreating owner.

He turned back. "In the stable."

"Could you lend them to us?" asked Mayne.

"Of course," said the owner. "Give me a moment."

As they waited, Lenox leaned back against one wall, trying to remain unobtrusive, and pulled from the inner pocket of his jacket the paper he had spent the trip to the hotel reading. He wanted another look at it.

It was a short biography of Eli Gilman, which the consulate had provided to Mayne. It originated, apparently, from a garrulous journal of congressional events in Washington, D.C. called *The District Record*.

Several of the details within it had struck Lenox. He read the article again now closely, deliberately trying to slow his pace.

Promising Massachusetts Republican Eli Gilman to be resident at the establishment of Mrs. Patricia Baptiste, Georgetown, from March 1
Strong opponent of Fugitive Slave Act; Unionist

Districters, a cynical people once they see their first few crops of politicians come and go from elsewhere in these united states, generally expect little of first-term arrivals in the great chamber.

An exception may be expected, however, in the case of the fluent and well-connected **Mr. Eleazer Whitney Gilman**, whose surprise election over

Rep. Hannibal Granger proposes to provide an interesting flavor to the forthcoming session.

Born in Lawrence, Mass., in 1830, the son of a minister in that town and grandson of a captain in the Revolution, Mr. Gilman was a brilliant student at nearby Phillips Academy, where under the tutelage of Samuel Harvey Taylor he gained a reputation as a gifted scholar of Latin and Greek and an unrelenting debater. By letter, Taylor expressed no surprise at his former pupil's election. "We were luckier to have him than he to have us," the great educator writes, graciously, to *The District Record.*

At the age of 16, Mr. Gilman abruptly withdrew from plans to attend Harvard and instead made a two-year sojourn in the territories, often by foot, taking odd work where he found it, generally alone but occasionally in the company of a friend from Andover, Mr. Charles Bemis, of the notable New York family, now a junior lecturer at Yale.

Gilman has commented that these two years altered his political and philosophical ambitions. Upon their conclusion he returned to Harvard for a year of scientific study, having decided during his time in the West that he no longer wished to follow the trail of his father in the ministry—but rather that of his grandfather, who remained in service of one kind or another to his country throughout his life, finally as a pension administrator for the state.

In a series of fiery orations delivered at the Old Corner Bookstore in Boston, at 283 Washington Street, the young Mr. Gilman gained the stunned admiration of a crowd which included numerous prominent local citizens, among them Mr. Ralph Waldo Emerson, Mr. Alexander Williams, and Dr. Oliver Wendell Holmes.

These speeches, collected in a pamphlet called *A Young American's Travels*, sold through three editions and went into a fourth. Soon, insistent friends demanded that Mr. Gilman challenge Granger—a Whig stalwart—for his seat. Bolstered by the personal appearance of Mr. Emerson on his behalf, Gilman carried the ballot box, to the surprise of local prognosticators, at the tender age of 23.

"I do not go to the Congress to bide my time," he vowed in his victory speech to supporters. He is already planning a trip to our Southern neighbors in Tennessee and Alabama to investigate the state of slavery there.

Gilman is unmarried; asked if he would accept an invitation to Mr. Pierce's White House despite their political differences, he replied in the negative, evidence, perhaps, of a new firebrand spirit that some fear could bring warring factions to a head, but others hope could resolve the great issue of our "peculiar institution" once and for all. It shall be of interest to note whether other invitations from prominent Washington residents obtain a more favorable reception. What is sure is that Gilman will reside with Mrs. Patricia Baptiste, in Georgetown. For reasons of frugality, however, he plans to take his meals in the Congress.

Lenox was just finishing this fascinating document again—fascinating both advertently and inadvertently, he thought—when one of the hotel's stable hands returned. In a trice he sheared the lock on the trunk away, and after he had gone, they all crowded forward to see what they would find, Lenox included.

"Awful lot of clothes," Hemstock remarked.

"Yes. What a shock," Dunn said.

"I only meant to say—"

"Let us get to the bottom of the trunk at

least," Dunn said, "before we have any more commentary. Unless we find, for instance, a bloody knife."

"Fine," muttered Hemstock, loose in his dirty jacket, overdue for a cut and a shave. "Fine."

Together, Dunn and Pearce, the American, took an inventory of the trunk's contents, both inspecting each item as it was removed from the trunk.

"Jackets, two," Dunn said.

"Jackets, two," Pearce repeated, making a note. Then the pair looked at the jackets, checked all the pockets, folded them, and set them aside. "Next?"

"Pants . . . three pair."

"Three pairs of pants."

They went on like this until they had gone through the trunk entirely. Lenox stood where he could see the top of Pearce's list clearly. *Shirts—5,* it said, *papers—various.* And so forth.

It was the books and papers that made Lenox most hopeful. He knew that he was the most likely person present to find something useful here, being the most patient.

But it was a jacket he asked about. "Could I see that for a moment?" he said, as Pearce folded a plain black coat.

It had one of Mr. Wedgwood's pins on its lapel, the figure on one knee, pleading: *Am I not a man and a brother?*

Pearce shrugged. "By all means."

Lenox looked at the inside pocket. *H. M. Carraway, Lawrence, Massachusetts.* He rubbed his thumb over the satin label, and at that moment, for whatever reason, he felt the full impact of Gilman's murder. A mixture of rage and sadness rose suddenly in his heart. This was no doubt identical to the labels that had been cut away so cold-bloodedly on the 449. Lenox could picture the young politician proudly ordering his clothes from his father's tailor, as Lenox had from his father's—good sturdy material, well constructed, meant to last a lifetime. At least, a lifetime longer than a quarter century. Somewhere in Massachusetts, at that moment, a minister in a jacket that bore the same label was soon to learn that his son was dead. He wondered if Gilman's father was very proud of his son; no doubt. Lenox's thoughts flashed to his mother's wish that he give up this career, but it was painful, and he pushed it away.

"What are the books?" asked Mayne, as Pearce and Hemstock unloaded these from their carefully stowed corner of the trunk.

"Probably *Uncle Tom's Cabin*," said Dunn.

In fact, the first book he held up was something called *Leaves of Grass*, by Walt Whitman, its pages still uncut. None of the Britons knew the writer, but Pearce assured them he was well regarded on the other side of the Atlantic, where this book had been released not long before.

"Never got to read it, poor fellow, did he," said Hemstock.

"He read these often enough, though," said Mayne, holding up a battered copy of John Donne's sermons.

There was a slim dark red leather copy of *The Tempest*, a two-volume copy of Alexis de Tocqueville, a brief history of England.

But it was the mass of letters and notepads that Lenox was most keen to see, as they unwrapped and set aside various items of food, dress, and personal grooming. He was hopeful, despite himself, that they would find some decisive clue and solve the murder of the young man whose life, whose speeches, whose choices, had been so full of now-commuted promise.

CHAPTER TWENTY-ONE

"How did you and Mr. Gilman first meet?"

Josiah Hollis raised his eyebrows—at least, as high as he could beneath the fresh bandage over his brow.

He looked markedly better than he had the evening before, when Lenox had left him in Thomas McConnell's office. The doctor on the ward at St. Bart's had released Hollis without cavil, and now he and Lenox were on their way to Mrs. Thompson's house. Hollis's possessions—in a dark traveling case fetched from the Greensleeves—were bound neatly to the back of Lenox's carriage. Hollis had agreed that it was necessary he find lodging elsewhere, since his attacker had obviously known where he, Tiptree, and Gilman had intended to stay. He hoped to find a room near the Thompsons.

It was all proceeding in good order—with the exception of one fleeting incident just now at the hospital, which Lenox had tried to put out of his mind, had even tried to convince himself he had seen wrongly. But couldn't, quite.

"We met in the Minnesota Territory," Hollis replied. "He was on his travels, and it was winter, very cold—colder than an Englishman can rightly imagine, I would think."

"I have been to a few cold places," said Lenox.

"Then perhaps you can. Regardless, he was in no wise dressed for the weather." The carriage bumped over a stone, and Hollis winced, putting a hand to his head. "He came to St. Paul and slept in a church there. I was speaking at a tavern nearby. He was in the audience and approached me afterward. We sat to supper—even my most sympathetic listeners there, Mr. Lenox, were not prepared to go that far—and from that day forward I counted him my friend."

"Then this journey had been some time in the planning."

"Only since his turn to politics. I think it surprised him to win his seat, but once he did, he wrote to me immediately—I was in Maine then, working on my autobiography, on the strength of an advance from a publisher in Boston—and proposed the trip. I accepted."

"I hear a great deal of Portland, Maine," said Lenox in a careless manner—a gentleman of the world.

Hollis looked surprised. "Then you can count yourself better informed than I am. I have never been."

"Is Portland not a—one of the great cities of America?" Lenox asked.

"I would not necessarily call it one of the *great* cities," said Hollis.

Graham and his blasted rum riots. "Oh. Well. Is the autobiography complete?"

"Nearly so," said Hollis. "I came here hoping to seek its publication in London. It would be a financial boon. I was supposed to meet with a gentleman in Drury Lane yesterday."

"Have you written him?"

"Not yet."

They sat in silence for some while, Lenox gazing out at the streets. They halted near the Strand for a while as two men in soft caps endeavored to shift a large crate onto its side. Evidently it had fallen off a dray. They finally managed it, only for the part that had been facedown in the muddy street to spring open, revealing dozens and dozens of black silk hats, a waterfall.

Boys darted in and started grabbing them, the men shouted, a constable appeared, activity subsided; the life of a city.

"Atlanta and Minnesota are very far apart," Lenox ventured.

"Yes, that's true. Since I obtained my freedom I have spent as little time in the Southern states as possible."

"For fear of being returned to your—to—"

"My owner?" Hollis looked at him. "No, sir. I am legally free. I have no owner. But I am conscious of the possibility of recrimination for that fact in the South."

And yet he had met it here, not there, Lenox thought. "How did you come to be free?"

Hollis glanced at a pocket watch—silver, the young detective saw. "That is a long story. I will tell you at some other time, perhaps."

Lenox smiled. "And if not, I can read your memoir."

The Thompsons greeted them with the information that the march in Hyde Park had now been not canceled but postponed. Another blow for Hollis. The organizers of the London Anti-Slavery Society feared another attack, Mr. Thompson said. They proposed instead a series of salons before Hollis left again for America.

"I had thought to leave by the earliest ship."

"I can see why," said Mr. Thompson. "But I hope we may entreat you to stay."

"If I may," said Lenox, "I would not board any ship upon which you are scheduled to sail until we know what happened. Your assaulter knew you would be at the Greensleeves. He may know what berth you intend to travel by."

Hollis saw the sense in this.

The Society was also planning a full public repudiation of the violence against Gilman in the press, Thompson said, and had printed a second run of his pamphlet, anticipating high demand once it was in the papers, beginning that afternoon no doubt, that he had been murdered: a member of the United States Congress.

Lenox stayed for a few minutes, but he had much to do, and after his coachman had fetched Hollis's belongings into the house, Lenox excused himself. As he traversed the town toward Scotland Yard, he reflected upon what he had heard.

He had thought of the case as belonging to Paddington, being about the peculiarity of a body on a train. But the matter belonged to a much wider sphere—it was, he supposed, an assassination.

That gave him a chill, and he took out his trusty brown leather notebook. He wrote some words at random as they came to mind—this always helped him—and among them included that one, "assassination." Eleazer Gilman was perhaps a fatality in the long, undeclared war between the states, South and North, slave and free. Lenox thought of what Edmund had told him about the delicate situation there now. He hoped Gilman would be one of the last fatalities. A peace might come. It all seemed very uncertain, though. By 1856, he supposed, in a couple months' time, things could look very different indeed.

These thoughts took him all the way to the Yard. With the permission of the American consulate, Mayne had set aside a desk at the Yard where the two inspectors and Lenox could examine Gilman's correspondence and journals at their leisure. It was on the busy first floor, where a great deal of administrative work took place. To his surprise, he found Hemstock sitting at the desk, reading.

"Hello, Inspector," Lenox said, coming up behind him.

Hemstock turned. He had a flask in one hand and a letter in the other. "Eh? Oh! Lenox. How are you?"

"Curious to see what you've found," said Lenox.

"Not much. There are ten letters in all. Five friendly, three threatening, and two merely confirming meetings. I've divided them up."

"That's a good start. Where is Dunn?" asked Lenox.

"He didn't tell me where he was going." Hemstock took a sip from the flask, his belly pushing against the desk as he tipped his head back. "I thought perhaps I'd give these a look before you arrived."

Lenox felt a brief flash of sympathy. Hemstock was not unlike some of the boys that Lenox had known at Harrow—heirs to great estates, barely qualified to operate a fried potato cart. It wasn't Hemstock's fault that his father had been a hero. The son ought to have been running a pub somewhere into slow, genteel default. In any event he was giving the case his best now.

"And the journals?" said Lenox.

Hemstock put his hand on two of these,

one blue, one black. The latter had the seal of Congress embossed on it in gold. "One is a diary with his schedule. The other is full of Gilman's personal experiences. I cannot find anything interesting in either, except that there is a list of the people he had seen in the north and those he intended to see in London."

Lenox nodded. "Perhaps I shall start with those, then."

"Feel free. I mean to go find myself a bit of grub," said Hemstock, heaving himself up from the chair. "Take the prime pew."

"Thank you, Inspector," said Lenox.

"Not at all."

Lenox sat down. If Hemstock had stayed even a moment longer, Lenox might almost have told him—out of sheer puzzlement and desire to discuss it—what he had seen at St. Bartholomew's. As they had been leaving, when Hollis had thought he was unobserved, he had reached out and taken from the front desk an inkwell and a brass pen, not a cheap-looking one, and put them in his pocket. Theft: pure theft.

CHAPTER TWENTY-TWO

An hour and a half later, Lenox thought he had excavated three firm suspects from this modest handful of documents.

It was quicker than he had any right to expect. He glanced at the clock, eager to get home and talk things over with Graham. Just after two. He was engaged to dine out that evening and wondered if he ought to cancel those plans. No; that would be rude. He tidied the papers, stood, and departed, nodding to one or two men on the way out.

Leaving the Yard, he discovered that what had dawned as a clear day had turned gray and menacing, with a whipping wind. He pulled his overcoat up around his neck.

Just outside the Yard was a fellow in a blue serge jacket selling newspapers, tobacco, and baked potatoes. Lenox, who had skipped lunch, stopped and bought one of each.

"Rain, do you think?"

"If it don't turn snow," the man said, counting change with fingerless gloves.

"Snow! In October?"

The man paused and looked up at the sky. "Coin flip's chance of it," he said. "In '49 the whole last week of October was a blizzard.

Couldn't get a cart through the streets, could I? No. And could I sell newspapers? Not to a soul. Hungry December that was."

"Then I hope it will only rain," said Lenox.

The man handed him his change. Lenox tipped him a farthing, and the man touched his cap. "Kindly, sir."

Lenox hailed a cab; only when he was seated, and chewing his first welcome bite of the warm, salty, buttery potato, did he realize that the newspaper he'd bought was reporting Eleazer Gilman's death.

MURDER AT PADDINGTON SOLVED! it announced in a bright headline.

A bit of a fib, that.

The papers had amassed a good deal of information on Gilman, however, including several details Lenox didn't know. (For instance, that an audience at court actually had been arranged for him, possibly even with the Queen.) He read the three articles the paper contained. None mentioned Tiptree or Hollis by name, though one did say, "Gilman had planned to speak at the march in Hyde Park in the company of a former slave, known for his true-life tales of captivity and escape."

He stepped down from the hansom at the end of Hampden Lane and walked the few hundred yards up its thin, meandering course to his own house, passing the familiar colorful storefronts on the way, interspersed with rows of quiet houses, each intimately recognizable to him. The flowers had finally been taken in at that of the widow Mrs. Cochran, a green thumb who had lived here thirty years and minded every one of her neighbors' growing things in addition to her own. Maybe it really would snow. Lenox felt a queer kind of loneliness suddenly, perhaps because of the overcast sky, perhaps because of . . . well, but what? Then he realized it was the memory of Edmund's warm, jolly morning room, and the contrast it made to Lenox's own quiet residence. He was sure it cut both ways—that there were many a father and mother in the houses around his who would have longed for an hour alone in his study with a book and a glass of wine—but in his case it was cutting one way, and it never *helped* when you knew something cut both ways.

He thought: Do I want a family? And realized, with a kind of strange and unexpected intensity, that yes, he did.

Perhaps his mother had intuited before he knew it himself what he would need next in life. Mothers could be like that, irritatingly.

He went up his steps and inside. To his surprise, he found that his neighbor was in his study, hands in pockets, looking at the bookshelves. "Hello, Deere," Lenox said, putting down his papers and unfurling the scarf from around his neck. "How are you?"

"My older friends call me Grey, you know," said the young lord. "I've been meaning to tell you."

"Do they!"

His name was James Grey—but his father had died when he was barely ten, and he had very early in life succeeded him as the 19th Earl of Deere. In the circles in which they moved, an acquaintance with a title was usually called by the title, not the name.

It was not a problem Lenox faced, of course; he had no title.

"I was wondering if you wanted a quick game of chess. But I see that you are busy."

This was true, yet Lenox realized that Deere (as he went on thinking of him) had never asked him to play before, not so directly as this.

"Of course," said Lenox.

They discussed whether there would be snow as they set up the pieces, and Lenox brought Deere up to date on the case.

"An audience with the Queen?" said Deere.

"Yes—and there were no names in his diary that you would not have recognized." Deere sat in the House of Lords. "Palmerston, Aberdeen, Gladstone, Disraeli, Lewis."

"Goodness."

"Those are only some. Half the cabinet, half the shadow cabinet. He meant business, Gilman."

Deere whistled. Viscount Palmerston was

Prime Minister at present. (Parliament was made up of two chambers, the House of Lords and the House of Commons, and could draw its ministers from either—Palmerston belonging, as a Viscount, to the former.) He had replaced the Earl of Aberdeen only that January. Sir George Cornewall Lewis was the Chancellor of the Exchequer, an office both Gladstone and Disraeli had previously held as well. Gladstone, for his part, had the unusual distinction of being the MP for Oxford University.

They began to play their game. "Were you there on Gladstone's budget day two years ago?" asked Deere.

"I wasn't. Why?"

Deere smiled, looking down at the pieces on the board. "It was memorable. He began his presentation. Very long they are, those presentations. After an hour his private secretary came forward with a silver cup of sherry and a dish with an egg in it. A spoon, too, I suppose. Gladstone put down his speech, beat the egg into the sherry, and drank it very slowly."

Lenox laughed. By tradition the only alcohol allowed in the chambers of Parliament was the "budget tipple"—the drink of the Chancellor of the Exchequer's choice, usually something simple like whisky, to see him through a long speech. Even the Queen could not drink in the Parliament. Gladstone, a dry but theatrical soul,

188

had taken advantage of the fact that he could. He would likely be Prime Minister himself, soon enough; in part because of that theatrical flair.

They played a tight game. Deere liked to castle early and then build a fortification of pawns and bishops, Lenox had learned, before deploying his rooks and knights with a bit more dash. Lenox himself had less strategy: He played the board, which sometimes resulted in fine attacking moments but also often left unexpected vulnerabilities in his back line.

He would make a poor criminal in this regard, as Deere had pointed out.

For a few moments Lenox was sure victory was his—he was up a rook—but then one of the young earl's bishops darted out of its protective shelter to even the board and put Lenox in check, and thenceforth, though they fought it out hard, Deere was fated to be the winner.

Lenox sighed when he at last knocked over his king. "Well played," he said.

"And you. I was careless."

"Would you like a cup of tea before the next game?"

"Ah! Very much."

Lenox rang for Mrs. Huggins, who was inordinately fond of the earl, and ordered a pot of tea. Deere lit his pipe, sat back in the comfortable armchair by the window, the small card table between them, and looked out at the gray day.

Lenox waited patiently. He had interviewed enough witnesses to know when some disclosure was forthcoming. The only dread he had was that it would force him to side in a secret against Lady Jane—something he did not think he could do, as sincerely as he considered both halves of the couple his friends now.

But he should have known Deere better than that.

When at last the lord spoke, it was to say, "I'm in a devil of a spot, you know, Lenox. I would appreciate your advice on how I'm to tell Jane something."

"What is it?" asked Lenox.

"It's my regiment. We're going to India just before Christmas."

Lenox raised his eyebrows. "So soon! I thought you had twelve months."

"So did we. But Catlett's regiment was to go, and he has fallen ill. He asked me as a special favor to take his place."

"What a pity."

"Yes. It means I shall have two years here when we return, but I do not console myself with that fact—I think Jane shall still be very upset. Besides which, we may be at war then, for all I know, in which case the promise of those two years evaporates."

"Could you not take her with you to India?"

Deere shook his head. "I would not wish to.

She is too happy and busy here—and she would come, if I invited her. We should scarcely see each other, and she should have to muddle along with the other officers' wives—all lovely women, and courageous to come to India, of course. I don't think Jane would dislike them. But it's difficult to join an entirely new set of people."

"Of course," Lenox said.

Deere looked unhappy, pipe in hand, eyes out upon the street. "She'll kick hard, I imagine," he said.

Funny how some men always reverted to the language of horses. Lenox could forgive him, though. Indeed, most military officers wouldn't have thought twice about their wives when assigned overseas—might have missed them, but wouldn't have spent time worrying over their feelings. Duty was duty. Deere, though, with his amiable sweetness of spirit, was different.

"How long will you be gone?" asked Lenox.

"Five months."

"It's not quite so long as last time."

"No, that's true."

"Well—you ask me my opinion. I think you should tell her the situation outright and then take shelter." He smiled. "I'm afraid you're in for it."

"Ha! Yes, I'm afraid I am. Head-on, then, you think?"

"Anything else she might well perceive as a condescension."

"Hm." Deere nodded, still staring out the window. Then he looked across the chessboard at Lenox. "Take care of her while I'm gone, would you?"

"Of course," said Lenox staunchly. So this was the true reason Deere had come over. "And really, five months, Grey—it will go before you know it. You can celebrate Christmas in May. I don't think the Savior would take it unkindly, even, a delay like that."

CHAPTER TWENTY-THREE

And then all at once, just past five o'clock, there was a driving snow across all of London.

Inspector Dunn was predictably displeased. "Don't see why we had to meet in person," he said darkly to Hemstock, staring out at the blizzard. "It will take all night to get home."

He wouldn't even look at Lenox. The three of them were waiting—with Graham off to one side—in a handsome marble vestibule outside the office of Sir Richard Mayne, on the top floor of Scotland Yard, which commanded wide views of the river and the south bank. There was already a patchy topcoat of snow on the steeples and chimneys. The sky was ghostly.

"Did you find anything in Manchester or Liverpool?" Hemstock asked.

"It was productive," Dunn said curtly.

Lenox took that to mean that he had not. He could not help but observe—indeed, it gave him a fierce private pleasure to observe—that the breakthroughs in the case had been his so far. The murdered passenger aboard the 449 from Manchester to London would still be anonymous if not for him. Josiah Hollis undiscovered or dead, in all likelihood. Their pursuit at a thwarted end.

He had known more peculiar cases, he reflected, but none quite so unorthodox in structure. Usually in a murder investigation, one began with a victim and traced him or her to a murderer; in this one, they had begun with an anonymous victim, and it had taken all the ingenuity they had to find out the man's name.

It meant that despite having done so much work, most of the case nevertheless lay before them. That was the murderer's cleverness, he supposed.

Dunn and Hemstock were bartering barely disguised incivilities, but went quiet at the sound of an approaching footstep on the stair. Sir Richard. The three men stood, and he gave them a nod before leading them into his office.

"Where are we?" he said without preamble, moving around to his side of the desk, pushing papers to this side and that, brow furrowed, looking for something.

Dunn delivered a brief and disappointing narration of his trip to the north. Hemstock followed this with a fairly accurate description of the documents. Lenox nodded along, and when Hemstock was finished made a point of complimenting him for his insights. He might as well try to be sure that someone liked him.

And what did the documents show, Mayne wanted to know.

"His correspondence was wide and impressive,"

said Lenox, "as Mr. Hemstock discovered before I began.

"Here, for instance, is a copy I made of a letter from the Prime Minister to him from two months ago: *I have received the letters of introduction most kindly supplied by Mr. Ralph W. Emerson, Mr. George Dallas, Mr. Horace Mann, and some half a dozen other august members of your political*—you take the point. Nearly all of the letters start that way. Gilman laid his groundwork well. The Prime Minister adds that he shall be happy to see Gilman on such and such a date—yesterday, in fact, it would have been, as it happens—for the space of thirty minutes."

"High connections."

"The highest. Here is a list of the people with whom he was to meet. You will no doubt recognize most of the names."

"So Viscount Palmerston is your primary suspect," Dunn said.

"No," Lenox said. "I am merely describing the situation to Sir Richard so that he may judge it for himself."

"Go on, then, please," Mayne said.

"There is also a second type of letter." Lenox handed it over. "Take a look for yourself. Mr. Hemstock will have seen it already."

gilman you *****r-loving filth stay out
of England there's plenty here won't

take it silent if you march, the white was placed by GOD himself to rule over the rest. signed, a proud AMERICAN of the Patriots Abroad

"Why is 'American' capitalized?" asked Dunn.

Mayne shook his head slowly, looking at the letter. "How many of these are there?"

"Three," Lenox replied. "He would have received all of them before his departure. Here is a more formal one."

> To the attention of the
> Honorable Mr. Gilman,
> We have our disagreements, but as fellow Americans we would hate to see you come to grief in Great Britain. Physical violence is abhorrent to our cause. Reliable intelligence informs us that you may be in danger of harm if you insist upon travel to London. Moreover it is unacceptable and traitorous that a representative of the United States would protest her actions on foreign soil.
>
> Yours most sincerely,
> *The Knights of America in England*

"I am not sure they would hate it as much as they declare," said Mayne. "The idea of violence against Gilman."

"I am of two minds," Lenox said. "I agree with you, but on the other hand I hardly think they would have announced their intentions so blatantly if they really meant him harm. There is even the chance that it might be a well-meaning caution, I suppose."

"Or they might not have counted on Gilman bringing the letter across the ocean with him."

This was Dunn. It was a fair point. Lenox nodded. "Yes."

Mayne rang for his secretary, Wilkinson. "Fetch Stevenage if he's still about."

Lenox waited for an explanation of who Stevenage was, but when none came he gamely pulled out the two journals with which Gilman had traveled, blue and black.

He held out the black one. "It was this which gave me the greatest pause, however."

"His journal?"

Lenox nodded. "His diary consists primarily of scheduling information, but the journal is different. It is full of scribblings. There is a much-blotted draft of a bill formally requesting the United States to free its slaves, and declaring Great Britain's withdrawal from all financial transactions touched by the . . . what are his words . . . *barbaric institution*."

"Well, he's quite correct there," said Mayne, taking the journal.

"There are also his observations of shipboard

life. A few sentimental reflections on a young woman named Margaret Murphy of Lawrence, Massachusetts, into which I hardly think we need to pry. But you will see the pages I have flagged. Look at the last one, to start. Crabbe was Gilman's correspondent at the American consulate. Son of a hero of their revolution."

Mayne opened the book, turning it halfway so the three investigators could read with him. The writing was quick, dashed off on one of the last pages—perhaps the very last shipboard morning, or not long before. It was so clearly of the penmanship with which one writes to one's self that Lenox, seeing it, felt a heartache. How very alive people were before they died!

To consult—Scotland Yard/Crabbe
- Anonymous letter postmarked Essex
(police at march?)
- gray-haired man shipboard—Lyman?
Liman? Strange behavior
- KAE
- Hollis safety/Patriots Abroad/Carel
Seaman

"Do you know what they mean?" Mayne asked, handing the journal back.

"The anonymous letter I take to be the one you have read, which encouraged him to seek out

198

protection at the march. The KAE—that must be the Knights in the second letter."

"Ah," Mayne agreed, putting them together. "The Knights of America in England."

"I have no idea about Lyman, or Liman. But you will remember that the man who bought all the newspapers and tobacco from the young newsboy had gray hair."

"Yes."

"I stopped by the consulate on the way here. The name is unfamiliar to them. We will need to seek out the manifest for the ship upon which they sailed, I think. Or else Hollis may be able to give us some information."

"And Carel Seaman, as he is called?"

Dunn spoke. "I know the man. He was brought up before a judge on a charge of assault last year. He and two friends set about an Indian traveler in Covent Garden. They might easily have killed him, though he survived."

"What was their motivation?"

"Racial. He did not make way for them on the sidewalk."

"Anything else? Lenox?"

"Seaman hails from Maryland. That is all I can add to what Mr. Dunn says. But I may have the articles about the attack on file at home."

In fact, he knew perfectly well he did: Each morning, he and Graham competed over matching sets of newspapers, clipping every article on crime in London that they could find, for an archive they were slowly but certainly building together. Lenox would guess that it was already the most complete of its kind.

He had recommended a similar one to Mayne the year before—but the commissioner had called it a waste of the Yard's time. That sat sore from the man who had banned snowballs.

He was across from Lenox now, holding his fingers to his mouth, eyes narrowed. "Finally we have proper suspects to investigate," he said. "Well done, Hemstock. Lenox."

"Thank you, sir," said Hemstock.

There was a knock at the door. A huge block of man, with a thick brown mustache and an expression that looked as if its owner would brook very little impertinence before resorting to violence, followed the knock inside without awaiting an invitation.

"You requested my presence, sir," he said.

"Hello, Stevenage, yes. Who are the Patriots Abroad?"

Stevenage—as this man, dressed in a blue suit, every inch the police officer, was evidently named—seemed to scoff. "Nasty but unimportant. A loose affiliation of alcoholics who get their joy out of threatening people."

"They come from America?"

"About three-quarters do. The rest are British. They meet down in Canary Wharf. Conspiring, I suppose, though I wouldn't trust them to plan my niece's birthday party. They do manage about a dozen prostitutes and a tavern or two."

"What about the Knights of America in England?"

Stevenage didn't look surprised at the name. "A slightly more respectable group, but with the same essential purpose. They meet in the Strand and wear tailored jackets. Actually I believe all of them are Americans. Merchant class. Not violent that I know of. Though most of them came to England because of a murky past in America, or so I've been told, so anything is possible. The leader hails from New Orleans. Quite happy at the moment with President Pierce, though they take a still harder line than he does."

Lenox, surprised at the easy expertise this man had, said, "Are you an authority in American matters, Mr. Stevenage?"

"No," the officer replied, without any indication that he wished to elaborate.

"Stevenage knows every gang in London inside and out," explained Mayne. "He is our encyclopedia."

"We keep a proper encyclopedia as well," Stevenage added. "The cemeteries being full of indispensable men, and all that."

"Is either group capable of political violence?" Lenox asked.

"What, this Eleazer Gilman I assume? I'd not

have thought so. They're very good with letters—threaten every abolitionist who comes to London, every Negro in particular. Not particularly enthused about the Irish, for that matter. But never actively violent so far. They are chatterers, you see. It's a hobby with them. An ugly hobby—no more. Five years they've been at it and never plucked a hair from an abolitionist's head that I heard of."

His tone implied that he would certainly have heard if it had been. "I see."

As if acceding to the fact that the groups of whom he was speaking weren't wholly harmless, he added, "I will say that Seamen is a man I hate to have on the loose. Unpredictable."

"Do you have a list of the places where they meet, these two groups? The membership?" said Lenox.

"I can have someone run it up. It will take fifteen or twenty minutes."

"I'll wait," Lenox said.

Mayne nodded. "Very good, Stevenage," he said. "Thank you. The three of you had better start with Lyman, or Liman, then, I suppose—and after that, Seaman and his people, too. Dunn, you take them. Lenox, you take the two patriotic groups."

They all assented.

Mayne sighed. "I always feel snow is a bad sign in these matters. Covers up too much. Everyone ducks inside. Still, push on."

CHAPTER TWENTY-FOUR

The women charged with managing London's social life were evidently made of heartier stuff than the timid souls who monitored the city's stabbings and shootings.

"Canceled! Don't be silly—it's two streets over."

These were the words of Lady Jane, who seemed galvanized rather than deterred by the snow, full of gaiety.

Lenox had waited alone for Stevenage's men to return with the names of the gang members, while Dunn and Hemstock hurried home to beat the snow. He had planned to pore over the names, cross-matching them with his archive, if he stayed in, but found that apparently he was still committed to an evening out after all.

And indeed, the house of Mr. and Mrs. Bronson and Susanna Geddes, which lay parallel to Hampden Lane—four streets over, in fact, but who would count—sparkled brightly in the snow, every window full of candlelight and motion, a small brilliant jewel set into the row of otherwise subdued and shadowy houses. Black carriages gathered outside, glossy horses leading them, steam rising from their nostrils.

Deere was with his regiment; Lenox, almost

before he could take off his coat, was taken on his usual bachelor parade, like a giraffe being led its turns through the zoo.

He greeted Deborah Tilton first. She had seemed one of Edmund's more promising candidates, until it had emerged that she was *already married,* which showed (Charles argued) that Edmund was the greatest dunce in London. With her was Lady Constance McKnight, who was just "out" and enjoying the attention of the boys her own age so much that Lenox, at twenty-seven, felt ninety, and Fiona Panday, who as usual talked exclusively and inconsolably about her aunt, who controlled the money that would be Fiona's when she married.

This was only the first wave of attack. Across the room he saw a whole legion of further potential wives, and saw them see him, some of them, he couldn't help but feel, with less than absolutely maximal excitement. At a party like this everyone was hoping to see someone or other; and so often it wasn't you.

Just as he was facing up to go and meet them, though, having been in the house for only fifteen minutes or so, he heard a mischievous voice behind him call his name.

"Mr. Lenox!"

He turned and saw a tanned, pretty face. It took him only a quick blank moment before he recognized her: Kitty Ashbrook.

His heart, strange independent creature, took a leap.

He bowed. "Miss Ashbrook! How do you do? I had taken you at your word that we were not to marry," he said, "and yet here you are, pursuing me."

"Is this what you call pursuit!" she asked.

"No. But you look so lovely this evening that one must almost propose out of good manners, Miss Ashbrook."

She flushed, seemingly to her own surprise, because she then laughed. "In that case every gentleman here is a brute, since not one of them has proposed."

A friend, involved in another conversation, was pulling at her, but as she was being tugged away she glanced over her shoulder at him and smiled prettily, a smile of whose effect she must be conscious, he supposed, but which was so easy, so natural, that it seemed just possible she had no idea how fetching it looked.

He had stood and watched her go for some length of time he couldn't name—a minute? a year?—when he heard his brother's voice, as familiar as his own, call him out of his reverie.

They joined together and soon were in the mix of Edmund's party. Everyone was rosy-cheeked and full of excitement about the snow, exchanging happy nerves about how on earth they would get home, and soon rising higher still in spirits due to Mrs. Geddes's cowslip wine.

To his surprise—though he shouldn't have been surprised, he supposed—he happened to see two of the men with whom Eleazer Gilman had scheduled meetings. It was a strange sensation when his personal world and professional one crossed. It must be for everyone, of course, but particularly for him. Already a fellow he'd known at Oxford had cut him that evening. He had learned to ignore that sort of thing, but it sent Edmund into a loyal rage.

The first of the two men who under happier circumstances would have met with Gilman that week was Wilton Sheridan. He was a handsome, athletic chap in a high collar. Lenox always spotted him by his thin mustache, which was waxed out to two perfect, glossy auburn tips, rising toward his ears.

Sheridan's father had been a rich man; like Charles, Sheridan was a second son, though unlike Charles, he concerned himself primarily with sport—specifically, horse racing. He held a seat in Parliament, which served him nicely as a hobby when there were no races on, as Lenox had once heard him say. By such slender threads of concern the lives of millions hung in an aristocracy.

Lenox asked him for a quick word. "Yes? Oh, Gilman!" said Sheridan, when they had gone off to the side. "What a pity. I saw that."

"We are trying to figure out what might have

happened. Do you know why he wanted to meet?"

"Something about slavery. So my secretary said. I am always willing to meet with these Americans. Good to have connections over there—big place, America."

"Had you expressed an interest in slavery?" Lenox asked.

"Me? No. But my father—well—we sold out of Jamaica just in time, the year '30 or so. Shame. There was a lot of money in sugar down there."

There had been a law until recently that England could only buy its sugar from Jamaica. "I see," said Lenox.

"I visited once as a lad," Sheridan volunteered, and took a draught of his cowslip wine. "I think they seemed jolly happy, to be honest with you. The slaves. They had good food, housing. Clothes. A church, if they wanted it, but they've their own songs and all that sort. I don't know why we wanted to rock the boat. Still, there you are. Wilberforce."

"He was a force of nature," Lenox said.

"They're very simple. They only wish to be happy and easy, you know. Ever so lazy. Father never tolerated them being beaten or anything of that sort—not for a moment. Beastly. Anyhow, I will admit I only went there once. It could have been worse at other places. No doubt it was. It's always some newcomer who ruins it for everyone. By the way, was that Kitty Ashbrook you were speaking to? A fine girl, that. Very fine."

Sheridan's blitheness stood in stark contrast to the more useful information provided by the second person there that Gilman had been planning to meet. This was a dour Member from Kent, in tiny round glasses, called Fry. He was widely considered a rising political star. Lord knew why.

"He was desperate to meet the Queen," Fry said.

"The Queen? Why?"

"To plead his case, I imagine. I cannot see what I could have done to help him, but I would have tried. Disgusting, the whole thing. Buying and selling people, in 1855. It's a disgrace."

Lenox was slightly taken aback by his ardor. Fry was a conservative, and his side had made the economic argument for slavery for years, while Sheridan, like Edmund, was a liberal, of the party of Wilberforce. He supposed that opinion had moved near unanimity, except in the case of personally interested businessmen. The abolition of slavery probably meant one less pony in Sheridan's string each autumn.

"Why did you accept the meeting?" Lenox asked.

"One does. If the letters of introduction are worthwhile. It happens a few times a month—

usually an American or a Frog. I can't remember anything about Gilman. You are free to stop in and ask my secretary about his letter though."

"I wonder why he thought the Queen would help him," said Lenox. "She never interferes."

"Behind the scenes she does. And she has that absurd goddaughter. Excuse me," Fry, who had been peering around the room the whole time he and Lenox spoke, suddenly said. "I see someone whom I had promised to visit with."

Then, to Lenox's astonishment, for he'd always thought Fry a tart and unpleasant fellow, he put an absolute beam of happiness onto his face and made in a straight line toward the other side of the room.

Left alone, Lenox noticed that Lady Jane was not five feet away. He took a glass of wine from a tray and went over to her.

She turned and both saw Fry approach a group of women, among whom happened to be Kitty Ashbrook. Together they pondered this spectacle together for a few moments.

"I wonder what it is like to be beautiful, as she is," said Lady Jane.

"Gallantry demands both that I insist you are and that I ignore the subject of your appearance entirely, since you are married," said Lenox. "But—being forced to forfeit one kind of politeness or the other—I will say that you are very beautiful, of course."

She laughed. "You're kind. But a woman knows by the time she's sixteen what the world thinks of her, down to the eyelash. It is why I hope never to have a daughter. Catherine Ashbrook is unusually beautiful. Watch the room move with her."

"What do you mean?"

"Watch."

Lenox did, and after a moment he perceived, to his astonishment—he, who prided himself on his skills of observation!—that Jane was correct. Conversations shuffled a tenth-step to the left if she moved, drew to the door when she seemed to, or the hearth when she sat.

"She knows, too, then."

Lady Jane narrowed her eyes, considering this. There was no envy at all in her mien. "Most of it, I imagine. Not all."

"I had not quite noticed it myself."

She laughed. "A very becoming way of telling on yourself—that you hadn't noticed at all! But now you will value her twice as highly, so I am glad, since I would like to see her often, which I will when you are married."

"I valued her before this conversation."

"Yes," murmured Lady Jane. "You did. I'm glad of it. I should also like a good line of credit with your mother."

"Yours is probably better than mine with her."

"No. She never liked my mother."

Lenox frowned. "I don't think that can be true. They are always so cordial to each other."

Lady Jane laughed. "I can only teach you so much about the behavior of my sex in one evening before I shall be forced to charge, Charles."

"She looks as if she's going to marry Fry."

Kitty was laughing happily at some joke the dry old stick had told.

But Jane was having none of it. She turned to him. "Charles Lenox. Can you really be so witless? Miss Ashbrook's eyes have only followed one person as the room's have followed her. And that is you."

CHAPTER TWENTY-FIVE

That absurd goddaughter. After he had gotten home and sat up for a while—so late that he was fairly sure even Graham had gone to bed before him, a rare occurrence indeed—that phrase came back to Lenox.

It had been Fry who'd said it. And the queen did indeed have a black goddaughter. Her absurdity was a matter of opinion; Lenox had yet to meet a person whose unalterable existence was absurd to them, and he would have to guess that Sara Forbes Bonetta—that was her name, he remembered clearly now from the articles about her, his memory prompted—did not consider her own existence absurd.

And Fry's own existence was the very reverse of absurd to him, of course. As was Wilt Sheridan's: more intimately concerned a thousand times over with the health and lineage of his horses than with that of his father's slaves in Jamaica. With his waxed mustaches, for that matter—Sheridan.

The absurd goddaughter had once been a princess in a tribe in Africa. Another tribe had captured and enslaved her when she was five, killing her parents. They had prepared her for human sacrifice. So the story went, at least. Then some Briton in that area had rescued her from this fate and made a present of her to the Queen. (A present! Like a mangosteen, or a porcelain place setting.) She must have been ten or eleven now, and if there was callousness in the young naval officer who had made her a present, at least the girl had lived.

Lenox wondered if perhaps it was in the favoritism shown this small girl, who lived at court with the full perquisites implied thereby, that Eleazer Gilman's hopes had resided. He must ask Hollis.

Lenox was warm in his chill study. Wrapped in a smoking jacket, he had his feet propped up against the ledge of his window. The snow had stopped. Now there was only the eerie emptiness of Hampden Lane beneath cloudless moonlight; ahead, the whispering late hours, his own in which to think.

After a long time he turned back to his desk, where he had laid out the documents Stevenage had given him. They detailed the activities of the Patriots Abroad (the less respectable of the two groups, or at least the less affluent) and the Knights of America in England (whose rolls included self-exiled merchants of the American middle class).

Not a very *knightish* place, America. Wasn't the premise of the whole project that they no longer had knights? Still, an American had received a lordship from the Queen the year before, by special dispensation, and the time it took to travel between the countries by ship shortened annually. During the revolutionary period the crossing had taken anywhere between six weeks and sixteen, depending on the season and the weather. (That had acted tremendously to the colonials' advantage.) Now it rarely lasted longer than two. Perhaps one day the countries would be reunited. He tried to imagine as far forward as he could: 1950, say, a time of instantaneous travel, and America and Britain a single nation once more . . .

He stopped woolgathering and settled in to read carefully over Stevenage's useful summaries.

The Patriots met in some configuration nearly every night in the White Horse Tavern, near Whitechapel. The Knights congregated in a tonier establishment, a restaurant without an official name but generally called the Stilton, where they had a private room and a tun of wine reserved for the second Monday of each month.

He scanned the names of the members of each group. There were some two dozen Patriots, roughly the same of the Knights. No crossover, nor did any name jump out at him except the unusual ones—a fellow who evidently went through his days encumbered with the name Christmas Byrd, for example. (In a crossword you would have put *goose*.)

With a sigh, he began the toilsome labor of cross-matching these names to the ones he and Graham had gathered from the newspapers over the years. He found no matches in the first ten or so names. Then he must have—he supposed—fallen asleep, for when he woke, it was with a confused start. His soft desk chair protested ferociously at the way his body shifted, squeaking beneath him and clattering against the desk.

After a moment the door opened. "All well, sir?" said Graham—still dressed, of course, bother him.

Lenox rose, rubbing his eyes, and smiled. "I thought I had stolen a march on you. But perhaps we both ought to get to bed."

"It's rather late, yes, sir."

His eye fell on the paper he had been studying. "These are the names of men who may have threatened Gilman." He sighed. "I feel no tremendous confidence that any of them are involved. But the rope is running out of our hands."

The case should be his, he could tell that now; he had enough information that he ought to be able to pick up the scent again, find the sham conductor who had slipped through his fingers, the gray-haired man who had attacked Hollis and sent Willikens off after buying out his newspapers and tobacco.

He had the clues. Only he didn't know where they went.

"I have been researching Mr. Gilman further, sir."

Lenox rubbed his eyes. "Have you? What did you find?"

"There isn't a great deal of other information, sir. All of the articles from the papers on file at the British Library were about the declaration of censure he hopes Parliament will pass against America."

Lenox nodded, thinking. "I saw his outline of the idea in his journal. He was a determined chap, anyhow."

After a brief further exchange, Lenox climbed upstairs to bed, falling asleep quickly and dreaming confused dreams in which Kitty Ashbrook appeared, and then Deere, all of it taking place in a house he could not name somewhere far from his own—a place with a bad feeling in it, in America, perhaps, or India. It was threatening snow, someone told him, someone just behind him and to his left. He saw his father, and then Edmund.

He woke in the darkest part of the night, overheated in body and mind.

He went to the window, pulled the curtains apart, and opened the latch slightly. The cool air was an instant relief.

But a feeling bedeviled him from the dream, which it took him five minutes of total silence, standing before the window, to name: loneliness.

There were a few flurries in the air again. At some length Lenox saw a figure pass beneath him on Hampden Lane. It was a tall man in decent clothes, certainly not at first glance the type to seem as if he would be out at—Lenox glanced at the clock—three o'clock in the morning. Perhaps something was preying on his mind, too.

It sent Lenox's thought to that evening at Paddington. The carriage; the horror of the strong young body torn open and slumped over. The stationmaster. Hemstock. The labels. And that blasted false conductor, fooling them all and making away as cleanly as you please on—

And in that instant, just as the man walking below slipped beyond view, Lenox's instincts came alive. Quickly he drew the window shut, locked it, then took the stairs to his study as quietly as he could manage, a candle in hand.

He went over to his desk and looked at Stevenage's report on the Patriots Abroad.

There it was: *the White Horse Tavern.*

Could it be a coincidence? He turned over his own notes, taken from his meeting in Mayne's office. He found what he was searching for. The porter at the Great Western had reported seeing a solitary man with dark hair leaving on "a bright white horse." He had been clear on that, Dunn said.

Those were not so very common. Uncommon in London, actually.

Lenox gripped the paper, reading the names again. He wanted badly for this theory to be true, which was a warning to be cautious about believing it to be true.

But it was a coincidence—and in the past five years, he had grown to dearly love coincidences. Or what seemed to be coincidences. They were the coin of his realm. For where he found a coincidence, six times out of ten it was no such thing at all but rather an odd sort of magnetism between two facts, such that the two magnets only had to be drawn closer and closer until they snapped together, seemingly at random—as if by coincidence.

The white horse, the White Horse Tavern. It struck him as very definitely possible that the way the murderer had departed had been a purposeful statement—of whatever dim ideas they had about racial purity (a *white* horse) and their own trumped up notions of symbolism.

He sat back, thinking about the Americans, trying to collect himself. He had always wanted to visit America, Lenox. He imagined it as a strange hybrid beast: a place that in some ways— fashion, importance, money—was still a colony subordinated to England, but in others a vast empire that seemed, between its promise of land and opportunity, certain to surpass this country. A strange place, in other words. In New York, he had heard, some of the houses were very nearly as fine as a home in London. But travel not far at all, less than a day, and you could be alone for twenty miles in every direction.

Standing at the desk, Lenox felt alone for twenty miles in every direction himself—far from the evening before and the dawn to come, far from the person he loved, wherever she might have set her head to rest in this great world, the person he hoped would bear his children, and whom he might still not even have met.

Far from himself in a way, in that queer hour; for it had stung when that chap from Oxford cut him. It still hurt that any fool with a coal baron's half-foot in the upper class could look past him because he had chosen this odd profession—which he could scarcely wait to pursue, in his current state of excitement, when the next morning arrived.

CHAPTER TWENTY-SIX

Night two. Hemstock looked wistful, as if he wished it had been he to draw the duty of sitting in a pub. Instead, for the second evening in a row, he, Lenox, and Graham were in a coffeehouse directly across the street from the White Horse Tavern, hoping, in Lenox's case with mounting desperation, that something would happen.

The snow was gone. It had risen as high as fifty degrees that afternoon, though the mercury was quickly dropping back toward freezing, and the puddles in the muddy carriage tracks on the street had begun to harden and craze.

"Another round of coffee?" Graham asked after a long period of silence, rising.

It was nine o'clock. "Not for me," said Hemstock.

There were five of them on the job in total at the moment. Three here, and two others being paid out of the Yard's coffers.

One was Walter Swain, the impoverished young apple picker who had ridden on the 449 between Tamworth and Nuneaton. He was sitting in a slouch hat and his own clothes—none too clean—in a table in the window of the White Horse.

On the windowsill next to him was a short stub of candle. If he saw the man who had been passing himself off as the conductor—the murderer of Norman Haase and Eli Gilman—Swain was to light it.

The other was little Willikens, who had temporarily given up his post at Paddington. (He had protested that his business would suffer, and so Lenox's own footman was selling the newspapers and tobacco from Willikens's cart, telling anybody who asked that he was an older cousin, covering for Willikens while he had the rheum.)

The boy was seated by a hot potato cart outside. Lenox's snack outside Scotland Yard had given him the idea of hiring it. He was wrapped in a new rough-hewn suit of clothes and coat he had chosen for himself, each at his insistence several sizes too large, and sticking close to the warm grate over which the potatoes were baked and buttered. If he saw the gray-haired man who'd bought his stock on the day of the murder, he was simply to come inside the coffee shop and tell them.

Dunn—off somewhere pursuing his own leads, related to Carel Seamen and the man called Lyman or Liman—had wanted no part of this business. Mayne had been hesitant, too, until he was won over by the enthusiasm of Stevenage, who had said that in fact the members of the

Patriots Abroad *did* keep two white horses at the White Horse Tavern, proud fools that they were. Whether they represented racial purity, or nothing at all, or some confused muddle of the two (which seemed most likely) was unclear.

"One more whole night of this again tomorrow," said Hemstock gloomily.

Lenox didn't reply right away. They had been here between 8:00 p.m. and 1:00 a.m. the evening before, with one of Stevenage's constables. He had confirmed at least nine members of the gang by sight—he was local—but neither Swain nor Willikens had spotted their man.

Nor had Lenox, of course. His eyes were constantly tracking the street for the charlatan conductor.

He realized that he must do something to lift Hemstock's spirits. Graham was at the counter, ordering coffee and, from the look of it, toasted cheese.

"Tell me," Lenox said, "if you weren't at the Yard, what do you think would you do, Hemstock?"

"I? What a question."

"Only wondering."

"Well. I should like to run a country inn."

"A country inn?" Lenox mused on this for a moment. "Yes, that seems a nice life."

"*Seems,* to be sure," Hemstock said, pointing a pudgy finger in the air as if he had caught Lenox in a fallacy, and sitting up higher in his chair. "But consider this: When have you met an innkeeper whose wife didn't run him very close—nag him from drinking his own beer, at that?"

"They do exist, probably."

"Yes." Hemstock sighed. He sat back in his chair again, as if his dream had gone in a puff. "And not a murder in sight."

"Do you dislike murders?"

Hemstock looked at him as if he were insane. "Yes. I jolly well do."

"Well, I know that. We all dislike murders. But do you dislike *solving* them, being involved with them?"

"Why do you think I came to you for help?" asked Hemstock. He shook his head, bewildered. "Cor. Your type. Dunn. I'll never understand you lot."

It was only at this exchange that Lenox thought again that Hemstock wasn't necessarily lazy, or stupid—though he was both in at least some measure. He was mostly just badly out of place.

"You might quit."

"Yes, any day I expect to inherit a great fortune," said Hemstock, gazing across the street at the window where Walter Swain sat. "I can hardly wait."

(It was lucky for them that Swain fit so seamlessly among the White Horse's clientele, which drew from three categories: members of its ownership, the prostitutes they managed, and down-and-outers with a penny or two in hand. Swain, in the character of the last, was drinking cider rather than gin to keep his head moderately clear. So he told them, anyway. He had proven trustworthy so far, but few Londoners could be trusted to stay too sober alone in a bar for five hours with an unlimited budget and no company. Few humans, in all likelihood.)

"It can't cost very much to set up as an inn-keeper."

"No, I have the savings by," Hemstock admitted. "But once they're spent, they're spent, you know—can't come back. If you fail, you're back to being a young jack, traded out."

"I see."

"I've never lived anywhere but London, either."

"Where would you set up this inn if you had your preference?"

"Gloucestershire," Hemstock said immediately. He rattled his flask, which had not refilled itself since he last checked it a few seconds before. "No question."

"You are very partial to Gloucestershire?"

"I couldn't give a fig for Gloucestershire. It shouldn't even be spelt that way, in my opinion. Damned nuisance."

"Then why pick it?"

"There's a coaching inn called the Fox and Grapes there, on the road north from Gloucester itself. I happen to know the fellow who owns it. He'd sell to me, I think. Little house above. Prettiest river you ever saw nearby, too. Full of trout."

"You fish?"

"I don't mind sleeping with a fishing pole near me from time to time," Hemstock said, and laughed his coughing laugh at his own wit.

Graham returned with the coffee and food. Lenox hadn't known he was hungry, but realized now that in the course of his long day, which had involved dead end after dead end as they tried to identify the members of this gang across the way, he had forgotten to eat. There was a Welsh rarebit, and he fell upon it with pleasure. Even Hemstock consumed a pickled egg.

The hours passed slowly, until at last they all dispersed and went home, Willikens and Swain (at Lenox's insistence) to lodgings nearby, each with a private room—a luxury that made them both suspicious, to the degree that in the boy's case it had taken the active ire of Stevenage's constable to get him to use it rather than sleeping in the streets.

A restless day passed, until the next night at eight they reconvened.

They had known it was inevitable they must attract the notice of the coffeehouse's owner. Having reconciled themselves to this, they set out to win him over, and succeeded without overmuch difficulty. He was a Mr. Collins, a red-cheeked, constantly moving chap of fifty, with bright white hair, and through constant custom, good tipping, and a titillating hint at their official business, they had made him into a friend and confidant.

But they hoped to keep their repeated presence there obscure to all but him, and this evening sat at a different table, at a different angle, than the night before.

It was much colder out. Willikens claimed he was perfectly warm, but Lenox went out at twenty past eight to buy a potato and check for himself.

It did seem warm enough there—just by the low fire, next to the good smell of soft potatoes and butter. Still, he was concerned enough about the situation that he missed what Willikens was trying to say to him as he handed over his change.

"What was that?" Lenox asked.

The boy repeated his words, with a soft, unflappable urgency, which would have done credit to a seasoned police officer. "This. Is. Him."

It was all Lenox could do not to let his head fly up. But he managed to thank Willikens with a decent simulation of nonchalance and open his potato in its wax paper to take a bite.

He was dressed down himself, Lenox. Very slowly, he glanced over and saw a man with surprisingly distinguished gray hair curling out from underneath a top hat, approaching them from the west in a long brown mackintosh. The man stopped and waited on the corner, not ten feet off, while two carriages moved briskly past under the yellow gas lamp and then crossed over to the White Horse.

They had planned for this. Lenox hurried inside and gave Hemstock and Graham a sign with his right hand.

Two fingers. The older man. Headed into the tavern.

Each now had their job to do. Graham went to find the constable on his beat who had promised to assist them if they actually saw anyone. Willikens waited fifteen minutes, hung a Back Shortly sign on his cart, and retreated to his room—whose privacy and warmth he had come to enjoy, Lenox had gleaned this evening, and blast it if he wasn't going to have to figure out where the boy lived and solve *that* problem, too, but it wasn't one for this very moment, he must focus, focus . . .

The young detective's heart was racing. He had been right. Or adjacent to right; they were at the least far closer than they had been before tonight to discovering the identity of Eli Gilman's killer.

Then, not five minutes later, after some comings and goings, Swain's candle came alight.

That meant both the conductor and the gray-haired man were present. After two days without a sign of either, both had appeared in immediate succession. The Patriots Abroad must have been meeting, Lenox realized. Swain's candle went out after thirty seconds but following a short interval flared alive again, as if he were playing with a lucifer match.

This was exactly what they had instructed him to do, so that it would not appear conspicuous when he lit the candle.

"We must go across," Lenox said in a low, urgent voice.

"We should wait for Graham to come back with the constable," said Hemstock.

"There isn't time."

"Time? They'll be in there for hours. Anyhow— no—look, we're twigged!"

Lenox flew out of his chair, for just at that moment, two men appeared on the low rooftop of the tavern. It was the sheerest luck that Hemstock had seen it—he might have missed them so easily. Lenox had.

"Damn it," said Lenox. "They spotted us."

They ran outside. Hemstock took a small pistol from his hip pocket.

"Stop! The law!" Lenox cried at the two men on the rooftop.

But there was nothing compelling them to stop, and after the briefest of glances backward, the two men set off along the rooftops.

Yet that glance! In it, Lenox had seen the face—the face of the murderer. Next to the gray hair and brown coat of his accomplice.

They ventured out further into the street, Hemstock and Lenox, a mismatched pair. They were helpless to do anything. The men were already two houses down, running, full running, a clearer admission of guilt couldn't be imagined, they were *caught,* but they were going to get away, because they were close to a dense cluster of rooftops, each with its own ladder. It would have taken twenty men to cover all the exits.

It was maddening. So close; so far.

But then, all of a sudden, in a huge surprising jerk—it must have been the ice, Lenox realized!—the dark-haired man, closer to the edge of the rooftops, lost his footing.

Lenox didn't see him fall, but he would never forget the hard, heavy sound of the body landing upon the ground halfway down the street ahead of them.

The man with the gray hair looked over the edge, then back at them. His expression was feral with panic, fear, and self-preservation. After an instant he was off, picking his way very carefully this time along one rooftop and then disappearing down a stairwell and into the warren of the houses—gone, Lenox already suspected, forever.

CHAPTER TWENTY-SEVEN

A difficult week ensued for Charles Lenox— sleepless, agitated, full of regrets. Again and again he thought of ways in which he ought to have ensured that Eli Gilman's killer could have lived to meet justice. A constable at the White Horse. Someone on the roof to prevent such an easy escape. It gave him no pleasure that justice had likely been done; he wanted the full facts.

Still, they were now all but sure that they had a name for the gray-haired accomplice: one Bert Smith, it would appear. The Yard had interviewed each of the so-called Patriots Abroad independently, and while they maintained a united front, to a man hotly denying any knowledge of the circumstances of Eli Gilman's death, Stevenage suspected that the gray-haired man was the one person among their number they hadn't been able to locate: Robert Smith, who went by Bert.

They searched his rooms near the White Horse and found them abandoned, with only a few unilluminating odds and ends left. He had no close family or friends.

As for the murderer himself, that was easier.

Winfield Bell, slayer of eminent American, plummets to death!

***Full report inside; 16 individual
illustrations of fatal chase
Inspectors Dunn and Hemstock lauded***

That was merely one headline that made the papers about the man named Winfield Bell.

He had been an American, Bell, raised in Charleston before moving north at the age of fifteen to New York. There he had become involved with a gang of criminals operating from what had once been called Stuyvesant Meadows, now Tompkins Square. They knew this because Scotland Yard kept a file of all foreigners suspected of having fled America to avoid hanging; Bell disappeared shortly after the 1852 death of a shopkeeper, a murder for which he was the prime suspect.

"A shame that nobody checked for his name in the rolls of the gangs here," Mayne said as they were reviewing the case together, the small team investigating the Murder at Paddington.

It was a dry, clear, cold day five days after Bell's now infamous fall.

"It would take hundreds of hours," said Stevenage. "Besides which, any of them with half a brain change their name when they come here."

"Bell must have had a quarter of a brain, then," said Mayne.

"Less than that after the fall," Hemstock said.

"Hemstock, please," said Mayne.

"What! You try and stop seeing it."

Mayne shook his head but apparently forgave the insubordination on the grounds of Hemstock's clear distress at the recollection. "Anyhow. The case may be resolved, but I would like to know more about Bell's motivation. We cannot have every American politician who comes here murdered."

"For their part, the Patriots are scared witless," Stevenage said. "They've stayed silent, but they know they're being closely watched. I don't think they'll move a finger without asking our permission."

"Haase's family will be paid a pension out of the railway fund," said the man off to the side. Lenox glanced at him. He always looked familiar, somehow. From the theater some time perhaps. "It was voted yesterday."

"I'm glad to hear it," said Sir Richard. "His daughters were distrait. Poor girls, quite as they should be. And what about Hollis?"

"He departs in a few weeks," Lenox said. "I shall see him before then, I hope."

"He's recovered?"

"Mostly," Lenox replied.

"Good. Then see him out of the country as fast as possible, please." Mayne closed the file he had. "The sooner this is behind us, the better. Find the gray-haired fellow one way or another, Smith. I don't care how you do it. Dunn, you're in charge of that. We need to give the Americans a satisfactory ending to this nasty business."

"Very good, sir. Though as far as I can see it's all a matter of them killing each other."

"Be that as it may. Go on, then, thank you. Lenox, stay back, would you."

Lenox nodded good-bye to the other men as they left. Mayne didn't look up; he was writing something. Nor did he speak when they were gone.

Lenox waited, until at last Mayne handed him the paper upon which he had been writing and returned his pen to its stand.

1: G. L. Pritts
2: Y. Goodin
3: J. Colbert
—>
4: S. Brush
5: J. Barker
6: C. Noel
7: J. Dunn
8: B. T. Jones
9: Q. Jones
10: R. H. L. Creeley

"What is this?" said Lenox.

"A list of my best inspectors." Mayne pointed

at the sheet and then looked Lenox straight in the eye. "The arrow is where you would be."

Lenox studied it. "Dunn is your seventh-best man?"

"That's your first question? Yes, he is. And what's more he would be higher up than Noel if he weren't so hard-headed. He's logical, at least."

"I'm flattered," said Lenox.

"Are you? My hope was that you would be insulted. Shouldn't you like to be first?"

"I suppose so."

"You might, if you come and work here." A lengthy look passed between them. There was no need at all for Lenox to explain to Sir Richard Mayne why he could not. But Mayne was apparently counting on Lenox being monomaniacal enough to overcome his bone-deep class aversion to working for hire. "Consider it."

"I will. Thank you, Sir Richard."

"Fair warning: You will otherwise soon find me less amenable. Not out of spite. Your involvement has worked well twice. Three times if you count the Dorset business—though that was his own. Still, one time it will go wrong, and thirty people will arrive at my office to ask why the dilettante brother of an MP was allowed to interfere in Yard business."

Lenox nodded. "I understand."

Mayne stood up, ready to turn his attention to

other matters, but took the time to add, "Dunn isn't *wrong* about you, you know. He's wrong in how he says it. But he's not wrong." Then he looked up. "What's more, if you come, I can give you a budget to study crime. You needn't take cases you don't wish to. Merely consult. Build up that archive you're always discussing. But with two or three intelligent clerks under you, good grammar school lads."

Lenox walked home, cold and full of complex feelings. He felt an overwhelming resistance to the idea of working for Scotland Yard, among the Dunns and Hemstocks of the world—but those last words of Mayne's, the promise of building something real and lasting, tempted him more than he wished to admit. What an edifice he could construct with more help and more time!

More immediate than any of this, however, was a determination to find the second man— not that he *be* found but that Lenox himself do it. (There was vanity for you.) The papers could detail Winfield Bell's history with ostensible solemnity—their prurience showing right through the light topcoat of sobriety—and elegize Eleazer Gilman as a peaceful representative of an allied nation. They could decide that the matter was resolved.

But for Lenox it was not.

He returned home to find a friend and neighbor

at his chessboard. Not Deere, though. It was Lady Jane.

She looked pale, out of countenance. "Hello, Charles," she said, rising. "I hope I am not intruding?"

"Never in life."

She sat down again with her quiet, graceful smile. Mrs. Huggins had given her tea. She poured him a cup, and he took a grateful sip, his ears and nose still cold.

"I came over because I have some business with you," she said once he had sat down.

"Do you? Not chess, I hope. Deere—Grey, rather—beats me often enough to suffice for both halves of the marriage, I should have thought."

"No, I loathe chess. Life is too short to play chess. Who told me that?"

"I cannot say."

"Duch, perhaps. Anyhow, listen. Now that you have pushed this fellow off the chimney tops—"

"Jane!"

"I'm sorry—now that he has *fallen*"—and here she winked—"I wonder if you might really settle down to the business of Catherine Ashbrook."

"I didn't push anyone off a building."

"I shall be sure to tell her that."

"You're going to drive me around the bend. Anyhow why does it matter now?"

"Because she is not short on suitors," Lady Jane said. She seemed serious. "I do not impose her upon you, Charles—if you do not find her congenial. But if you do, I beg you would let me take the reins of your social calendar, just for these first weeks of November, before everyone goes off on their holidays."

He hesitated. He remembered with vividness that moment standing in front of his window late at night, the loneliness of it; the hunched man passing solitary down the snowy street.

"Very well," he said.

She was well bred enough not to dwell on her victory. "Good. And now I must ask for your help."

"Anything, of course."

"It's about James."

"Oh?"

"They are going to ask him to leave. A wife in his regiment told me." Lenox's heart fell. Deere hadn't told her himself, then. "My question is how can I convince him to stay."

"To stay?"

She nodded. She looked like misery incarnate— at least, to Lenox's closely watchful eye. "I will tell you something that I cannot tell even my other friends."

"What?"

"When he is gone—well, you cannot imagine feeling as alone as that. It is the very worst thing. He can't leave. He can't. And he won't ask me to come to India. I'll ask, and he'll say no, and I'll have to listen."

It had been many years since he had seen tears in her eyes for herself, perhaps even since some adolescent game in the gardens that had gone against her, so self-possessed was she in general—yet there they were, plump and unfallen in the corners of her eyes.

He set down his cup of tea. "I'm so sorry, Jane. I can try to speak to him."

"Could you?"

"And if it doesn't work, we may hope that it is only for a short time."

She wiped her eyes. "Yes. All right. But would you try? I'm sure he'll stay if he sees how very much it means to me. I'm sure he will."

CHAPTER TWENTY-EIGHT

When Lenox looked back upon that November and December of 1855, it was for the month's Mondays and Thursdays. It was upon these days each week that Kitty Ashbrook and her mother received callers between ten o'clock and one in the cozy, elegant, light-filled rooms they shared in Eaton Square.

On the occasion of his first visit, it was Lady Jane who brought him. "I haven't been invited," he said when she proposed it.

"You must join us here in the second half of the century, Charles."

"I'm more modern than you. Graham has just acquired a clothes press that runs by steam. Our ironing days are over."

"I was unaware that your ironing days had ever begun."

He frowned. "Well, not *mine,* specifically."

"Mrs. Huggins!" she called out gently.

They were in Lenox's breakfast room. The housekeeper appeared after a moment. "Yes, ma'am?" she said.

"Are the girls downstairs using a steam press? Or ironing?"

A stony look came onto Mrs. Huggins's face.

"I can attempt to ascertain the answer to that question now if you wish, ma'am."

Lady Jane glanced over at Lenox, eyebrows raised. "Mrs. Huggins, I wouldn't have it in my house, personally," she said. "There are limits."

"It's a disgrace," said the housekeeper.

"Mrs. Huggins!" said Lenox.

She looked implacably firm—ready to lose her job. "I cannot apologize, sir."

"Nor should you," said Jane indignantly.

"I mean to say, perhaps she should!"

"She can't."

"I cannot."

Lenox looked between them in consternation. "This treachery! From two of the people closest to me!"

"The curtains come out more wrinkled than they went in, sir," said Mrs. Huggins.

"I don't know that we should be in such a headlong rush toward the second half of the century, Charles," said Jane.

"I couldn't have put it better, ma'am," said Mrs. Huggins.

When the housekeeper had gone, Lenox gave up and said that he would go to the salon; he could not hope to beat Lady Jane in a battle of wits.

Jane had been correct that his introduction into Kitty's household offered no difficulty. Miss Ashbrook and her mother, a trim and sympathetic widow of forty-four, herself very likely to marry again soon, one thought, greeted Lenox with great solicitude, insisting that he come again, which he did.

The mix of people there was lively and included many of the mother's friends. But it was plain— if concealed in a very fetching way—that they were in London to get the daughter married. They had her looks, her manners, and her ten thousand pounds with which to do it—and that seemed to be a very good combination to many a gentleman. Eight or ten of these passed through on each of those Monday and Thursday mornings, often in the company of sisters or mothers. They ate toast with preserves from the orchards of the ladies' cousin the Lady Cumberland; they lingered beside a charming small fireplace and made chat. They complimented the scenes of cottage life framed on the wall nearby, which might have been painted from Miss Austen's novels.

At the center of this mannerly commotion, Kitty Ashbrook sat tranquil. She was sympathetic, witty and friendly and well read. She was dependably polite.

Yet it was easy to glance off her surface. Only on the third formal occasion they met did Lenox glimpse the human beneath again, as he had when they danced.

Jane had ceased to come with him after their first visit, and for just a few moments, this time,

Kitty and Lenox stood alone by the fire, Mrs. Ashbrook entertaining two gentlemen at the windows by pointing out who else lived near them in Eaton Square, house by house.

"Do you go to a dance or a supper every night?" Lenox asked during this rare opportunity for private conversation.

"Nearly," she said, holding a teacup and saucer as they stood. "And you?"

"I? No. When I was younger, perhaps."

"Of course, a gentleman may dine out anytime he pleases, and expect to find congenial company—at his club. Women are not quite so fortunate. We must roll the dice each new night."

"That's true. Yet I think you must enjoy being out."

She smiled, a bright and even smile, exceedingly pretty. "Say rather that when you have seen me I have been enjoying it," she replied.

She was dressed in a green velvet dress, with a diamond pin holding her chestnut hair back from her forehead. "I am fortunate, then."

"Or else you bring good fortune." Though she had rarely been even this direct, he felt what he had occasionally felt—a sense that he was favored, yet no possible way of moving into greater intimacy. Except that now she added, "I often find that I look for you when I arrive at a dinner party."

"Do you?" he said—stupidly. It was not at all a gentlemanlike question, uttered only because he was taken aback.

"I do," she said. "You are generally not there, alas. Yet I cannot seem to pass eighteen hours without the pleasure of Mr. Campbell's company."

Lenox grinned. Campbell was at the window, and in age more suited to the mother than the daughter of these rooms—though his aims were fixed squarely upon the latter.

"Since you are so kind, I will say that I do the same. And I will add you one better."

"Oh?"

"Because of you I have been reading Thackeray."

"Have you?" she cried.

"Yes, and it takes an inconvenient amount of time, too—since the novels are so very hard to put down."

"How lovely!" This was the first moment when he felt as if their gazes met naked. "And you find him agreeable?"

"Agreeable? I don't know if that is the word. He is not easy on his fellow man."

"At bottom it must be agreeable to see the world in its true nature," she said. "For who could wish to be told a lie?"

"Some readers, I think."

The bell rang. She smiled at him with some

strange and real warmth and gave his hand a quick squeeze. "There I suppose you must be correct," she said.

During subsequent calls they revisited this subject, and with this key unlocked the last door of formality that had been bolted in front of them. By early December Lenox would have said they had grown genuinely close, as close as good friends, yet still far apart enough that he often found he was heartsick for her. He began to ask Lady Jane (whose prestige in the social world this winter, though Lenox was only dimly aware of such motions, had never been higher) to find a way for him to be invited to certain evenings at which he knew she would be present.

Was that love? He thought it might be, yes. On the whole, he thought it was. He was in love with her beauty; of that there was no question, for each time he saw her now he marveled at himself for ever thinking her merely pretty. On some mornings, visiting the Ashbrook apartment, he felt a sudden (and of course impossible) urge to take her in his arms, to press his face into her hair and kiss her slender neck.

And he was in love with her mind. He knew this because they exchanged letters, and the letters were as of lively an interest to him as could be. Her charm to him did not rest exclusively upon her looks.

Yes: This must be love. What he didn't yet know was how much love and marriage had to do with each other, or how well he had to know her before he declared himself.

It was Deere in whom he confided that doubt, as they were playing chess one evening.

Deere was to leave the country shortly. The decision had been taken, and Lady Jane, in this one case, had turned out to be mistaken— even her influence could not overcome the duty that Deere felt toward his Queen's commands. His wife protested that they were not even her commands, but he could not see them any other way. It was a funny, stubborn purposeful self-delusion, upon which, Lenox faintly discerned, much of the character of the officer class must have depended. Deere was so liberal-minded in all other ways, yet so fixed in this one.

"I suppose the question is whether you can imagine life without Miss Ashbrook," Deere asked Lenox.

They were in a very evenly matched contest, and for some time the young detective didn't reply, contemplating his move. At last he pushed a pawn one place forward. He had improved.

Then, as it was Deere's turn to lean over the board, Lenox took a moment to fill his pipe. It was a frigid evening. They had warmed brandy next to them, and were sat close enough to the windows that it actually made some difference.

All the way on the opposite end of his study was the large, blazing hearth, filling the room with its inimitable scent of burning firewood.

"I can, of course," said Lenox. "I am living it now. Aren't I?"

"No," said Deere. "Because you have the hope of seeing her tomorrow. And the tomorrow after."

"Yes. Yet I do not know that there is one single person for each of us, for whom we are destined. Do you?"

"I believe I do," said Deere lightly, still not looking up from the board.

"So did Gillham. Not to draw the comparison with you—but to myself."

There was a divorce in the papers at that very moment—the handsome, tempestuous Earl of Gillham and his beautiful, tempestuous wife. The law was still such that only aristocrats were permitted to divorce.

"You are no Gillham," said Deere.

"Thank you."

"He's much better looking." The young lord moved a piece and then looked up, gazing frankly at Lenox for a moment. He had a face full of interest in others, its thin features, which might so easily have turned contemptuous and unkind in one so privileged as an earl, transformed into gentleness because they were continually animated with empathy. "You may yet come to believe that there is one person for each of us.

And it may be Miss Ashbrook for you. I suppose only time will decide."

"Of course."

"As I said, I do. But of course, I married dizzyingly far above myself in temper and intelligence and goodness. I admit freely that my luck may have colored my opinion." He gestured at the board and picked up his brandy. "Go on, Charles—your move."

CHAPTER TWENTY-NINE

As the weeks before Christmas passed, a debate was occurring at a level of mild heatedness between engineering experts, and argued much more ferociously by the nonexperts who waged their war in the letters section of the newspapers.

It was this: London was certain to have *some* underground means of transportation built within these next ten years. But should it be a system of underground trains, or should the proposed tunnels be filled with water and have barges running between stations?

"It makes me think this country is mad," said Josiah Hollis.

He and Lenox were walking up Three Colt Lane together. They were to take luncheon together at a teahouse Lenox knew near Canning Town. Hollis had moved into lodgings not far away, near his friends the Thompsons as well as a significant number of other Quakers. They were among his most supportive allies here in England, it seemed. The Quakers had always been among the staunchest abolitionists. It had been a Quaker dwarf who convinced Benjamin Franklin to turn anti-slavery—making him, along with John Jay, the most famous of what

America called her Founding Fathers to protest the institution.

"The argument for the barges is that they would cost less, I believe," said Lenox.

"Until the water begins to break down the soil, and thousands of bodies buried during the Middle Ages begin to float up."

"Goodness, you've a morbid imagination, Mr. Hollis."

"So would you, had you lived my life."

This was their second meeting since the capture of Winfield Bell. The bandage was gone from Hollis's head. Hair had grown—patchy but healthy—over the scar. There had been no further attempted assaults upon him, though he had given two public lectures and participated in half a dozen salons at which he was the primary speaker. A poor substitute without Mr. Gilman's corresponding efforts, he said, but he was nonetheless glad the weeks had not been wasted.

"And yet I fear it's a far cry from what you envisioned when you set out from Washington," Lenox said a bit later, as they walked.

Hollis nodded, then was silent for the length of a block. "It bothers me not to have an explanation of their motivations."

Lenox shrugged. "They are a group of bad men, and at least two of them, probably more, were outraged by Gilman's presumption in coming here. His visibility gave them time to plan. It seems uncomplicated to me—tragic, but uncomplicated."

"Yes," said Hollis.

"You must not underestimate the tremendous popularity of Miss Stowe's novel, either," Lenox said.

"*Uncle Tom's Cabin.*"

"Yes." This was something he and Graham had discussed. "It has been the bestselling novel in every shop month upon month. The ground for an anti-slavery movement is strong here. Anyone strongly pro-slavery must be alarmed."

"Yes," said Hollis thoughtfully, "I have had that sense."

"You seem as if you had a caveat to add."

"Only that I am not sure England's influence is so great as my friend Gilman hoped. He was an optimist; I am a pessimist. I fear bloodshed will precede any resolution to the question of slavery."

"You would know better than I."

Hollis glanced over at Lenox. "The owners of the plantations in America have too much to lose."

"Yet you carry on trying."

"I carry on trying," Hollis affirmed, nodding once, cane still behind his back. He stopped. "I believe this is the address you mentioned?"

Later in that week, Lenox happened to be playing cards at the Oxford and Cambridge Club when Wilt Sheridan came in. He was the MP whose father had owned those hundreds of slaves in Jamaica, the one with whom Gilman had been scheduled to meet.

Lenox wasn't sure why—there could be no point in bringing up anything with Sheridan that didn't have to do with horses—but out of some irresistible impulse, he said, "Sheridan, I wanted to mention. I dined with a former slave on Tuesday. An American."

"Did you! Gilman's slave, you mean?"

"Not Gilman's slave, but—yes, Gilman's friend. I thought I would let you know that you are well out of that business. I know you said they seemed happy to you when you visited Jamaica as a child, but the tales he told me were so horrible that—well, I know you are a broad-minded sort. It's up to us, I suppose. Our generation."

"This was in your capacity as detective?" he asked.

"Yes," said Lenox.

"I see." Sheridan smoothed the sides of his mustache upward, grimacing his cheekbones to make it easier. "They shall settle it in America one way or another, I suppose. I don't think our generation will have much of a say in that. At any rate I want no part in the problem."

He lifted his glass in salutation, clearly unmoved by Lenox's little speech, and returned to his friends. Lenox didn't regret the attempt. Let anyone who pleased call him a detective, and see if he cared.

The next days went quickly, until as he always did he went to Lenox House on the twentieth of December.

He and Lady Jane traveled together to Sussex, both wrapped in heavy rugs. She had seen Deere and his regiment off two days before. The particular object of her ire at the moment was Captain Catlett.

"Fallen ill, my foot." Her carriage moved over the rattling ground just south of London, on the way to Sussex. In four hours it would drop her at her father's house, and then Lenox would be just half an hour from his brother, his mother, his family. "He has a mistress in Carnaby Street—everyone knows it."

"Does he! Do they!"

"Yes, including the Queen, probably. And for this my husband must travel to India. The military is intolerable. Thank goodness for you Kitty Ashbrook isn't in the army."

"Do you wish you had gone?" Lenox asked.

"That's the worst of it, you know. I don't. I wish I were with him, but no, I am happy to be in England for Christmas. Is that not disgraceful!"

"Not at all."

She looked out through the window. "I feel a horrible sort of wretchedness when I think of him opening the presents I packed so carefully—alone in his little cabin at sea on Christmas Day."

"He will toast you quite a lot to his friends."

"There's that consolation."

"And we shall toast him."

"Yes," she said.

"I might even win at chess, if I stick to playing my nephews."

Christmas was very dear to the heart of Markethouse, the small town that had lain under the protective gaze of Lenox House for some six centuries. During the next week, Charles spent a great proportion of his time out and about, the town green's lampposts festooned with wreaths, Edmund on the church steps handing out a Christmas goose to every family that wouldn't have had one otherwise, frost dotted in white paint on the window of the local pub. It was a bright, cheery week. Molly's sister and her family were staying at Lenox House, too, and so as a group they were some dozen in all, loud, a nightmare for the servants no doubt, usually a child crying in one corner of the house and two laughing in another and a fourth investigating the pigs (they would all insist upon sneaking away to visit the pigs at any conceivable opportunity).

In the happy occupation of the previous several days he had nearly put Kitty out of his mind. On Boxing Day, however, Lenox received a letter from her.

25 December 1855

My dear Charles Lenox,

I believe I promised to write you in Sussex when last we met. Here I discharge my obligation. Strictly speaking I needn't add anything, I suppose, but of common manners, I will say that my mother and I are happily situated in Hampshire with my cousin Martha and her family. I am the much-adored aunt here, and I confess that it is nice for once to be an elder, rather than a youth, in the eyes of the world. Only temporarily, of course. As Augustine said—make me good, Lord, just not yet.

Do write and let me know how you are; and I shall be disappointed if you are not with us at Eaton Square on the day the year turns. 1856! I had just gotten used to writing 1855 on my letters. Hadn't you? Every year one says it, but then every year it's true.

As I am, in friendship to you,
Kitty

Inside, unmentioned in the letter, was something that made Lenox's heart skip: a lock of dark hair. He studied it in his hand, and then before he knew what he was doing pressed it to his lips, before quickly returning it and the letter to the envelope and tucking them in the front left pocket of his jacket, just over his heart.

CHAPTER THIRTY

It was New Year's Eve when Lenox finally arrived again in London. He was happiest to see Graham, who had taken six days in Oxfordshire to visit his family. Now they were back in their usual places at the breakfast table, going through identical stacks of newspapers across the table from each other.

Each had a cup of tea, and it was a day when one wanted a cup of tea, for outside it was again awfully cold, so cold that even a minute outdoors began to cause a strange dizziness. The Thames had frozen.

Lenox wrapped a hand around his teacup and felt its warmth. There were charities for those without a home; officers of the church traveled poor areas, offering shelter to anyone outside, or blankets and hot soup if they would not come.

Yet he had felt the whistle of the cold cruel wind through tenements ten miles east of here, and guilt occupied him. In the end, which of them was a Christian who lived in warmth while others were freezing? And yet who was virtuous enough to trade away their place in that warmth?

In the midst of these contemplations, he had lost pace with Graham. Hearing the crisp shear of his scissors (Graham's articles were always cut very precisely; it was his that went into the archive, not Lenox's), he turned his attention back to the papers.

There had been a rash of petty thefts in Bethnal Green.

"Have you ever felt inclined to steal, Graham?" Lenox asked. "As a boy perhaps?"

"I do not remember it if so, sir," said Graham. "Although there was an orchard near our house where all of us took apples now and then."

"You can hardly call that a career of crime. Edmund once stole another boy's cricket bat. I think we both thought we were going to be taken to the Tower of London and beheaded. There's an awful lot of beheading chatter when you have a tutor just down from Oxford and writing a history of the monarchy."

"Did Sir Edmund need a cricket bat, sir?"

"No—but the other boy was a scrub and a taunt."

"I wonder if he still has it, sir, your brother."

"I don't think so. I recall hazily that we left it in a pub or a shop somewhere, somewhere that it would be found and returned to the boy. Geoffrey Gogg. He had painted his name on the handle in black."

"What prompts the question, if I may ask, sir?"

Lenox took another sip of the dark and fragrant tea, slowly waking out of the deep sleep he had fallen into after his cold journey home from Sussex. "I suppose because of this article. But it has been on my mind. Due to Hollis, actually."

"Indeed, sir?"

"Yes. We were at lunch not long ago, you may remember. As we left, I saw him slip one of the teashop's spoons into his pocket. Nothing special—a spoon you might find anywhere."

"It might have been absentmindedness, sir."

"No. It was the second time I saw him doing such a thing." Lenox paused. "And yet in all other respects he seems an honorable man."

"Strange, sir."

Lenox nodded. "Mm. Well, he has gone back to America now. I shall never know why he did it, unless by some unlikely chance our paths cross again."

It was a long, quiet day. Lenox relished the solitude after the bustle of Markethouse, sitting in his study and catching up on reading. As for Graham, with most of the staff given the day off, he was organizing Lenox's wardrobe to his satisfaction, a job that was never finalized but that brought him great joy.

It began to get dark early—at only half past four or so. Lenox fell asleep in front of the fire before dinner. When he woke he was cold, even as the embers burned next to him, and he knew that it must have fallen off another few degrees outside.

This was why it surprised him when not long afterward there was a knock at the door.

Graham went to answer it. Lenox stood, curious, near his desk, almost venturing into the hall. It was a bad day to be outside.

Graham entered a moment later. "You have a caller, sir, who wishes to present himself to you."

"A caller!" said Lenox.

"Yes, sir."

"Who?"

"He would not confide that in me, sir."

Lenox gave Graham a look of consternation. "Is he respectable?"

"Very, sir. Though he seems angry."

Lenox thought. "I will meet him in the hall I suppose. Will you stand close by?"

"Certainly, sir."

In the hall was a man of perhaps thirty—a gentleman by his dress and bearing. Yet Graham was correct, the man's expression was full of a strange furor.

"Good evening," said Lenox. "I do not believe I have the pleasure of knowing you."

"Nor shall you," said the man.

With dark hair and dark eyes, he was good-looking in an overweight, brutish kind of way. "You have come to see me, not the reverse."

"I will not trouble myself by remaining here

long. I have come to demand that you leave off your attentions to Miss Catherine Ashbrook."

"Miss Ashbrook?"

"Yes."

"Now I must ask your name," said Lenox. He drew himself up, crossing his arms. "It is already the demand of a blackguard—made anonymously, it becomes also one of a coward."

Rage flared in the man's face. "You have heard what I said. I cannot answer for the consequences if you disregard me. Or if you call me a coward again."

He turned and went back into the cold, slamming the door behind him.

"Quick, Graham—what do you see of his carriage?" said Lenox, running up to the window.

Graham had already gone into the breakfast room, across the hall from Lenox's study. "A coat of arms, sir—but impossible to make out."

Lenox crowded in behind him. "Four horses. We shall have to ask Mrs. Huggins if he was here before. You heard the exchange?"

"I could scarcely prevent myself from doing so, sir."

"What an absolute madman!" Lenox shook his head wonderingly. "If I'm murdered, give them a description of that person."

"I will, sir."

"You're supposed to reply that I'm not going to be murdered."

"Ah! Of course, sir. In all likelihood you won't be murdered."

"In all likelihood!"

Graham nearly smiled, and Lenox did; the exchange with the visitor had been absurd enough that he needed some kind of relief after it.

Four horses, and a coat of arms: money. A title, too, probably. Anyone who had one might put their family's coat of arms on their carriage, but in general only those who held or stood to inherit titles did so. If it were a second or third or eighth son or daughter who did it, they were either quite pretentious or came from the very, very upper reaches of the aristocracy, the children of dukes and royalty.

Bewildered and a bit overawed, Lenox returned to his study. He was to dine in half an hour or so, but he was composing a letter to Deere, who had written from Gibraltar. (*Nobody on board plays chess*, Deere had written, *nor of course is any of the gentlemen in the stateroom my wife—meaning that the diversions of Hampden Lane are still, whatever the joys of shipboard life, unsurpassed on these travels as yet.*)

Lenox had become deeply involved in his reply once more, with all the news he had of London and of Deere's friends, when he heard another knock on the door.

His body went taut. This was really too much— an impossible intrusion. Graham was in the hall, and Lenox immediately went to the door of the study. He was ready to see this impudent person off very harshly.

But to his surprise, the visitor sounded—sounded, at least, from the study's doorway—like someone different.

Lenox glanced at the clock on the wall. Half past six, and now two unexpected visitors on the last and coldest day of the year; strange indeed.

Graham came into the study, and from his bemused look it was clear that he was no less surprised than Lenox. "It's not the same chap?" Lenox said.

"No, sir."

"I hope this one's not as angry," Lenox said.

"No, sir." Graham held out a card. "He's a detective. He called two days ago hoping to meet you, but was informed by Mrs. Huggins that you would be away from London until today."

Lenox took the card from Graham. "A detective? He called himself that?"

"Yes, sir."

"But not one that you know? It seems impossible."

"If I'm not mistaken, sir, he's American."

CHAPTER THIRTY-ONE

A small, neat, prematurely gray gentleman trailed Graham into the study. He wore a practical gabardine suit and had a hat under his arm. He walked with a just perceptible heaviness in his left leg, as if he carried an old and familiar wound in the hip.

"May I present Mr. Winston Cobb, sir," Graham said.

"Good evening, Mr. Cobb," said Lenox, and they shook hands. Graham withdrew. "Charles Lenox."

"I'm pleased to meet you, though sorry to call upon you on a holiday."

"Not at all. I only hope that I can help you in some way, given how cold your trip here must have been."

"Starting with a cold passage across the Atlantic!" said Cobb, and smiled gratefully. "Fortunately I have a heavy cloak, which your butler was kind enough to take from me."

"Goodness, have you sailed here from the States? Please, sit. May I offer you a glass of brandy, or a cup of tea?"

"If it's not too great an imposition, I would be most grateful for coffee, most grateful. I have the American habit, and my day has been a long one."

"Of course. The days are often longest when the light is shortest, as my father once remarked."

Lenox went into the softly lit hall and asked Graham if he might get them some coffee, and perhaps something to eat as well.

"Right away, sir," said Graham. He disappeared through the small door near the front entrance that led down to the kitchen.

Alone in the hall, Lenox borrowed a moment for himself, trying to assess the situation. Then he shook his head and went back in. He couldn't parse it.

Cobb had sat down on the blue leather sofa in the center of the room and was setting out two groups of papers on the table. For a dreadful moment Lenox wondered if he was a salesman.

"How can I help you?" he said.

"I am here on behalf of the United States government, Mr. Lenox. My charge is to provide them with an account of the deaths of Mr. Abram Tiptree and Representative Eleazer Gilman."

"Gilman!"

Though he reacted with surprise, the name had never been far from Lenox's mind. Indeed, he thought of it daily, contriving to discover some clue that might lead them to Robert "Bert" Smith, the accomplice of the murderer Winfield Bell. But even as Bell's body had been falling, Lenox had considered the case essentially solved.

"Yes—Mr. Gilman," Cobb said.

Lenox was conscious that he must be cautious. He had immediately taken to the small American—he had no side, as the saying went, nothing officious or arrogant in his manner—but his aims were still unclear.

"What I can tell you is that I was there on the night the body was discovered, and that the same man pretending to be the conductor of the 449 later fell from the rooftop of the White Horse Tavern."

Cobb nodded seriously. "I have heard something like that, and am glad to have your confirmation. Well—I have found it best, since I arrived here earlier this week, to declare my bona fides immediately." He gestured at the papers he had laid out. "If you would care to study them."

"Of course."

Lenox took up the larger of the two sets of paper. In a scrolled Gothic script, it said at the top:

Commissioned, hereby, for a term of three (3) months, as a Federal Marshal, United States Army Sergeant (ret.), Winston Cobb who, in the execution of his duties, agrees, First,

Thereafter it enumerated a long list of duties. Lenox read through them carefully. The government had temporarily relieved Cobb of his duties as a member of the Militia of the District of Columbia and provided him with wide latitude and a (quite generous) daily payment of fifteen dollars, plus matching funds for his expenses when in England, out of the United States Treasury, in addition, of course, to travel to and from London.

It was signed by no less a dignitary than President Franklin Pierce. Apparently his philosophical differences with Gilman's party ended at the water's edge.

Lenox turned to the second document. This proved to be a scrupulous and thorough set of papers of identification issued by the American consulate in London, which had received by separate ship a detailed physical description of the newly commissioned marshal and a password that he was to give them upon his arrival. Two signatories attested that he was the man the government in Washington had sent.

"This looks like they have made a very serious business out of Mr. Gilman's death," Lenox observed.

"Indeed they have, Mr. Lenox," Cobb replied gravely. "As well as Mr. Tiptree's."

"I thought Mr. Pierce was an opponent of all for which Mr. Gilman stood."

"All—except America, I think," said Cobb. "He was a United States congressman. We do not take the death of one of those lightly."

"May I ask without offending you what the Militia of the District of Columbia is?" Lenox asked.

"Of course you may. It was our Thomas Jefferson who created it, Mr. Lenox. He was the first president to live regularly in the District. The American army of his time was small, and he wished to create a standing guard for the city and its politicians—in particular the president—so that they would not be susceptible to surprise attacks by small foreign parties. Or domestic parties, for that matter."

"I see! And you came to this militia through the army?"

"Yes, I did. President Jefferson recruited the first officers of the militia himself, and they have generally drawn on the recommendations of their friends from the army and navy when they selected new members. There is some prestige in the uniform—I hope."

"I see," said Lenox. He looked across the table at Cobb. "But you are not a police detective?"

"No." Cobb met Lenox's look, and a deep intelligence flashed somewhere in his eyes, lurking some long distance behind his good manners. "However, it has occasionally fallen to me to investigate crimes. Including murder. It is something of a specialty of mine."

"How interesting."

"I should hasten to add that my presence implies

266

no rebuke at all to the work done by Scotland Yard. Or yourself as a private consultant, for that matter, though it was not until I met with Mr. Hemstock and Sir Richard Mayne that I came to appreciate your role in the case fully."

Lenox nodded. "I should speak with those gentlemen before you and I discuss this matter."

"Ah!" Cobb reached into his jacket pocket. "I thought you might say that. You may still do so if you wish, obviously, but this might save us each some time."

Here the American produced a letter from Mayne enjoining Lenox to help. He recognized the handwriting of Mayne's assistant, but it had a postscript, under seal—*Americans are bloody serious about this. Tell him all you can. Mayne.*

As Lenox read this, Graham knocked and entered with coffee, sandwiches, and toast. Cobb was very earnestly grateful—in that particular American way, which made such sincerity tolerable.

"Very well, then," said Lenox, going over to his desk. He took a key out of his pocket and retrieved his papers relating to the Gilman murder. "But it may take an hour or more to tell the whole story."

In fact it took four. Cobb was a determined and curious questioner, Lenox a willing respondent, and they discovered they had a great deal in common—so much so, as they exchanged stories of investigation from that capital and this one, that by the end of the evening there was a real amity between them.

It was just shy of 1856 when at last Cobb left, having taken down perhaps a dozen pages of notes. Lenox was tired, and a little perplexed, but not unhappy. He told Graham about the long meeting. They were involved enough in their conversation that the clock took them by surprise when it struck midnight. They wished each other many happy returns through yawns, and soon Lenox retreated to bed, for he had a New Year's breakfast to attend the next morning at Lady Jane's.

He woke at the first light, however; no problem in rising. But with his awakening he felt a strange unsettled suspicion in his mind.

What had caused it? Something pressing, yet indistinct. He stared through his window at the view of distant trees, swaying against the pale morning sky.

Was it about Bert Smith? No; he thought not. He felt the answer close at hand, and he spent some time chasing it fruitlessly through his thoughts. It was nothing Cobb had said, for Lenox had done most of the talking. Cobb had had very little new information—was still in the stages of gathering it.

He had to fall asleep to find it again. His alarm rang at eight o'clock, jerking him from an unexpected second slumber, and he realized he knew what it was that had been on his mind.

Gilman: That was the problem. They had missed something. He knew it by instinct. None of it added together just so—with that click of perfect transparency one felt in some cases. They had gotten it wrong—not all wrong, no, it had been Winfield Bell whose face he saw in Paddington Station and at the White Horse Tavern.

But they had gotten enough wrong that Lenox knew, prompted to relive the case by Cobb's visit, that someone, somewhere, had gotten away with murder.

CHAPTER THIRTY-TWO

M issed what, sir?"
Lenox and Graham sat across from each other at the breakfast table, their old battle stations. There was a pot of tea between them. Each had a cup, and their newspapers lay to the side, neglected, as Lenox tried to formulate what he meant. He was dressed for the breakfast next door, though wishing he could skip it.

"It's the bones of the thing," he said.

"Sir?"

"*Why* kill Gilman? The answer seemed so clear that I never questioned it: Bell and Smith were driven by racial prejudice. They're pro-slavery, anti-abolition. But scratch deeper and you realize that if that were their motive, their actions make little sense."

"How so, sir?"

"For instance, why write a letter to Gilman, then go to such lengths to conceal whom they had killed?"

Graham raised his eyebrows slightly. A hit. "Perhaps they didn't expect Gilman to bring the letter."

"Very well. Yet you must admit a strange tension between their writing him directly and then the ruthlessness with which Winfield Bell murdered the conductor, Haase, and then impersonated him, in order to eliminate any sign of who Gilman was. The very labels on his clothes." Lenox warmed to his subject. "Were they trying to make a public statement of politics or avoid notice? It must be one or the other—it cannot be both. And for that matter, why Gilman? There must have been a dozen emissaries of the abolitionist movement in America this year alone. Stevenage said the Patriots Abroad threaten them all."

"Did you not say that Gilman was the most illustrious, sir? They may have wished to instill fear in future visitors."

"True." Lenox continued to stir his tea, for the distraction of it rather than to any practical end. "It just . . . doesn't seem right. That's all I know."

"Perhaps it's the arrival of Mr. Cobb that makes you think so, sir."

"I suppose that's possible."

"And yet . . ." Graham was frowning.

"What?" said Lenox.

"Your doubts make me wonder, sir: Why make attempts on the life of all three?"

Lenox snapped his fingers. "Yes! Graham, you wonderful fellow—yes, why on earth would these patriot fools, or whatever they're called, elect to kill *all three* of the party? It triples their danger. More than triples. And at separate times, in separate locations. Abram Tiptree, the secretary, as soon as they arrive, in Liverpool.

Gilman on the train from Manchester to London nearly a week later. And then, shortly thereafter, Hollis. Deeply irrational if they wished to send a message. Only Gilman could have mattered to them."

Graham nodded. "It's strange."

Lenox stood up. "And if Gilman's death was to make a point, why cut out the labels of his clothes? Why attempt to leave him to be discovered the next day on the train, so that he might have been mistaken for a vagrant, or a nameless gang member from Manchester?"

"I don't know, sir," said Graham.

"It must be because something was at stake larger than anger at Gilman's politics."

"Such as?"

"I don't know." Lenox took a last sip of tea and began to gather his things to go out. "A wish to silence him, perhaps? What I know is that I have been criminally idle in not going to Liverpool. Abram Tiptree was murdered first. I have neglected that fact for too long."

"Then you don't think it was Bell, sir?" said Graham.

They had moved into the hallway, and Lenox was wrapping a scarf around his shoulders. "Oh, it was Winfield Bell. I saw him—conversed with him—in his guise as conductor. And Willikens confirmed that it was Bert Smith who bought all of his stock."

"That is also strange, sir," Graham observed, helping him into his coat.

"What?"

"That Smith, the accomplice, should clear the newsboy away from the platform."

Lenox nodded. "Yes. And do you remember what Willikens said? *He tried to talk normal, but he was shamming it.*"

"His accent, sir?"

"Yes." Lenox shook his head. They were standing at the door. "I can't make head nor tail of anything they did, now that I actually, properly think it through. These are deep waters."

"How can I help, sir?"

"Could you find out what you can about Bell? Without risking your own neck, please. Don't go speaking to his friends at the White Horse."

Graham nodded. "Very good, sir."

Lenox sat through a breakfast at Jane's house that in other circumstances he might have enjoyed, but now yearned to have over. As soon as he could excuse himself he did, and ventured out to see Cobb.

It was slightly warmer than the day before, but still very cold. Ragged clouds unraveled across the pure blue sky. Lenox was confounded but energized; once he had hailed a cab, he took his seat and went back to the very start of his notes from this case.

He must not assume he understood a single fact

about it clearly, he reflected—must return to the very first questions he'd had that night on the platform at Paddington.

The hansom jounced out of Mayfair on the uneven cobblestones and made its way into the heavy traffic of Regent Street, which eventually made a great swooping curve at Piccadilly Circus. From here it was a short trip to Cobb's lodgings in Leicester Square.

It was a section of London that Lenox visited infrequently—he was not an avid theatergoer, which was the main reason to stop there, and paid no visits at all to the well-known brothels off the square, being still, at bottom, no matter how urbane he became, shocked in his country boy's Sunday heart that they existed so openly.

There was a porter at Cobb's lodgings, which, though not quite a hotel, had many of a hotel's amenities. He took him to the American, who met him with gladness but surprise. He was dining on eggs and kippers, dressed in a sober blue suit, the slight halt in his step perhaps more pronounced when he rose to shake Lenox's hand. A day of activity, out in the cold.

"Was there something you forgot last night?" he asked curiously.

"No—it is that our conversation has made me rethink things. Entirely, truth be told, or almost entirely."

"My heavens! You'll have to sit down."

Lenox did. "I still think Winfield Bell our murderer," he said, "and Bert Smith his accomplice. But I'm confident of very little else."

"Please, go on."

And so Lenox detailed, in slightly more orderly fashion than he and Graham had flung their thoughts together, all that struck him as out of kilter about the murder of Eli Gilman as they currently understood it—and as the papers, with declining frequency, reiterated its particulars.

As the young Englishman spoke, Cobb, breakfast finished, lit a pipe and listened, with an open, intelligent concentration.

At last, when Lenox had finished, he nodded slightly. "My mind has been following the same track as yours."

"Has it!"

"Yes. Though you must remember that I have the advantage of coming in after the fact, and thus being able to see the whole field of play without prejudice or confusion—at least, I hope."

Lenox had reached an age—or perhaps more importantly, had confronted enough obstruction from recalcitrant inspectors and sergeants at Scotland Yard—at which, while he was still confident in his ideas, he was more generous when they were wrong than perhaps he once had been.

"You have seen more already than I did the whole time," he told Cobb. "I'm heartily sorry—and very glad you came."

Cobb shook his head. "It was you who pieced together Mr. Gilman's identity, and you who led Inspector Hemstock to the White Horse, Mr. Lenox. At every turn I seem to discover some tidy piece of detective work that turns out to have been yours."

"Then perhaps we can join our efforts."

"With pleasure," Cobb said seriously, and to Lenox's surprise reached out a hand.

Lenox shook it, with a sense of reinvigorated energy and obligation. It was New Year's Day, after all.

CHAPTER THIRTY-THREE

The two men devised a plan. Cobb had been preparing to go to Liverpool that day. They decided that he would carry on, while Lenox reopened his investigation into the case here.

First, though, Lenox returned home, for in his haste to catch Cobb he had left several letters and invitations unanswered to which he wished to reply. Besides, he wasn't dressed warmly enough. He took the omnibus again. It was one of the more and more common kind painted a bright cherry red. When he had first moved to London, just several years before, they had been of different colors depending on their destination, a rainbow of vehicles trailing their way through the city. He rather missed that.

After a brisk twenty-minute ride, he walked the short distance from Grosvenor Square to Hampden Lane. About to duck into his house, he noticed that there was a soft light flickering in the front room next door and turned his steps there, almost without thinking, to see Lady Jane.

No matter how much she insisted otherwise, he knew she had been in low spirits. It had not truly abated even over Christmas, though she had put on a creditable simulation of seasonal gaiety.

He knocked on the door. Kirk, her butler, a

large young fellow with a round face and the look of an all-county ale drinker, escorted him inside.

"Charles!" Jane was in her light blue morning room, writing letters on a small rosewood secretary. She had on a white dress, with a gray ribbon drawing it in around her rib cage. "I wish you the happiest of new years."

He bowed. "And you. Am I interrupting?"

"I hope so. It's a letter to my father, and I never know what to tell him, because the only news he really wants to hear about is who's won the snooker at the Carlton Club. And they still won't have me as a member."

"You would be the first woman."

"Someone must be. Anyhow, what are you doing? Nothing, I suppose? Not a single thief caught yet today?"

"It's still morning. Although I have been busy, since you mention it."

She stood up and crossed the room to a rose-colored sofa, inviting him to sit.

"Tell me all about it, please," she said. "Put my mind to some use other than wondering about the weather in the Aral Sea, or wherever on earth James finds himself this morning."

So he described Cobb's visit the night before. Lady Jane expressed surprise at Lenox's reconsideration of the case, which she had followed in the newspapers as everyone else

278

had. She remarked that the assassination had in fact had the opposite effect than presumably the assassins had hoped: It had reignited the debate about whether Great Britain ought to pass a resolution of the kind that Gilman had come in part to propose to lawmakers, or even ought to break off trade with America.

They talked about this some while—before Lenox said that he wished he knew more about Bell, the murderer. "He's a mystery to me."

"Yet one sees so much about him."

"It may seem so, but it's always the same few facts. That he was dishonorably discharged from the American navy, that he moved here—to avoid prosecution, they say, though that is speculation—and that he fell into crime."

"And Lady Elaine."

"Yes, and that."

This was a relatively new personage in the whole saga. Lady Elaine (no known last name) had been Winfield Bell's consort—probably, in common law, his wife. She was a lifelong resident of the east side. The name was an affectation. She was, nonetheless, at least somewhat grand; she managed the tenement where the prostitutes under the "protection" of Bell's gang lived.

They had been well known as a couple for at least three years. Not well liked, however. Even in Whitechapel, where very few people were inclined to speak about each other to the police, plenty had been willing to describe the general rottenness of Winfield Bell and his Lady Elaine.

Dunn had interviewed Lady Elaine at length and concluded that she knew nothing of interest. Now, though, Lenox mentally added her to his list of witnesses to revisit.

The question, as he told Jane, was how Bell had leapt from his low-grade fever of criminality to the full raving illness of savage and calculated murder.

"The influence of the White Horse?" she suggested, naming the tavern that had quickly become infamous.

"Perhaps," said Lenox. "Perhaps. By the way—I had nearly forgotten myself, but I received another visitor yesterday evening, too."

"Who was that?"

"I hoped you might be able to tell me. He wouldn't give his name. He only came, stood in my entranceway, and instructed me to stay away from—can you guess? Kitty Ashbrook."

Lenox said this lightly, but Lady Jane's eyes widened. She was cradling a cup of tea in her hands. She took a sip, and as he observed her, sitting in the gentle slanting yellow light of the late morning, he felt grateful that he had a friend like this—that her eyes widened, that she was as concerned as he, or more.

She quizzed him for an exact physical description.

"A coat of arms," she said finally, a puzzled look on her face. "Was Graham sure?"

"I think so. He's not often wrong."

"No, he's not." She set her tea down on the small flute-edged end table next to her. "But I don't know who would behave that way over her."

"Who are her suitors?" he asked.

"You would know as well as I."

"I did not recognize him, certainly."

Lady Jane frowned. She was unaccustomed to aught but victory in the social battles she waged. "We must find out who he was. I shall call on her mother this afternoon."

"I like her, Mrs. Ashbrook," said Lenox.

Lady Jane nodded. "Yes, I do, too. She is hard done by, yet uncomplaining. To lose a husband at her age, too late for more children, yet early in life, and two years of mourning to endure—that is no easy thing."

"I have not had the courage to ask how Catherine's father died."

"Catherine! You are on intimate terms."

Lenox blushed. "Perhaps that's true."

"Are you in love with her?"

He didn't answer right away but turned and looked through the window, eyes narrowed in thought. "I can't be sure. What does love feel like?"

She smiled tenderly. "It doesn't feel like that question."

"Then perhaps I am not."

"I would not encourage you to marry without love, you know, Charles. But do you feel—are you capable of love, just at this moment in your life I mean, do you think?"

He looked back into her eyes. It was the nearest they had ever come to discussing the fact that he had once declared his love for *her*—and the additional unspoken fact, nevertheless known to both of them, that on that occasion he had felt no doubt at all.

"I think I am," he said. He thought of his joy at getting Kitty's letter over Christmas, with the lock of her hair. It sat in a small gold box on his desk now. "Yes, I think if I knew she loved me— if I felt safe in her love—mine would come forth readily."

"Have you declared yourself?"

"No. Indeed, she has committed herself more than I have, I think—unless I am mistaken."

"How could you be mistaken?"

He told her about the letter, though not about the lock of hair. He meant to keep that to himself—always—in case they married.

Lady Jane said it sounded as if Charles were very much in Kitty's heart.

"I hope so. As much as I would hate to prove you and my mother right at one time."

"What do you feel when you think of her?"

He thought of her: her kind eyes, long hair,

and slender shoulders, her bright even teeth, her smile. And his heart skipped as he realized, yes, she was a person he knew, whether she was forthcoming of herself or not, he knew and understood her—and loved her.

"I think I do love her."

Lady Jane reached over and squeezed his hand, then let it go. "Good. Do you know, they never spent much time in London before this. I think your visitor must be some country acquaintance of theirs, sure that he has first claim on her. But if you love her and she loves you, you shall have her. I promise you that."

He laughed. "What a veritable Athena you are, Jane, intervening in the affairs of us mortals. Thank you. I should prefer to know who he was before I see her again on Thursday. Not that I would ask her—but for myself, I would like to know."

CHAPTER THIRTY-FOUR

In 1560, the French ambassador to Portugal, Jean Nicot de Villemain, sent a present back to his king. It was a healthy young plant, and along with it he sent some seeds for further cultivation. The plant's use was medicinal—promoting a clear mind and preventing the plague, it was said—and the young ambassador, who had previously been known mostly for negotiating a marriage between a five-year-old French princess and a six-year-old Portuguese prince, became famous throughout Paris for his discovery. The great Linnaeus himself named the plant after Nicot de Villemain: nicotine.

The last Lenox had checked, the plague was not abroad in London—in general one knew very quickly when it was around, as he understood—but he did feel deeply in need, after he had stopped by his house, ordered his carriage, and departed, of clarity of thought.

With the window of the carriage just ajar, he lit the scarred but (thanks to Mrs. Huggins!) shining old pipe, with its circlet of gold binding bowl and stem, that had belonged to his father.

With this done, he threw his undivided concentration upon the murders of Abram Tiptree and Eli Gilman, and the assault upon

Josiah Hollis. By the time he had reached his destination, the questions he had cumbersomely formulated with Graham, then articulated more clearly with Cobb, had grown clear in his mind. He knew—he thought—exactly what he wanted to know.

He entered a small stone police waystation in Coke Street, which served as a local headquarters.

"Mr. Lenox!"

This was the voice of Constable George Batch. "Hello, Batch," said Lenox, with real friendliness. "How have you been?"

"Quite cold. You?"

"Cold on the trail of Winfield Bell. That's why I'm here."

Batch frowned. "Bell? Isn't that all finished by now?"

In the course of their three nights of surveillance of the White Horse Tavern, leading up to the climactic sightings of Winfield Bell and Bert Smith, Lenox, Graham, and Hemstock had come to know Batch quite well—and Lenox to admire him as a smart, straightforward, physically intrepid young agent of the Metropolitan Police.

Stevenage had noticed the same qualities. They were in the East End now, not far from the infamous Whitechapel, where the poorest of the poor scraped by. It was here that Batch hailed from—a true local—and here that he primarily worked. Stevenage had relieved him of the burden of a regular beat and given him the more serious job of helping to track the gangs, patrol the streets as he wished, and assist in special cases, like the one involving the White Horse.

"Not quite finished," Lenox responded. "In fact I was hoping I might ask you, or an associate, to make a quick trip back to the tavern. I don't feel quite easy going on my own."

Batch laughed. "No, I doubt they would give you a very warm welcome." He glanced at the clock on the wall. "I can spare an hour if you like."

"I would be grateful."

"Let me fetch my coat."

They had spent so long staring at the White Horse, which lay on the busy corner of Whitechapel Street and Back Church Lane, that Lenox felt he knew it by heart: dark green paint, gold lettering, swinging sign painted with the white horse. In summer no doubt a few shrubs outside, but certainly not on this January morning.

He was counting on it being quiet, and when they entered, they found that it was. An old woman was mopping the floors and wiping the tables; a few patrons, each alone, sat nursing gin.

The bartender was younger than anyone else there—only seventy-five or so. "Help you," he said to Batch, politely but firmly.

"Yes," said Batch. "We need to see the stairwell leading up to the roof."

Lenox expected some resistance, but Batch must have been well known; the man just nodded and led them to the back of the bar, past the dartboard and the tabletop skittles ("devil among the tailors" they called the game in these parts), past a last table with a pair of dice sitting in a diagonal of sunshine, waiting for the evening, and into a private room.

PATRIOTS ABROAD, a silk banner proudly announced, in the colors and style of the American flag. It was hand sewn.

"This is their private room?" Lenox asked the bartender.

The courtesy extended to Batch was not his to call on, apparently—the bartender didn't reply, and Lenox didn't ask again.

The old man did show them to a narrow door, about half the width of a normal door. "There you are," he said, and turned and left the room without another word.

"Well?" said Batch.

"Up we go."

It was a bit strange to be in the White Horse for the first time. Lenox had not been part of the initial search for the gray-haired accomplice, his focus in those frenetic first moments resting with the two people he felt were under his protection, Swain and Willikens. Nor had he returned, however—and there he could blame himself for slackness.

The rooftop of the White Horse was laid with an ancient worn-down brick, smooth enough that you might easily slip even were there no ice there at all. A thrill of horror ran through Lenox.

Batch must have felt it, too. "Bit unsettling," he said.

There was a rail that came up to about Lenox's chest. Higher than he expected. He leaned on it, looking out at the buildings that stretched for miles toward the West End. It was a clear view—new tenements, old brick façades, white stone balustrades. Each of the buildings housed some story, sad or cruel, upward or downward, a story involving cupidity or generosity, love or meanness. All of them had an element of poverty.

How long could a society last when so many of its members clung to life in it so tenuously? It had been different when Lenox's parents were young, he thought—but London had grown so huge and unwieldy and dense in the last fifty years. The world even now was very different than the one into which he had been born.

Lenox and Batch tracked Bert Smith's possible routes over the rooftop until Lenox had satisfied himself on that point. There were a dozen points of egress into the busy lanes behind Whitechapel, each the matter of scaling a few windows.

"It would be easy even in the ice," said Lenox.

Batch nodded. "Yes."

"Yet I see where we made a mistake," the young detective murmured, hands in his pockets.

"Where?"

"Eh? Oh." It wasn't what he had been thinking, actually, but he said, because he liked Batch, and because it had just occurred to him, "Very strange that they would go to such lengths to conceal who Gilman was on the train, yet then Bell would come out on a white horse, as memorable as you like."

Batch, with his fleshy, shrewd face, shrugged. "You must bear in mind that you are dealing with extremely stupid people."

Lenox emitted an involuntary bark of a laugh. "I've no doubt. Still, I would be curious to see these white horses. I never did."

"I'll ask old Rutherford if you like."

"The bartender?"

"The very one."

"Good, let's go inside."

Batch didn't need a second invitation. "Oy," he said to the man behind the bar when they had reentered it. "Where are the white horses?"

"What white horses?"

"From the stables."

Rutherford shook his head. "Ain't none."

"How's that?" said Batch.

"Quoit died about nineteen month back— Whitey before that. Been looking for a replacement but none's come up, you know."

"You mean they haven't found one to steal," said Batch, though in such a genial tone that it could have been mistaken for a joke.

"Don't know about all that."

A voice piped up from the end of the bar. "They call them girls as is available white 'orses," it said, and then a drunken cackle came from the gap-toothed, grizzled pile of dark clothing on one of the stools.

"Shut your trap," Rutherford ordered.

"The prostitutes?" Batch said.

"No longer—not any longer, guv," said Rutherford. "Saw an end to all that, didn't he— Bell, I mean."

"And Smith," said Lenox.

Rutherford merely turned away, toward a small stove that had a copper kettle on it. He poured himself some black, bitter-smelling liquid from it into a tin cup with a big round handle.

"Rutherford," said Batch, "what about Smith?"

"What about him?"

"Did you know him well?"

"I only work here. That's the God's honest, Constable."

"You must have at least seen him, then."

Rutherford opened his eyes wide, as if to say *you'd be surprised.* "You didn't?" asked Lenox.

"Not till that day," said the bartender, and took a draught of the scalding coffee. "Excuse me, please. I've food to start preparing."

"We'll excuse you when we're ready," said Batch.

Lenox didn't want to suborn Batch's clear authority here—goodness knew how one won it—so he asked a few more questions in aid of making the constable's point. The answers revealed nothing of use. But he had learned two things already during this short trip, he thought, which had changed his understanding of the case for good.

CHAPTER THIRTY-FIVE

Mayne had told Cobb that while he would offer whatever information and support he could, he wanted no part of the case to fall back upon the Yard. They had moved on from Eli Gilman and Winfield Bell.

Thus it was that late that evening, after eleven o'clock, Lenox, Graham, and the American congregated in Lenox's study—only the three of them. It had been a long day for Cobb, no doubt, but he was sharp-eyed and fresh.

He told them that his trip to Liverpool had been informative. He spoke to both Lenox and Graham, not just the former; Lenox had told Cobb about how integral Graham's role in the solution to the case was, and Cobb, with that springy democratic reflex Lenox had noticed in the few Americans he knew, had immediately folded Graham into his confidences.

"I went to the docks. Nobody there would speak to me. At last, out of frustration, I went to the army garrison. I had a single letter of recommendation to its commander, from my own superior at the militia. I'd been hoping I wouldn't need to use it."

"How do they know each other?"

Cobb took a sip of water. "Well, it was funny.

He took the letter, read it—an old man named Whitworth, scars all over his face and hands—and then burst into laughter." Cobb smiled. "Apparently Brig—my commander, Brigadier General Adams—and this fellow, Whitworth, met in the War of 1812. In battle."

Lenox raised his eyebrows. "Did they!"

"Whitworth poured me a brandy. Then he recounted the whole thing in perfect detail—as if it had passed not an hour ago. A warm battle, he said, which is how these old veterans describe it anytime they've sustained a great number of casualties."

"And then?"

"He made me promise to pour Adams a brandy. Said he thought they'd fought each other to a handsome standstill—would be happy to shake his hand one day, when they'd both reached the other side of the grave, and relive it shot by shot, maneuver by maneuver. Said he could remember every rock of the field they held. He bet Brig could, too. I said yes, I thought so. After that he dismissed me pretty perfunctorily, but he sent along a man of his, and all at once the doors that had been closed to me were opened."

"What luck."

Cobb nodded. "Yes, and I heard a good deal about Tiptree. Shall I read you the exact account of the incident?"

"Please," said Lenox.

So Cobb read aloud. *"Mr. Abram Tiptree, resident of the District of Columbia, United States, arrived in Liverpool on the clipper ship* Clarissa *14 November 1855, traveling from New York. He was in the company of his employer, Mr. Eleazer Gilman (now staying Quilt's Inn, Upper Frederick Street), and their associate Mr. Josiah Hollis (ibid). The* Clarissa *arrived at Slip 3, Queen's Dock, at a little after 6:00 p.m. Some passengers from the ship had already debarked in rowboats, including Messrs. Gilman and Hollis.*

"Mr. Tiptree waited in the company of their trunks for a porter. Sailors on deck were stowing the ship for dry dock. Mr. Tiptree was alone. At approximately 6:15 there was a loud cry then a thump; sailors rushed to discover that Mr. Tiptree had fallen from the gangway into the water. He was retrieved from the water and rushed to Royal Liverpool Hospital. He lingered in a comatose state, having sustained a wound to the left side of his forehead, for several days before dying.

"No witnesses on the docks or the ship saw anyone unusual. Sailors reported that Mr. Tiptree had been unsteady at sea. The coroner determined the cause of death as misadventure. The case is closed."

"A loud cry and a thump," said Lenox.

"Yes. It seems obvious to me that he was murdered. Then again, it's possible it might have been an accident. One can see the viewpoint of the police and the coroner. There was no reason for them to believe that anyone wished Tiptree any harm."

Graham had an observation to make. "More than once while in your employment, sir," he said, "I have been mistaken for you as I stood by your luggage. It may be that the attacker thought Mr. Tiptree was Gilman."

Lenox nodded. "Yes, and his trunk said 'E. Gilman' on the side. Did you see Tiptree's trunk?"

"No," said Cobb, "it's been shipped back to his family, unfortunately. Still, I think Mr. Graham's theory makes sense. It explains the lag between the attack at the dock and the attack on the train—some time would have passed before Bell and Smith realized that in Tiptree they had killed the wrong man."

Lenox felt pity for the young secretary—gone so young, and not even the star of his own death. "Shall we take it as a working theory for now?"

"I think so," said Cobb. He swung his right arm gently through the air in the mimic of an attack. "The left side of his forehead—that is exactly where a blow would have caught him."

"Yes."

"Unfortunately, that is the full extent of what I found. The *Clarissa* has already shipped back out. Still, I was glad to have gone. And I am curious how the two of you fared."

"Graham?" said Lenox.

"I have discovered little today, sir," he said, "but I am hopeful that my meeting with Winfield Bell's common-law wife—the woman known Lady Elaine—will offer more."

"She'll talk to you? She wouldn't give up anything to Dunn."

"Yes, sir. I offered her a financial incentive. I understand her position as the procuress of the Patriots Abroad may be in jeopardy without Bell. She jumped at the chance to talk."

Lenox frowned. "Be careful, Graham. They'll cut your throat and leave you there if they know you have money."

"I have taken precautions, sir," said Graham.

No more needed to be said. "Good, I'm glad."

"And you, sir?"

"I went to the tavern. I discovered two things there."

"What?" said Cobb.

"The first is that the tavern hasn't owned a white horse in nineteen months. At least if we believe the account of the bartender there, which I was inclined to do. This brought home to me—how do I put it?—how outlandish it is that we are expected to believe Bell took all that time to disguise who Gilman was, then bolted away on a white horse as an homage to his group of friends, or to his racial preferences."

"People do foolish things for their politics," said Cobb.

Lenox nodded. "Yes, no doubt. But then where did he get the horse? Did he hire it? You would have to look around a bit for a white horse—ask here and there, draw attention to yourself. I tried."

"It might have been worth it to him. It was a grandiose plan."

"Even if you set aside the horse, there is the second thing I discovered at the tavern. Of that I feel no doubt at all."

"And what is it?"

"Winfield Bell didn't fall to his death. He was pushed."

Cobb's eyes widened. "Pushed!"

Lenox nodded firmly. "There's a stone wall on the roof. It came up to my chest. I'm five foot eleven inches without shoes on. Bell was smaller than that—it would have come up another two or three inches on him, say to his shoulder."

"So he would have been unlikely to fall over because he slipped."

"It would be impossible," Lenox replied. "It would have taken me at least ten seconds of serious effort to climb up and hurl myself over. It couldn't have happened accidentally unless I were—oh, six and a half feet tall, no matter how icy it might have been. He'd have fallen straight back onto the rooftop and picked himself up again."

"Bert Smith," Graham murmured, arriving

quickly at the conclusion Lenox had spent much of the day reaching.

"Yes. Suddenly he seems to be the crucial figure. Nobody can tell us a word about him. He was a relatively recent addition to the Patriots Abroad—the bartender hadn't seen him before; at least so he said. And he had no great friends among them except Bell. So who is he?"

"And what were his motivations?" Cobb said.

"I have no idea. But what I do think—what I feel convinced of—is that Winfield Bell was serving Smith's goals, not merely his own. I would guess that it was Smith who hired a white horse for Bell to flee on. And I would guess that as soon as Bell was caught, Smith shoved him over the edge of the rooftop and disappeared. Now we merely need to figure out who on earth Bert Smith is, and why he engineered this awful scheme."

CHAPTER THIRTY-SIX

Their American visitor turned out to be an idiosyncratic fellow, at least in his unobtrusive way. The next day he came over early (Graham was already out visiting Lady Elaine) and after repeatedly declining breakfast, at last he requested—at Lenox and Mrs. Huggins's joint insistence—a glass of cold milk and a piece of brown bread; but only the crust.

"I'll eat the middle part," said Lenox to Mrs. Huggins.

She shot him a fierce look. He suspected her of fearing Americans. "I shall return directly, sir," she said.

She did so—with a plate so heaped with brown bread crusts that it would have taken a month to eat them all.

"Thank you very, very much," said Cobb.

"Are you sure it's enough?" Lenox asked.

"I think it should be more than sufficient—thank you," said Cobb earnestly.

"And there's plenty more if it's not," added Mrs. Huggins.

Lenox sighed internally at the loss of his little joke. But he liked Cobb, a serious, modest man, but one whose modesty never devolved into meekness. Their conversation was lively with disagreement and disputation.

And Lenox had realized, with dawning excitement, that Cobb's own stores of knowledge about crime were as evolved as his, if very different. "This reminds me of a murder in Blackpool in 1845," Lenox might say, and Cobb would nod, listen, and say that it reminded *him* of an attempted murder—with several witnesses— in Pittsburgh, not eighteen months before.

A meeting of minds, in other words. For Lenox, who had encountered so much resistance in his vocation, it was a welcome change.

As Cobb worked his way through the pile of crusts, Lenox read once more through all his notes about Bert Smith, hoping to find something in his careful observations from his interviews that he had missed before. Cobb, meanwhile, was going over the list of contents of Gilman's trunk. Two of Hemstock's men had brought it there this morning, and now it stood in Lenox's dining room, where they had set up at the long table, which was spread with piles of paper.

They worked steadily and unstintingly. At around half past ten, Lenox glanced at his watch. "Would you mind if I left you for an hour?" he said. "I want to ask someone a few questions."

"Of course." Cobb looked at the clock over his shoulder. "What time do you expect Mr. Graham to return?"

"Soon, I hope—though knowing him, it might not be until this evening, or even tomorrow."

Cobb held up a sheet of paper. "I have a question about Gilman's schedule."

"Yes?"

He handed the paper, which was divided into three columns, to Lenox. "Am I right in saying that in the left-hand column are important members of the government, and in the center, people acquainted with Her Majesty, belonging to the court? I deduced as much from the book you lent me, but I may be wrong."

Lenox scanned the lists. There were about a dozen names on the left, starting with the Prime Minister's, and five in the middle. "No, that's correct. What about these names in the rightmost column, though?"

"That's my question."

Lenox looked at the names: Wilton Sheridan, MP for Camberwell; Forsythe Witt, MP for Rivington-on-Tyne; Samuel Jonas, MP for Spall.

He felt a quick anger at seeing Sheridan's name—his horses, his wax-tipped mustache, his casual manner. But he could not see anything sinister in the person, only superb indifference to others.

He knew Witt and Jonas by reputation, nothing more. "They're all Members of Parliament, as you obviously know. Shouldn't they go in the first column?"

Cobb shook his head. He tapped the book that he had asked Lenox to show him: *Who's Who*, which had come out annually for six years now and quickly become famous, a compilation of the background, education, and careers of Great Britain's most prominent men.

It was a wide-ranging publication. Lenox had grown up with *Debrett's*, which listed the peers, but the *WW* (as everyone called it) included peers as well as artists, politicians, civil servants, and judges, and there were aristocrats it omitted. The only criterion was notability: achievement in life. It reflected, Lenox thought, a new attitude that had started to weave its way into England's fabric and must feel familiar to Cobb: the belief that a person's birth was secondary to his or her qualities.

"All eleven men in the left-hand column have extensive entries," Cobb said. "So do the ones in the middle. Only one of the three on the right does—Forsythe Witt, and that's because of his career in shipping. It scarcely mentions his political career."

"Yes," Lenox said. "He was only returned to Parliament as a Member last spring. The rich man's retirement—a seat on the green benches."

"Would it be correct to say that all three are backbenchers?"

Lenox nodded. "The very definition of them."

"Then why would Gilman have arranged

meetings with them, when the rest of his contacts were of the highest caliber?"

"It's an excellent question. I don't have an answer."

At that moment there was a knock at the door. Lenox excused himself and answered it—concomitantly with Mrs. Huggins, since Graham was out—to find Lady Jane.

"Why have you sent over for all of my brown bread, Charles?" Jane asked. "Are you trying to starve us out?"

She was curious, not irritated, but Mrs. Huggins looked guilty. Lenox gave her a glance. "Our guest only eats brown bread and milk," he told Lady Jane.

"Is he four?"

"No, I would put him at forty or thereabouts. Mrs. Huggins?"

"I believe I hear Ellie calling me, sir, excuse me."

"She heard no such thing," Lenox said, when the housekeeper had vanished downstairs. He turned back to Lady Jane. "Did you come just about the bread?"

"I was going to ask if you wanted to have lunch, but now I see that you have company."

She said it in such a light, offhanded tone that Lenox knew immediately—for he understood the people he loved by an instinct that preceded logical deduction, the same way he sometimes understood clues before he knew why—that she was lonely.

"As a matter of fact, if you could accompany me to Paddington Station for ten minutes first, I can give you lunch at the coffeehouse there."

She looked glad. "Such glamour that would be! But are you really on your way? I'm not inconveniencing you?"

He pointed behind her. "No, no! You can see for yourself that I called for the carriage a few minutes ago. Here it comes round from the stables."

At Paddington, Lenox and Lady Jane stopped at the stationmaster's small brick hut. None other than Mr. Joseph Beauregard Stanley was there. Lenox asked him if he was off the night shift, and Stanley said that they'd been kind enough to give him mornings, since he was still perturbed by the events of the 449.

Lady Jane said she didn't blame him; the stationmaster blushed, apparently not having registered her presence, and asked in a hurried way what had brought Lenox back. Lenox said he was in search of Willikens.

"He'll be on Platform 1 this time. The 222 from Glasgow arrives in nine minutes. But you'll have to look—he has a new coat."

They found the little boy sorting and tidying his newspapers and tobaccos and breath-sweetening mints. He was still in the suit Lenox had given him; he declined all other clothes, seemingly out of some superstition, even when Lenox said it would be terribly hot in the summers; that was a problem for summer, the boy said dismissively, and Lenox realized that life had taught the lad not to look as far ahead as most people did.

He greeted Lenox without any particular favor, and Lenox did not feel he ought to ask about the room above the station in which Willikens was now boarding, or the breakfast and supper that his landlady, Mrs. Hudson, was meant to give him.

Instead, he said, "I need to ask you again about the fellow who bought all your papers."

"Bert Smith?"

"You know his name?" said Lenox.

Willikens pointed at the newspapers. "Yes, there's been a bit of news about him."

Lenox hadn't known he could read. "I need to ask you if you remember anything else about him at all. A scar—perhaps on his face, or hands?"

"No scars on his face or hands."

"Take your time," Lenox said.

"No scars," Willikens repeated firmly. "I told you everything else."

Lenox knelt down. "Joseph, I need you to do me this one last favor. Close your eyes and think. We'll watch your papers. Just think."

"Who is that lady?"

"Don't talk . . . she's . . . it's very rude—"

"I'm Lady Jane Grey," said Lady Jane, and put out her gloved hand.

Willikens raised his eyebrows. "You're not."

"I'm almost sure I am."

"You hosted a ball for the naval fund last week at the Longleat Club with the Duchess of Marchmain."

Lady Jane laughed. "Did I? I suppose I did."

"It was in the papers."

"Willikens!" said Lenox.

"Fine, fine," said the boy.

He shut his eyes, and they waited. To his credit, he kept them closed, and in his tight little face, lightly freckled, the muscles of concentration flickered.

At last he opened them. "Nothing," he said. "Well—one thing. I do remember coughing when he leaned over. There was a kind of powder off him."

"Powder? Talc?"

"Something like that, maybe. Musty and white, like."

"Did it get on you?"

Willikens shook his head. "Not really. Maybe. But I don't think so—it just filled the air for a moment and then went away."

"Hm." Lenox made nothing of that whatsoever, unless perhaps Bert Smith had shaved to disguise himself. He sighed. "Well, thank you anyhow. If you think of anything else, send word. Otherwise

I'll see you next time I'm here. Or you can always reach me at the address on that card I gave you."

"Righto. How many papers do you want before you leave?" Willikens asked, and Lenox thought that took some cheek. But Lady Jane bought one of each, and some mints as well.

CHAPTER THIRTY-SEVEN

Having had a happy luncheon with Jane, Lenox returned to Hampden Lane. He was hanging up his hat when Mrs. Huggins appeared.

"Did you give Cobb something to eat?" he asked her.

She looked horribly unhappy. "I tried, sir."

"But didn't succeed?"

"He said he didn't want to impose on me and that he would get his own lunch—and he went and returned with *three apples,*" she said.

"Then everything ended well. How is he coming along on the bread, though?"

"Sir," she said, and gave him a look of such betrayal that he felt guilty.

"I'm sorry, Mrs. Huggins. Why don't you bring in something light for the two of us now?"

He had eaten a hearty bowl of broccoli and potato soup served with crusty bread and plenty of butter at the coffee shop with Lady Jane—an ideal meal in this weather. But he would eat again to make the housekeeper happy.

In the brightly lit dining room, covered in stacks of paper and loose objects that the staff had been instructed not to touch, Lenox and Cobb traded reports of their progress. Cobb was still making his inventory of the contents of the trunk.

"I am all curiosity for Mr. Graham to return," said the American.

"As am I," said Lenox, "but I don't know that we should look for him until much later today. He's methodical."

In the event, Graham proved Lenox's prediction wrong. He was back not twenty minutes later, cheeks red, the cold rushing in the front door and down the hall behind him—most welcome in this case.

"Graham!" said Lenox.

The valet made straight for the dining room, unpinning his cloak and removing his hat on the way, sensing, no doubt, that the two investigators were eager for his report.

"How do you do, sir?"

"Very well—and you?"

"It was a satisfactory morning," said Graham, taking a seat.

Lenox felt a surge of excitement. "Why? What did she say?"

Graham took a twice-folded piece of paper from his jacket pocket. "I wrote down everything I could after I left," he said. "But two facts I found particularly salient."

"Go on."

"The first is that Winfield Bell suddenly came into a great deal of money in September." Graham glanced between his listeners and was apparently content with their reaction, because he went on. "Mrs. Peck—though she goes by the sobriquet Lady Elaine, her name is Anne Peck—was sharing a room with Bell at the time."

"How did they fall in together?" asked Lenox.

"They met three years ago, just after Bell moved here, at the White Horse. As she recalls there was an immediate affinity between them."

"Sorry to interrupt. Please go on."

"Mrs. Peck complained that she had often been responsible for Bell financially. He was fond of drinking and gambling, and she was secretive about what work he did, if any. In September, however, he returned home with a pair of gold earrings for her. She was wearing them this morning."

"Did he offer an explanation?" asked Cobb.

"No. She assumed that he had been on a successful run at cards. But his behavior continued to change. For instance, he bought a new suit of clothes, and when she became sick in late September he paid for a doctor to visit."

"Sweet of him. Did she have any idea where the money came from?"

Graham shook his head. "None. In fact, she is convinced of Bell's innocence."

"Innocence!"

"Yes, partly because of the second piece of information she offered that piqued my curiosity. It would seem that, whatever his other faults, he had no special obsession with matters of racial origin."

"How do you mean?" asked Cobb.

"According to Mrs. Peck, Bell's best friend from the merchant navy was an African, who stayed with Bell every time his ship stopped in London. The two of them would go on long sprees, she said—a week or more."

Interesting. Lenox recalled that Bell had been in the American navy. This was one of the most common careers he met in his investigations, and it had struck him as deepening some prejudices irreversibly (against women, for instance) while loosening others (most obviously against other nationalities, since there was such a motley of people aboard a ship).

"But he was a member of the Patriots Abroad," said Cobb.

Graham nodded. "I asked about that. She said that he couldn't give a—well, she said it colorfully, but making the point that he had no interest in slavery, for or against. He was apolitical. I pressed her on that question. She insisted that he had only begun to frequent the White Horse because when he moved here, after his discharge from the American navy, he had a friend who was there every night. He was a game but passive member of the group, as I understand it."

"I should have spoken to her long ago," said Lenox. "Superb work, Graham. Thank you."

Cobb nodded soberly. "It is. But tell us—what

did you make of her honesty? Her story seems so clearly to Bell's benefit."

"On the contrary, it seems to me to guarantee that he was guilty of murder," said Lenox. "That is how he came into his temporary fortune."

"Yes. Yet it also makes it sound exceedingly unlikely that he would have murdered Gilman purely for reasons of racial pride or prejudice."

"I do not think Mrs. Peck would be capable of constructing the character she has given Bell from nothing," Graham said. "She is a lax talker—a drinker, incautious. My belief is that she was telling the truth."

"Does she mourn Bell?"

Graham shrugged. "After her fashion, sir. I would hazard that she is accustomed to sudden loss—death included. She has a new male friend already."

"From the White Horse."

"No. He's a police officer, she told me. With some pride."

Lenox was curious. "Did she say whom?"

"No, she refused."

At that moment Mrs. Huggins entered the room, trailed by a kitchen maid named Mercy. Between them they carried a banquet's worth of food and drink, as if by sheer volume they could overcome Mr. Cobb's taste—tea, buttered toast, a plate of soft cheeses, caraway biscuits, chocolate biscuits, and much more. Off to the side were a glass of milk, several brown rolls, and an apple.

Mrs. Huggins placed all of this on the table, with a face that seemed to say that she did so absolutely without judgment or intolerance. If a person wanted to eat a hundred apples it was all one and the same to her.

"Can I pour anyone tea?" she asked.

"I might as well give it a whirl, thank you so much, Mrs. Huggins," said Cobb, smiling, and Lenox liked him all the more in that moment, for putting her at her ease.

In the end all three of them took tea, and some of the color came back into Graham's cheeks.

Cobb was asking him further details about Lady Elaine, taking notes. Lenox, half listening, pulled *Who's Who* over. He read his brother's familiar entry—he himself had none—then looked up the name Ashbrook (no luck there), before turning to the page Cobb had flagged.

Witt, Forsythe, *financier; b. Newcastle, 9 April 1808; educated as bookkeeper and cashier, Travers and Co., 1818–1824; traveled in 1825 to Mandeville, Jamaica, as bookkeeper to Elfrid Robinson; remained in employ there 1825–1828, surviving two epidemics of cholera, removing in 1828 to St. Ann's Bay, Jamaica; there founded Witt and Co. Shipping; m. 1830* **Miss Alana Robinson**, *daughter of his former employer (d. 1851, in childbirth); who bore him seven children, five living; returned to England 1848, having survived further cholera outbreaks and a smallpox epidemic; m.* **Mrs. Chelsea Adkins**, *relict of Rev. Theophilus Adkins; returned in 1854 as MP for Rivington-upon-Tyne.*

Mandeville, Jamaica. Tuning Cobb and Graham out entirely now, he read the entry again carefully, starting from the beginning. As he did, a strange idea stirred somewhere in his mind.

CHAPTER THIRTY-EIGHT

When Lenox saw Kitty Ashbrook the next morning, for the first time since he had departed London for the Christmas holiday, their interaction was noticeably different.

The pretense of platonic friendship, the deflecting banter of the crowded ballroom—both of these had evaporated, replaced by a deep, immediate, and reciprocal gratitude that they were together once more.

"You are most welcome," she said when Lenox arrived exactly at ten, the first person there, indeed almost impolite in his promptness.

He felt the sincerity of her words. She was attired quietly, in a navy-blue dress with a small diamond necklace, and her rich, fragrant hair was clipped so that almost all of it fell over her left shoulder save a few bewitching strands curling down her neck.

Perhaps it was not that she had never looked so fine, but that her eyes had not searched his like this before; or perhaps that his had not searched hers.

He took both of her hands. "I am so very pleased to see you again, Miss Ashbrook," he said.

For once he was conscious of his own dress: the

gleam of his boots, the perfect turn of his collar. These were Graham's standards, not Lenox's. But he was appreciative of them now.

"I trust you passed an agreeable Christmas?" she asked.

"I did. Yet I missed seeing you here!" he said. "And you?"

She smiled. "We were quite gay. My cousin has a large family, and they squeezed us into it without even noticing, which is the nicest way, I think. Don't you?"

"I do," he said.

He might have been agreeing to anything on earth, for all he knew at that moment was the feel of her light, cool hands in his, the nearness of her face, her pale neck, her sweet eyes.

Why did he not kiss her? The question posed itself to his mind, and he thought—standing before the fire, the dainty prints of Bath and York Cathedral on the mantel just next to them, the broad windows overlooking Eaton Square casting a subtle loveliness of light into the room—that he would. The time had come. He could see it in her face, too, her spirit reaching toward his, and her body, her face, ready to follow at the slightest encouragement.

As he was leaning forward, however, the bell rang.

She dropped his hands with a squeeze and smiled apologetically. A frustration—yet one tinged with happiness, for deferral could only add a kind of charming unhappiness that contained the joy which would be theirs when at last they did kiss.

He hadn't thought until this very moment of the man who had visited him at Hampden Lane, ordering him to leave Kitty Ashbrook alone. Now he expected to see this gentleman when the door opened. Instead, as it happened, it was a friend of Mrs. Ashbrook, and Kitty's mother hurried in.

Soon the room was full of half a dozen people. Lenox still felt the electricity of his private moment with Kitty nearly an hour later, when he reluctantly departed. The carefully developed language of love was entirely insufficient, he discovered: the tingle of happiness on his face—no poem he had read had approximated that, what it had felt to be present in that room, alive with every fiber in him to Kitty's movements, the subtle ways she adjusted her body, the glances she cast at him more often than, it seemed, wonderfully to his heart, she would have if she could have helped it.

He thought: I am in love.

It was slightly warmer in 1856 than it had been in 1855, and, buoyed by his visit at Eaton Square, Lenox walked home. At any rate it was dry; a wet winter was what Londoners dreaded, when it grew so damp that a small gust of breeze froze your bones.

At a bookstore on Cate Street Lenox broke his stride. It was a sign that had caught his eye.

Travails of an American slave!
Hear the brutality of the masters; sufferings
of the enslaved; and more, from
MR. JOSIAH HOLLIS in person, seven o'clock
in the evening, Jan. 5

Curious. He'd been quite sure Hollis had already gone back to America. The discrepancy troubled him, and he decided he would go to the talk two evenings hence.

This afternoon, however, he had plans. He went home, changed into more comfortable clothing (and with the change, out of the dreamy mentality induced in him by Eaton Street and Kitty—Kitty Lenox, she might be called soon!), and went to fetch Cobb.

Soon they were in a hansom heading west. They were on their way to see Edmund. "Now you shall meet my brother," said Lenox, "and you may judge which of us is a truer representation of the decadence of our English way of life—as opposed to the invigorating purity of American capitalism."

Cobb shook his head sadly. "I fear that we are no model at the moment. We're trying to spread too much country across too little compromise these days. It will tell sooner or later."

"You don't think there will be a civil war?" asked Lenox.

"If there is, I am prepared to fight. I shall return to Vermont and enlist there. But to answer your question, I do not think there will be. The slaveowners will never dare secede, though it be their great threat."

"I do not think you mentioned whether you have a family," said Lenox.

He had not phrased it as a question on purpose, to give Cobb the chance to politely decline the confidence, but the American said, "I am recently married—in June of last year."

"My congratulations! And you find it a happy state of affairs."

Cobb smiled almost shyly. "Very. My wife is from South Carolina—Eliza—and she has turned our garden into something magnificent, complete with a little lamb for wool, and an icehouse. A very castle, you know—though you can see the next house over, two hundred feet off."

"Indeed, it sounds idyllic."

"It is, Mr. Lenox."

"Does your wife object to your line of work? Its dangers?"

"Less strenuously than she objected to this long absence."

"Ah, of course," said Lenox. "I have a friend who is enduring just such a thing. He is in the military."

They arrived at Edmund's house and found him in his study. He welcomed his brother very gladly.

"May I introduce you to Mr. Winston Cobb, who is a member of the militia that guards Washington, D.C.? Mr. Cobb, this is my brother, Sir Edmund Lenox."

"It's a pleasure to meet you," said Edmund, and he and the small, tidy American shook hands. "Welcome to London."

"Edmund, to hurry to the point, we came to ask about Samuel Jonas."

Edmund frowned. "Jonas? Whatever for?"

"Never mind. What do you know about him?"

Edmund had resumed his seat, and Charles and Cobb had taken the two chairs across from him. "Not all that much. He rarely comes into Parliament. Quite rich, quite idle. Never leaves the Carlton."

"What do you mean—that he rarely comes into Parliament, Sir Lenox?" asked Cobb.

Edmund smiled at this misnomer and said, without commenting otherwise, "Please, call me Edmund. What I mean is that he's only in Parliament every tenth day or so that it assembles. Here in England I'm afraid that's not uncommon. We're very lax about attendance compared to you."

"How did he make his money?" asked Cobb.

"The colonies."

Lenox felt a buzz of excitement. "Which?"

"I can't remember. Do you want me to look?"

"If you would."

Edmund pulled down his thin light blue parliamentary record, a diary and registry that only Members possessed.

As he leafed through it, he said, "Of anyone on earth to want to see—that great oaf—but here we are. S. Jonas. Yes, here we are. He was . . . let's see, he was briefly in South Africa, then a long while in Jamaica, and finally in Australia. Not a colony anymore, of course. I—"

Australia had been granted sovereignty to govern itself just a few months before, but nothing could have been of less interest to Lenox at present.

"When was he in Jamaica?" he said.

Edmund frowned. "It doesn't give exact dates. The biographies are very brief. You may look for yourself."

They did, and to his disappointment, Charles saw that his brother was right. It mentioned that he had spent "a good part of his thirties in Jamaica and America" but otherwise gave no detail.

Still, there it was: The three men, Sheridan, Witt, and Jonas, were all connected to Jamaica. Was it meaningful?

"You would not call him a powerful man in the House of Commons, then?" Cobb asked of Edmund.

"I would call him just about the least powerful man in the House of Commons," said Edmund, "which is to say that he has one vote—a goodly measure of power for any Englishman."

"I see."

"Counterbalancing that is the fact he will be turned out in the next by-election. It is quite a certain thing."

"Why?" said Charles.

"It's a close district, and he has a good challenger this time. Last time he didn't. I can't remember his name, the new fellow. One from our side. Not that it matters, for Jonas is the greatest layabout you ever met, and even constituents hear of such a thing sooner or later."

"Do you think we would find him at the Carlton now?" asked Lenox.

"I would bet a thousand pounds on it." Edmund scorned the Carlton Club, a beautiful building on St. James's Place, which served as both spiritual and second home to much of the conservative party. "Mr. Cobb, if you go there, have Charles take you over to the Athenaeum afterward for a cup of tea, so you don't leave these shores without the experience of a real gentleman's club."

They called at the Carlton; and Edmund would have lost his thousand pounds. As it happened, Charles knew the club's head porter fairly well, not least from the times he had dined with the Duke of Dorset there. He was a cordially peremptory fellow named Whyte, who spoke to them while making notes in his register.

"He's usually here, sir, Mr. Jonas, but not today."

"Yesterday?"

"Oh, yes," said Whyte. "And the preceding . . . say, fifty. But you are the second fellow looking for him! I did not give the other his address."

Lenox frowned. He would pay the thousand pounds himself rather than let Dunn solve this case before he did, if it were Dunn. "Could I trouble you for his address? I know information that may be in his interest."

Whyte picked up a piece of paper. "I had already written it down, Mr. Lenox. Best regards to your brother. I'm sure he's quite welcome anytime he'd like to cross the aisle."

CHAPTER THIRTY-NINE

Jonas lived in Elizabeth Street in Belgravia, not far, in fact, from Kitty Ashbrook. The address proved to be that of a handsome, substantial house, which had been divided into apartments for bachelors. Jonas's was number 2.

No one answered the bell; to Lenox's surprise, quiet Cobb pulled a shimmy from his pocket and in a jiffy had them inside a resplendent foyer, with a subdued landscape of London on the dark blue wall and a vase of hothouse tulips.

Lenox said to remind him not to fight the Militia of the District of Columbia.

Cobb laughed. "You may treat for a truce in advance, after the hospitality you have shown, Mr. Lenox."

There were three floors, each with its own proprietor. They reached the second and saw what was evidently Jonas's door, for there was a *2* painted on it in black.

Lenox stopped several feet short of the door. "It's open," he said in a low voice.

Cobb looked, and indeed the door was ajar. "Carefully, then," he said, and without hesitation stepped in front of Lenox and pushed it open slightly farther.

Lenox, young and eager to prove himself,

wished *he* had done this, but now that it was done he had no choice but to follow his American counterpart. A floorboard creaked as they entered, and they paused. But no replying sound came. If the house held Samuel Jonas, he was either hiding or dead.

His rooms were a mess. Clothes, old plates of food, newspapers crumpled rather than folded, pewter flagons fetched up from the pub and never returned for their deposit—all these lay strewn over the floor and tables and chairs. Lenox reflected that he would have gone to the Carlton Club, too, if he lived here. Yet it was a quite obviously expensive life he led.

There were touches of domesticity. On the wall was a pair of portraits that from their dress Lenox guessed must have been from around the turn of the century. Perhaps Jonas's grandparents. On either side of the portraits were framed pictures in cross-stitch. One was of Parliament, and the other was of a large white house with high white columns supporting a broad balcony that shaded a large front porch, with *Jonas Hall* in scroll across the bottom.

"I'll check the bedroom," said Cobb softly.

As he did this, Lenox investigated the large living room, checking behind the sofa, in the single closet, and through the swinging door— with his heart in his throat—that led to the servant's quarters.

These were small, a kitchen and a narrow bedroom. Lenox checked both thoroughly, and both were empty. There was a quartet of oranges, a luxury, out on the counter. He felt them: firm. Jonas had been here recently. But the servant's room looked unused. That would explain the mess as well.

"Empty," said Cobb when he came back into the living room.

"So are the kitchen and the servant's room." There was an unspoken moment of relief, a slackening of vigilance. "Then what do we make of the door?"

"Nothing good," said Cobb.

Lenox gestured around the room. "On the other hand, nobody could accuse Mr. Jonas of being overnice in his style of life."

Cobb shook his head. "No. I can't believe he represents an entire constituency of people but can barely hold together two rooms."

"I think his servant has left him."

"Why?"

"The quarters look unused. All of Jonas's meals have been brought in."

"There's a diary and some papers on the desk in the bedroom," said Cobb. "I didn't look, but perhaps we should."

"I think the open door justifies it."

The diary was empty of commitments—except, strikingly, for on this day. *Sav, 4:00,* said the entry, underlined twice for emphasis. "What could that mean?" Cobb asked.

"It's bound to be the Savoy."

"What's that?"

Now that was very hard to explain to someone who didn't live in England. In essence, long ago a member of the royal family had been given a tiny sliver of London as a duchy, and while it was still subject to the Queen's laws, it had strange, ancient laws of its own, too. The most famous of these involved debt. No writ of debt applied in the Savoy. That had made it a famous hideout for men who could afford the high prices there but not the tens of thousands of pounds they owed; George Mowbray, a cousin of Lenox's own, hadn't left the Savoy in ten years. There were always debt collectors waiting at the edges, even in the dead of night, looking for people who thought they could dart in and out of the Savoy's protection.

Lenox explained all of that as briefly as he could. "But do you imagine Jonas is in debt?" Cobb asked.

Lenox said that he didn't think so. "He could be arrested at the Carlton any time. But it may be that his meeting is with someone who is dodging the collectors."

"True."

"Debtors' prison is a fearful place. Have you read the books of Mr. Dickens?"

"I have. He may be the most popular writer in

our country, aside from Mr. Cooper," said Cobb. "And Mrs. Harriet Beecher Stowe, of course."

"If we ever manage to get rid of them, it's Dickens who will have done it," Lenox said.

It was just past one. The two men agreed that they must of course be present in the Savoy at four, though as Lenox said, there were a variety of pubs, lodging houses, and inns there. Their best chance was to be out in the streets a bit beforehand. For that they would need Graham—an extra set of eyes.

They looked through the rest of the flat—quite unabashedly, for there was something in its squalor that seemed to disqualify its inhabitant from privacy—without finding much. The rolltop desk held quite a lot of money, in pounds and dollars; even this was pretty casually kept. There was a half-composed letter to Jonas's haberdasher, ordering two new top hats "of the kind I bought in July." In short, everything gave the appearance that Jonas might reappear any minute and resume his normal course of activities. It was this—perhaps the letter—that hastened their search, and finally they left.

"Door open or closed?" asked Lenox.

"Ajar, I suppose," said Cobb, after thinking. "They trained us to leave everything as we found it in cases like this."

An unbidden thought flashed across Lenox's mind: Cobb was not merely a soldier, or a detective. He was a spy. Lenox believed that he was in London as a detective, and he did not doubt that Cobb was playing straight with him. But could he be wrong?

These thoughts didn't cause him to miss a step in the conversation. "Before you leave, I wish you would give me a list of these injunctions. I am trying to learn the profession, but it is uneven progress."

"With pleasure," Cobb said. "I feel no very great confidence at the moment myself, though. Jonas might simply have left the door open and have a meeting with a friend. The connection to Jamaica might be accidental."

"Perhaps," said Lenox.

He knew it wasn't. Something about the double line under the appointment; something about the crimes, and the people; something about Sheridan's stubborn ignorance; something about Winfield Bell's sudden fortune: All of it *felt* linked; all of it must be linked.

They agreed to meet at three o'clock on the steps of the royal chapel in the Savoy, a church built to order by one of the Henrys a few hundred years before, a miniature jewel of stained glass and paneled wood. From there they could explore the nooks and clefts and hiding places of the old district, in search of an answer, at last, to the mystery of who had murdered Eli Gilman and why.

CHAPTER FORTY

Gentlemen's clubs were well and good. Officers' messes, coffeehouses, restaurants, and tearooms, too, all had their place. But sometimes one wanted nothing more than a spell in a good pub.

Lenox, Graham, and Cobb had spent an hour trawling through the Savoy without luck. About halfway through the journey it had started to rain—a cold, driving rain, the kind that made you long to be indoors with a cup of something strong and an engrossing novel. At last they had taken refuge in a public house called the Duke of Lancaster, a winding burrow of a place with several rooms and two enormous fireplaces.

They sat at a table in the shadow of one of these six-foot hearths. The barmaid came round, and the three all ordered hot spiced cider with rum. Meanwhile Lenox shivered, with that horrid feeling of being cold and hot at the same time in wet clothes. Someone—perhaps his brother?—had once told him that a turkey without its feathers was hideous, clammy, pale, pimpled, trembling at the slightest touch. Those same physical symptoms were present when someone quit drinking or tobacco or opium suddenly—went, as the saying had it, cold turkey. Well, so he felt now.

"They must have met in someone's lodgings," Cobb said.

"It may also be that *Sav* stood for something else," said Lenox.

"Mr. Graham, would the Savoy have been your first guess?"

"Without a doubt, sir," and though Lenox was not sure whether honesty or loyalty played a greater role in this reply, he was grateful for it.

Their ciders came, hot and delicious. Cobb had a bacon sandwich; Lenox, a paper sleeve of chipped potatoes, warm, crispy, salty and filling. As for Graham, he had a slice of steak pie with his cider. The rain lashed the windows, fierce and relentless, the gray sky dimming even faster than usual. Lenox tried to remember the shortest day of the winter and failed. He hoped they were past it. December, wasn't it? Or was that wishful thinking? Still, it was a companionable little meal.

As Cobb and Graham talked, Lenox's mind turned to Kitty Ashbrook, and he thought of the contrast between this afternoon—welcome as it was—and her warm, inviting sitting room, the feeling of her light hands in his.

And then, in the midst of his idle thought, as the three of them sipped their cider, two men entered the Duke of Lancaster: Samuel Jonas, whom Lenox recognized faintly, but surely, and with him, as if by way of confirmation,

Wilt Sheridan, blithe Wilt Sheridan, with his mustaches waxed carefully to the tips and not a hair out of place.

Lenox nudged Graham and Cobb. "It's them."

None spoke further—all three recognizing that they were placed, as if some divinity had set them there on purpose, in the perfect half-concealed spot to observe what the two men did.

Jonas waddled to the bar. He sat down heavily, his thinning hair tossed up in wild torrents by the weather. He looked miserable. A day away from the comforts of the Carlton.

They couldn't hear the two men. "Graham?" said Lenox. "They know me."

Without further prompting, Graham took, with his usual knack, the most natural path in the world toward a spot at the bar just by the two men.

Lenox could see that Jonas had ordered a double brandy, Sheridan a glass of hot red wine. Their talk was very brief. Graham, next to them, ordered and sipped a pint of ale, studying—or at least appearing to study—a folded journal that he had drawn from his jacket pocket.

The two men finished their drinks, stood up, and left, just far apart enough that it was clear they were going separate ways. Lenox and Cobb had to wait for an agonizing few seconds as Graham sat, prolonging his ruse, before returning to them.

"Well?" said Lenox eagerly when he had returned.

Graham took his seat again, and said, in a low voice, "Forsythe Witt couldn't make this meeting. It was Jonas who reported that. Sheridan was quite put out. They are meeting at six at the Carlton Club instead. Sheridan objected to the plan but eventually agreed."

The two detectives absorbed this information. "Can we get into the Carlton Club?" asked Cobb.

"I can, at least," said Lenox. "I have to think of a friend who won't ask questions. Let me think for a moment."

He had an equal number of friends on each side of the House of Commons, Lenox, tilting perhaps toward his brother's party (and his father's, and his own) in proportion. Most of the conservatives were school friends. He searched his mind for one who wouldn't care about letting him in as a guest without wanting to know why. It was notorious for its privacy, the Carlton; the chances of getting Cobb in were slim, and Graham probably none.

Lenox glanced at his watch: 4:55. It would need to be someone close at hand, too, worse luck.

Forsythe Witt. Wilton Sheridan. And Samuel Jonas. One liberal, two conservatives. All three Members of Parliament. Roughly of the same age. Sheridan the only aristocrat among them, however.

Why were they meeting? What did they know?

"I can't think of the right person," he said, not quite listening to himself, for his mind was working.

"Perhaps Sir Richard?" Winston Cobb said.

In fact, Mayne *was* a member of the Carlton, but it was impossible to explain to Cobb why exactly the commissioner would have felt honor-bound never to use it in his work.

"There is also His Grace the Duke of Dorset," said Graham. "I think he would do it for you."

"Graham!" Lenox cried. "That's it!"

"A duke?" said Cobb. "My understanding is that they're—not indebted to many people, I suppose."

But Lenox was already standing up, for this one happened to be, as the visit to Hawkes's had again shown. The young detective had inadvertently learned many of Dorset's most important secrets in a case not long before, and that same case had produced a grudging sense on Dorset's part that Lenox, so socially inferior to him as to be beneath his notice in general terms, had the right to call upon his goodwill should he wish.

There was a line of hansoms just outside the pub. They stepped into one, having agreed to go together to Dorset House, with its beautiful views of the Thames, its masterpieces of art and craft and furniture, and its air of sorrowful majesty.

They had been in the cab for five minutes,

the rain still very heavy, the sound outside thunderous, when Lenox said, slowly, "I think I understand what's happened."

"What?" asked Cobb, who had been sharpening a small knife he apparently kept in his belt.

Lenox didn't speak for fully half a minute after that. Indeed, his eyes might have fallen closed. But at last he said, "Tell me where I go wrong. I'm not sure yet. Will you?"

Graham nodded; Cobb, too.

"Wilton Sheridan, Samuel Jonas, and Forsythe Witt. Three men who are roughly of an age, all of whom were in Jamaica at an overlapping period of their lives."

"Correct."

"An aristocrat, and two men who set out to become rich and did it."

"Correct."

"And those two both returned to England within the last five years and immediately expended some of that wealth to become Members of Parliament."

"Yes."

"It doesn't run cheap, a seat in Parliament."

"So far we know all of this," Cobb said, though not impatiently.

"My next thought, then, is how unlikely a friendship it is."

"Why?"

"Sheridan is a man of the turf who was in

Jamaica once, twenty years ago, by his account. Horses are all he cares about. The others are men of business. From that I think: What did *they* have that *he* wanted?"

"Have, sir?" said Graham.

"Samuel Jonas had land and money. He was a successful merchant."

"As was Forsythe Witt," said Cobb.

"Not quite!" Lenox had warmed to his theory as he began to explain it; he was all but sure, and a slow excitement started to suffuse him. "If you notice from his biography in *Who's Who*, he started with less than Jonas, Witt. He began as a bookkeeper and moved around Jamaica in search of work."

"Yes."

"What he did have was a *shipping* company. He had boats."

"And what did Sheridan have that needed to be moved in boats? Sugar?"

Lenox shook his head slightly, then looked at Cobb and Graham, seated on the bench opposite him. "Slaves."

CHAPTER FORTY-ONE

The card room of the Carlton Club justified the invention of the word "sumptuous"—and even perhaps the invention of the word "sumptuosity"—and probably, in all good faith, the return of sumptuary laws, which for centuries, until around the time of Queen Elizabeth, had placed a tax on furs and types of cloth that only the very rich could afford.

The room's chairs were of a mind-boggling plushness, the woods of table and bench darkened with age, the grandfather clock, with its heavy gleaming pendulum, a construction of ancient magnificence and intricacy.

Cobb had no doubt seen comfort, but there was no mistaking the way he took everything in subtly as they sat there, he, Graham, and Lenox—a citizen of a republic visiting a monarchy.

It was the three men's good fortune that the duke had been indignant at Lenox's suggestion that he might not be able to get all of them into the club.

"My father was one of the founders of the Carlton," he'd said.

"So I recall, Your Grace," Lenox had replied.

And indeed he did now remember that Dorset had his own tables at White's and the Carlton, never to be used by any other patron, no matter how busy the dining room might be.

"I myself paid for a portrait of him to be installed there recently. Next to Charles Fox." This was a Whig hero. "Goodness me. My second footman would receive a welcome at the Carlton. Certainly you and your friends shall."

He had ushered them in as if the club existed to serve his whims, then left them in the card room and gone to smoke on the next floor up (and perhaps complain about the world, to some friend who would commiserate about their equally unfavorable fortunes while sipping forty-year-old port). A discreet waiter—discreet almost to the extent that Lenox would have believed he was deaf and blind, if they hadn't spoken—brought them whiskies with soda.

From here they had a view of the grand staircase, but not such a direct view that they could not conceal themselves. Lenox, in particular, knew he would stand out to Wilt Sheridan, whom he had seen in every ballroom in London over the course of the last four or five years. He kept his back to the door.

It was ten to six. He felt a drumming anticipation in his pulse. They were close to an answer.

And after all the winding oddities of this case, it was a modest piece of cross-stitch that had told Lenox the story.

Jonas Hall. That was what the cross-stitched picture in Jonas's apartments had said, beneath a picture of a house. But as he had walked the apartment again in his mind—he had an excellent visual memory, Lenox—the house had looked . . . strange. Why?

It was snow white, with large columns and a balcony overhanging a porch. There were willow and magnolia trees. There was a well to the side.

It was, he had realized, an *American* house. There were English mansions in the Palladian manner, but only in America had this very specific style become popular—and more specifically still, only in the South, where the heat turned the shade of the front porch from a comfort into a necessity. Jonas Hall didn't sit in Kent or Shropshire or even South Africa, Jamaica, or Australia. Lenox would bet anything on that. It was in America.

Cobb had agreed, when Lenox described the house. And that completed Lenox's theory. It was roughly this: that some twenty years before, with slavery about to end even in England's colonies, a young Wilton Sheridan had faced losing the value of five hundred slaves. Instead of selling them at a catastrophic discount, or manumitting them, he and a pair of other Englishmen in Jamaica had devised a plan.

Forsythe Witt, a tyro in the already risky business of shipping, would smuggle the five hundred men, women, and children, despite the laws explicitly forbidding such transportation, to the shores of the United States of America. And if they were successfully delivered, Samuel Jonas, who must have either had American connections or made enough money to buy a plantation there, would take ownership of them at Jonas Hall.

The profits—of what? the sugar the slaves harvested? the tobacco? or simply of selling the bodies one by one?—would be split three ways.

It had been Graham who pointed out one of the most telling details of all.

"Both men ran for Parliament immediately, too," he had said in the carriage on the way to the Duke of Dorset's.

"I don't follow," Cobb had replied.

"Members of Parliament have certain immunities, sir," said Graham.

"Like the ones of the Savoy?" Cobb asked.

Exactly like that, Lenox thought. "Yes, though greater in extent, Mr. Cobb," Graham said. "Particularly in civil matters. The full details of their immunity are quite arcane, but extensive, I believe."

"It explains why Jonas would seek a seat and never vote."

It was a plan of such calculated malignancy that Lenox almost hoped he was wrong. Sheridan had always struck him as superficial but inoffensive; Lenox didn't know the other two men, but the idea of their plotting led to uncomfortable ideas indeed—about what exactly was happening, under the Queen's name, in the empire upon which the sun never set.

Now here they sat, waiting to see why the three men had needed to meet so urgently.

Wilton Sheridan arrived first.

"Sheridan, sir," Graham murmured. He had the best view of the hall.

"Where's he going?"

"The bar, I think."

The bar wasn't quite within sight of the card room, but it was just around a baluster, past what the club called Cads' Corner. This was a private alcove between the bar and the card room, with a few comfortable armchairs and an array of papers, more private than either the bar or any of the public rooms. With any luck the three men would meet there.

"Nervy business," muttered Cobb.

Lenox nodded. "Very."

He didn't bother to explain that for him—at least in his mind—it was particularly so because he was in the Carlton Club. If he made a scene here, if he were embarrassed, or thrown out, the great ten thousand would know it before the evening was over. Letters would fly to every corner of the isles, to the great country houses and the little cottages, to sisters and brothers, to first and second and third cousins, to nieces, aunts, friends. Charles Lenox had created a scene in the Carlton Club—tried to *arrest* a member, if you would believe it—on the very premises . . . the pinnacle of embarrassment . . . no, nobody had been able to convince him to leave that foolishness behind.

He didn't mind for himself. At least, he tried to convince himself of this, half-truth though it might have been. But he actually did mind on behalf of his brother, who must see so many of these people in Parliament, and on behalf of his mother.

And perhaps most painfully of all, though he was gone, Lenox minded on behalf of his father.

It occurred to him that they should have fetched a constable. He said so to Cobb and Graham.

"It's not too late," said Cobb.

A set of footsteps proved him wrong. It was Samuel Jonas, gut overhanging his tight breeches, hair only moderately less wild than it had been at the Savoy. Lenox watched him in a mirror and saw, now, a redness on his skin—not the kind earned temporarily by exertion but the kind that came from years under a hotter sun than England boasted.

Leaning to catch sight of them in the mirror, he saw Jonas and Sheridan shake hands. Neither looked very happy to see the other, however.

Six o'clock came, and the heavy sound of the grandfather clock nearly bolted Lenox out of his seat. The chimes passed, and all five now waited on Forsythe Witt: the successful merchant shipper, returned triumphantly to a seat in Parliament.

Why were the three men meeting? Surely it would be better not to. They must have had something vital to discuss. But what?

Then they heard something—perhaps the answer, Lenox thought—coming up the great staircase.

Lenox repositioned himself very slightly so that he had a better view of the mirror. Graham— opposite him, facing the open doorway—had a book open and an air of nonchalance. (He, needless to say, was the most correctly dressed of the three men for the room.) Cobb had gotten up and was riffling carelessly through a pile of old copies of *Punch*.

Lenox's plan, if they overheard nothing of value, was to follow Jonas out of the club. "Won't that be conspicuous?" Cobb had asked.

"I don't think it will, if we're careful. The Carlton will be busy at that time of evening."

"Why him?"

"The open door. He's a mess of nerves right now. He's obviously set in his ways, here seven days a week. I say we confront him with the theory and take him to Sir Richard before he knows what's happening."

"Kidnap him!"

"Not quite that," Lenox had said, smiling. "But not too far off."

Decent planning. But no planning had prepared him for the nerves that accompanied the arrival of Forsythe Witt. This gentleman came up the stairs, dressed impeccably, shoes buffed, neatly shorn salt-and-pepper hair and the beginnings of a similar beard on his chin.

"Hullo, Jonas. Sheridan," he said.

"Hullo, Witt," Jonas replied.

Witt turned to the barman. "A brandy, please."

Lenox was staring at him, mouth open, caution gone.

For Witt was a very different person now than he had been the last time Lenox saw him. Then, he had been standing atop the roof of the White Horse Tavern, having just witnessed the death of Winfield Bell. This was Forsythe Witt—but it was also Bert Smith.

CHAPTER FORTY-TWO

G raham," said Lenox, in a low voice. "That's Bert Smith, for God's sake. Could you please—"

But Graham was, as often, several steps ahead of him. "A constable," he said. "We shall be in a carriage outside. I have Sir Richard's card."

When Witt had received his brandy, the three men took to Cads' Corner—and thus out of sight—with their drinks.

Cobb gave Lenox a pointed look and walked slowly over to the bar. Lenox lost Cobb in the mirror—he had edged as close as he could to the three Members of Parliament—and so he was in the agonizing position of being separated by a wall from a murderer, perhaps three murderers, without being able to hear a word they said.

He tried standing near the doorway, but it was no use. The club was just settling into its busiest presupper hour, and the noise from each bar and from the entryway downstairs grew louder minute by minute

Then he noticed something. In one wall of the room, paneled and painted so as to be nearly invisible, was a servant's door. Was this how their drinks had arrived? It might well have been—he had been too excited to pay attention, and he made a note, somewhere in the back part of his brain, that the next time he was in a situation of high stakes he would be scrupulously watchful.

He went through the door. It led into a plain white hallway. This itself had two doors at one end and a staircase at the other, and he went to the first door and had almost pressed it open when suddenly, very clearly, he heard Wilt Sheridan's distinctive racecourse drawl.

". . . at some bookstore tomorrow."

Lenox stood by the door, barely daring to breathe. "Let him get back to America."

That was another voice. Sheridan answered by saying, "He seems to like it pretty well here, I suppose! And if Gilman knew, he knows."

"We can't know who Gilman told. Would you trust a slave? He would have told someone."

"We have a great deal riding on the hope that Gilman told nobody at all about Jonas Hall, so that he could blackmail us. Impertinent bugger."

That exchange had been between Sheridan and Jonas, Lenox suspected. And its subject must of course have been Josiah Hollis.

A new voice came in. "I tell you absolutely that we have to get the Lenox brother, too."

Lenox almost gasped—but didn't.

"You must drop that idea," said Sheridan.

This suggestion made Sheridan seem, at least for the brief interval that followed this reply, slightly less rotten in Lenox's eyes than he had been five minutes before. He was only human.

"Sooner or later I shall see him. It's absolutely inevitable. Collins said he was in the coffeehouse, jabbering about me. Or about—Smith. If I see him just once at Parliament, the whole game is up."

Collins! The coffeehouse owner! He had betrayed them. That was bitter—yet Lenox ought to have known that his allegiance would be to the tavern across the street, not to the police. It was a bitter failure, an amateur's mistake, and he remonstrated with himself even as he went on listening.

Jonas spoke next. "Then don't go into Parliament."

"I want to."

"It would draw too much attention to the Gilman matter if Charles Lenox died. Right now it's all solved and tidied away. We've gotten away with it, for heaven's sake, Witt."

"I'm telling you, I shall see him—sooner or later—and it will all be over. I cannot quit London for the rest of my life."

There was a pause, as the implication, Lenox guessed, became uncomfortably clear to the other two men: If Witt went down, so did they all.

"We are here to talk about the slave. Will those same men do the job again but get it right?"

"I don't want to—"

At that moment there was a creak. Lenox nearly touched the ceiling, he jumped so high. But it was only the other door in the hall, not the one he had been standing at. A servant came in and stopped.

Lenox put a finger to his lips. "Shh," he said, whispering. "Trying to win a bet."

The servant nodded and walked on—without a word, or even so much as a change in his expression. The commonest thing in all of Christendom must have seemed to him to be a faceless aristocrat trying to win some daft bet worth a servant's annual wages. He resumed his path up the back stairwell.

Lenox, not daring to get caught twice, let himself back into the card room. There were now two gentlemen there, both older, who looked at him strangely. "Wrong turn," he said, putting his hands up. "I'm meant to be dining with the Duke of Dorset."

"Through there," said one of the men.

"Thank you."

Turning his face to conceal it, Lenox went by the bar. He noticed Cobb, eating warmed cashews and looking at a racing form as if he didn't have a care on earth.

Lenox almost risked a glance back at Cads' Corner—but forbore and, without haste, made his way down the stairs, carpeted in a rich crimson so deep it required some nimbleness.

He left with what he hoped was a suave "good

evening" to the porter at the door. But he was trembling. It was the first time he had ever overheard his life directly threatened, and taken all in all he thought he would have preferred to have it said to him directly. There was something dreadful about the coolness of Bert Smith's—Forsythe Witt's—voice as he proposed killing "the Lenox brother." Him! Think how upset Edmund would be, his friends, his mother . . . even Kitty, he thought, glancingly. But of course, Gilman had friends and family, too, and he was gone, dispatched as casually as a brandy in the bar of the Carlton Club.

Lenox didn't know quite what to do with himself. Graham had yet to return. He hailed a hansom and asked the driver to stay there; he was waiting for a friend, he said. He gave him half a shilling as good-faith money.

Ten minutes later, Cobb came out. Lenox inconspicuously saluted him from the hansom, and Cobb got in.

"What happened?"

"They dispersed. Sheridan is dining, Jonas went to the card room, and the third one—Witt—stayed at the bar."

"Did you overhear them?"

"Barely a word," said Cobb, with a look of deep frustration.

"In that case it falls to me to tell you that I believe I owe you my life," Lenox replied.

Cobb raised his eyebrows. "Your life!"

"If you hadn't been assigned to come to England I would have believed to this day that Winfield Bell and his anonymous accomplice acted on their own. And I wouldn't have overheard a Member of Parliament making plans to kill me. Nor two others considering it."

Cobb's eyes had widened. Lenox explained the doorway that had enabled him to listen in on some of the men's conversation.

"Then they were meeting to plan what to do about Hollis," said Cobb.

"Yes. I would guess one of them must have seen the same advertisement I did. It's all over London—I've spotted it several places."

Cobb nodded. "They had everything to protect, if Gilman wrote ahead that he knew about Jonas Hall. Jonas mentioned it by name?"

"I think so. He may have called it simply *the Hall*."

"Then your theory was correct."

"That remains to be seen," said Lenox.

There was a rap at the door. It was Graham, with a constable named Conover. Lenox knew him by sight, as he did many London police officers—a gigantic, skinny ginger fellow, with freckles all over. He was about as dim as they came, but he had the right uniform on.

"I'm Charles—"

At that moment, however, a gleam of bright

light came from the Carlton Club. All four men looked up to see who it was, departing in the middle of the dinner hour.

It was Witt, in company with another man. Not Jonas or Sheridan. They must have split up.

"What shall we do?" asked Cobb.

"I think we must get him now," said Lenox, though he hardly felt the courage of his words. "Better than later."

Witt descended the few steps of the club with his friend, and Lenox stepped out of the cab and stood next to Conover. "Witt," he called in a quiet voice.

Witt stopped. He turned to the friend he had been walking with. "Parliamentary matter. I'll catch you up there. Shouldn't be a moment."

He came over to them and lit a small cigar, striking the match against a silver box, taking his time until its tip glowed a brilliant orange. Up close, he had a sinewy, defined face, starved out and pointed forward. A hunter's face—a brutal, intelligent face.

"You're Forsythe Witt?" Cobb said. "We'd like to ask you some questions about the two men you just met with. About Jamaica and Jonas Hall. About the old days, and the crimes the three of you committed together."

Witt studied Cobb for a long moment. Then his gaze turned to Lenox. For his part, Lenox was watching for the lean, elegantly dressed fellow to produce a knife or a gun. Perhaps to bolt.

Instead Witt shook his head once, as if thinking of a dozen regrets simultaneously.

Then he said exactly what Lenox should have expected him to say: the savvy thing. "If you spare me hanging and let me out of the country, I'll give you Sheridan and Jonas."

CHAPTER FORTY-THREE

Two long days later, Lenox stood in Carlisle's Bookshop amidst an excited crowd of people.

Carlisle was a bookseller, small publisher, and advocate for various causes. He ran an excellent bookshop and a still better salon. On this evening, at a quarter past seven, the fifty or sixty people in the room—Lenox, for his part, was alone—quieted, because Josiah Hollis was striding into the room, tall and grave, though nodding politely to the people he passed who greeted him. He held his hands behind his back.

He stood by as Carlisle gave him an introduction. After thanking the crowd and making a small joke about the weather, Carlisle said, "We are thrilled to be publishing Mr. Hollis's true account of his early years, and hope many of you will order from the private first edition of five hundred to be published later this month, before it goes into general circulation in March. We are equally thrilled that Mr. Hollis has extended his stay in London to help complete and edit the book so that it will be available sooner than transatlantic mail would allow."

Ah! That was the explanation for Hollis's ongoing presence in London.

Carlisle went on then, talking about the book

and its author in equally admiring terms. After a few minutes, Lenox's mind drifted. He was tired. Somewhere in London at this very hour, if all went according to plan, Wilt Sheridan and Samuel Jonas were being placed under arrest.

His fatigue was not purely physical. He had been involved in the grueling hours it had taken to interview Forsythe Witt and then verify his story. Yet it was more an emotional than physical drain he felt on his spirits.

He knew more about slavery than he ever had before. This was no imposition on him—only it had involved a kind of permanent disillusionment, for while he had been staunch in his position as an abolitionist, like the overwhelming majority of Britons, it had been a position largely formed in theory theretofore. After their conversations at the Yard with Witt—after hearing about the life of a plantation—it all seemed too terribly real.

His guesses about the crime had been right in some respects, it emerged, wrong in others.

The first part he had missed was that Witt had been much more than just a man with a few boats. He was an active slave trader in America. This was part of the service he had provided to merit inclusion in the triumvirate with Sheridan, who had slaves to offload, and Jonas, who had capital. Witt was the muscle and the talent. His birth was obscure, his fortune minimal, but he had been able to do what the indolent Sheridan and Jonas could only conceive. It also explained why it was he who had been chosen to play the role of Bert Smith. Of the three men, he was the only active one.

"Take us back to the start," Sir Richard Mayne had said at the outset of their interrogation. "Twenty years ago."

Though Lenox, Hemstock, Dunn, and Cobb were all present, Mayne was conducting the interview himself. Whatever he had done, Witt was still a Member of Parliament.

He smoked continually throughout the questions, creating a fug in the small room where they all sat around a plain table. "Sheridan was young then. So was I. Even Jonas." Puff. "Sheridan had about five hundred and forty hands on his plantation in Saint Elizabeth."

"Slaves, you mean."

Witt nodded. "Sure, if you like. Anyhow. Wasn't hard to see which way the cat was going to jump. They were going to be freed. They were Sheridan's inheritance. His elder brother would get the English property; the plantation was entailed upon the second male. Soon enough he knew it would be worth whatever you could get for the acreage. Not much at all.

"It was Jonas and I who approached him. Jonas had a cousin in South Carolina who owned a property with about thirty slaves. That's quite a lot in America. A prosperous family might have two or three. More than five hundred—well, that's a large, large number."

"How much does a slave cost?" Hemstock asked.

It was Cobb who replied. "Something like fifteen hundred dollars," he said.

Hemstock whistled. It was a small fortune in itself. "Multiplied by five hundred and forty," said Lenox, squinting up at the ceiling as he calculated. "Eight hundred and ten thousand dollars? Is that right, Mr. Witt?"

This was a *vast* fortune—enough, even split three ways, to make them some of the richest men in the world.

Witt shrugged. "As for your math, I daresay it's roughly right. But we worked very hard, you know.

"I started taking them over thirty or forty at a time. Of course, you have to keep them alive. That's not free. Then you have to find the right market. Sometimes for a large male you might get more than two thousand dollars. But a female is worth less, and a child less still. As time went on we figured out that the skilled ones sold for much more. A good blacksmith under thirty could fetch twenty-five hundred dollars."

"A child less still," repeated Dunn. "But they stayed with their parents."

Witt looked at him scornfully. "They're not *like* us; they don't care. They put on a show, but they don't care." Puff. "We were able to buy Jonas's cousin's farm and slaves off him, overpaid for it—since it can be difficult for the British to own land in America.

"Soon enough, his American slaves and our Jamaican ones were assimilated, without anyone noticing. We bought some of the surrounding land. We didn't farm it very hard, which some thought peculiar. Instead we had the cook train cooks, the blacksmith train blacksmiths, the cooper train coopers. And so on."

Sir Richard looked up. "To increase their value on the auction block."

"Yes."

"And Sheridan and Jonas were conscious of all this?"

"Jonas was. He was there, for heaven's sake—there more often than I was, for I traveled constantly. But Jonas loved the place. He took one of the slaves as a mistress. Filthy. Moved her into the house, wouldn't let anyone touch her, though he whipped her himself when she tried to escape. As for Sheridan, he only ever asked about the money. Obsessed by it, he was. Finally by 1836 we'd gotten all of his men out. But he never lost the fear that we were shorting him."

"Were you?"

"Here and there. About as fair a partnership as you're like to find in that trade. He held out a carrot for us, you know: seats in Parliament. To his credit he made good on them. Found us the races, at least. We had to win them on our own. Jonas is about to lose. If he did, I told him, I thought he should go back to America. But there was never such a one for London, now that he's back."

"Did no one in Jamaica notice?"

"People in Jamaica become less observant if you gave them a few dollars," said Witt. "More outlay, you see? Before you think we're so rich as all that."

So it went on. He was a brutally unsympathetic man. He recounted the death of slaves and friends without compunction or remorse. When they came to Winfield Bell, he was outright derisive.

"A fool." That was his verdict. "A few pounds he cost me. Not more."

"What was the plan, then?" Cobb asked. "Why did you kill Gilman?"

But here Witt stopped. It was the first detail that Cobb and Lenox hadn't told him before he'd told it back to them.

"Thus far I haven't seen a paper guaranteeing my safe passage off this island," he said. "When I do, I'll tell you whatever else you like."

Lenox, reflecting on this exchange as it had passed late two nights before, stirred only when there was a loud round of applause. Carlisle was coming offstage; Hollis inclined his head and approached the dais.

He thanked his friends the Thompsons first. He then gave a eulogy for Gilman and Tiptree, one that was moving to all present, or so it seemed at least to Lenox; tears stood in the eyes of the woman next to him as Hollis described the friendship the three had made on their crossing of the Atlantic, three men from very different backgrounds, Tiptree urbane and bright, Gilman fiery and brilliant, Hollis himself seasoned and wary, distant at first.

This formed a natural transition to his own history.

What had Lenox been expecting? Well, what he heard was a litany of horrors. Lives lived in intense heat, hunger, and pain. Flayings at the post—or in the case of pregnant women, Hollis said, facedown, their bellies in holes they had dug themselves, so as not to endanger *the master's property*—illness untreated, near starvation. Bodies that gave up life in the rows of sugarcane and were merely pushed to one side of the furrow.

"Were none of the slave owners kind?" one man interjected from the second row at one point.

The American took the question in good faith. "Some are, to be sure, sir," he said. "These I consider the most evil and least Christian of all— for they make the practice easier to justify, with their slight humanities."

Lenox admired the undramatic, unadorned,

straightforward way that Hollis told his story. It made him wonder if the book was just as plain—or if Carlisle would help to make it less political, more personal. The single moment when the whole crowded bookshop held its breath was when Hollis described his mother being caught out by the local patrollers one night while she was collecting herbs, and sold off as punishment.

He had still never found to whom, despite years of trying.

After the speech, there was a long line of people who wanted to meet Hollis. Lenox was content to wait. He sat, reflecting on the case. Not with satisfaction. As he had told Cobb, only the American's arrival had saved his life. And it had been Cobb, too, who isolated the three men involved in the plot from Gilman's calendar. That was the crucial thing to have missed, and Lenox a well-connected Londoner, too, with a brother and several other relatives and a dozen friends in Parliament, Lenox, who could tell Disraeli from a backbencher far more easily than Cobb might ever hope to.

"Mr. Lenox!" said Hollis, when at last the store had mostly emptied.

Lenox stood and smiled. "Good evening, Mr. Hollis. I was hoping to buy you supper, but now I see that you are grown very famous."

"Yes, I am pleased to have found a British publisher for my memoir. And after it appears here I will go to France, where it is being translated even now."

"My dear sir, congratulations!"

"But I would be happy to dine with you, if you have half an hour to wait."

"Please take whatever time you need," said Lenox. "As it happens, there is some further news about your attack."

"I hope nothing alarming?"

"Not at all."

"Then I shall be with you shortly."

Lenox went and ordered Hollis's book from Carlisle. He'd had a good night and happily took the order, thanking Lenox, who then waited among the tables full of gleaming red leather books, their pages still uncut—each still unread, with the chance it might contain any story at all. Thinking of Kitty Ashbrook, he bought a copy of *Ivanhoe* to be sent back to Hampden Lane.

CHAPTER FORTY-FOUR

A nd they're being arrested now?"

Lenox nodded. He and Hollis were dining in a public house called the Rose and Crown.

Hollis's entrance had drawn several stares, but they had ignored these, and now were warming themselves by a large fire after the icy walk from the bookstore. Hollis drank claret; Lenox, a strong cup of tea, for he was tired, and besides that not sure whether more work might lie ahead of him that night.

"That is the hope. Mr. Cobb, the American investigator, says the embassy is raring to prosecute them in America for importing slaves to the country."

"That is what I believe men call ironical," Hollis said.

Lenox nodded. It was indeed, for all that it had its own queer logic. "Regardless, they have committed crimes enough for the gallows here. Witt finally admitted all of that. In fact, he was rather proud. He instructed Bell to cut the labels out of the clothing in the hopes that it would be mistaken for a random death. He hired the white horse so that blame could plausibly fall on the Patriots Abroad if anyone saw Bell leave the scene. He bought all of the newsboy's goods so that nobody would recognize Bell as being out of place as conductor. He shoved Bell over the edge of the building when he knew they were caught and then disappeared. It explains why all of the Patriots Abroad were so vehement in their denials. They knew nothing. It was all between Smith and Bell."

"In its way it was ingenious," said Hollis, looking down at his food. "Witt must be a man of abilities."

"I think so, yes. Sometimes strong trees grow crooked and gnarled. My impression is that he kept Jonas and Sheridan together in their scheme; neither is notable for his character. But it's remarkable that you can look at it so objectively."

Hollis smiled. "If I took offense at every story of this kind, I would be a busy man."

Lenox nodded and took a bite from his own plate. The food was very good: beefsteak, mashed potatoes running with gravy, buttered peas and parsnips. "I suppose so."

"They found the perfect pawn in Winfield Bell."

Lenox nodded. "Exactly. The ostensible motivation was race. The real motivation was money."

"It might serve as a motto for our politics in America," Hollis remarked.

According to Forsythe Witt, it had been no difficulty at all to infiltrate the White Horse

363

Tavern under the stolen name of Bert Smith, playing the role of a former sailor in need of funds. He had known Winfield Bell for all of three weeks before he proposed the murder of Eleazer Gilman.

"When did you become convinced you had to kill him?" Mayne had asked Witt.

"His letter was to Jonas. An informant—I hope to meet him face-to-face someday, damn him—told a local pastor that many of the slaves on the Jonas plantation spoke with odd accents. Word made its way around after that, apparently. Eventually news of it reached Gilman and the other abolitionists in Boston.

"It was Tiptree's father who pieced the whole thing together. A businessman with interests up and down the coast. He started asking questions. Eventually they reached as far as Jamaica. It seems that even people there noticed that Sheridan's slaves had moved away in large numbers."

Moved away. Lenox had braced himself to ask the question during the entire course of the interview. "Are they all sold? The slaves?"

Witt had nodded. "The plantation house is empty."

"Do you have bills of sale? Records?"

"Would you have kept them?"

"So we have no way of tracking down these men and women who are held in illegal bondage now?"

"No," said Witt. "You don't."

Lenox had left the room. His sense of fury was almost narcotic—his sense of injustice, of rage.

Yet there were were six million human beings in America, and a million of them were slaves. Why should this make him angrier than that?

Perhaps because it was only human to care about the fate of a story whose participants you knew; perhaps because this scheme had been British; perhaps because he knew Sheridan; perhaps most of all because of how tantalizingly close these families had been to freedom—only to be not just taken back into slavery, but then separated.

Strangely, it had been Dunn who had come out into the hallway where Lenox was pacing. For the first time in their acquaintance his voice was dispassionate. "Infuriating, ain't it."

"Yes," said Lenox shortly.

Dunn had taken a pinch of snuff and walked over to the window, looked out at the glittering lights of London. "It's our job."

The "our" was a gesture of kindness. "Yes," said Lenox.

Dunn had glanced over. "Your Willikens was smarter than anyone else."

"How's that?"

"It was he who noticed that Witt's voice didn't sound right. And it was he who noticed the powder."

"Powder?" said Lenox.

"The Bert Smith we were after had gray hair. Witt has dark hair that's graying slowly. We can ask, but I would bet a shilling he used powder to make himself gray. All the judges and barristers have it for their wigs. It may even have been a wig, come to think of it."

Now, at the Rose and Crown, Lenox described this and more to Hollis, who was steadily eating as he listened. He had the air of a man who savored each bite of good food he took—but out of determination rather than pleasure. It was peculiar; after his talk, Lenox felt he understood less about the former slave than he had before.

"May I ask you a personal question?" said Lenox.

Hollis set down his knife and fork and wiped his mouth, picking up his glass of wine. "Yes."

"You stole an inkwell from St. Bart's, and a brass pen."

"Did I?" said Hollis. His expression hadn't changed.

"I merely wanted to know why. They helped you there, you know. McConnell helped you."

Hollis took a sip of wine. "Who will pay for this supper tonight?" he asked.

Lenox frowned. "I suppose I will."

"And as a gentleman, should I decline your offer?"

"No."

"I should—as a gentleman. It would be proper. But I won't. I didn't own myself for twenty-seven years, Mr. Lenox. This skin you see"—he rubbed his thumb and his first two fingers together, the very skin he meant—"was not my own. Can you imagine the feeling of that?"

"I don't think I can."

"Now it is my own—yet it is the reason we are dining at this very nice public house, instead of at your private club. Is that true?"

Lenox flushed—for it was. "What does that have to do with St. Bart's?"

"I expect to be killed sooner or later," Hollis said. "I have a wife and four sons. I mean to accumulate whatever I can in the time left to me, and however I can."

"So then, did you steal from the Thompsons?"

"No."

"Or Mr. Carlisle?"

Hollis looked offended by the question. "No."

"But why not them?"

"They invited me into their homes. Even if I loathed them, I would not steal from them. But I steal from the machine that made me. I gain particular pleasure in stealing from a rich man, or a miser, or a man who judges me by my race, or the phrenology of my skull. But I do not mind stealing from a hospital either."

"I don't know what to call that sort of code."

"Then you needn't call it anything."

They fell into silence. It was bred so deeply into Lenox that theft was wrong that he couldn't claim to understand Hollis. It was bred so deeply into Hollis that the world was unjust, on the other hand, that it was hard to call him wrong.

Lenox wondered if it was as simple as his wife and four sons; if perhaps the feeling of never being allowed to possess anything had led to a kind of insane desire for possessions, no matter how inconsequential. If the theft was even voluntary.

He broke the silence. "Thank you for answering. It was an impertinent question."

Hollis looked down and started eating again.

"To finish the story," Lenox went on, "Winfield Bell leapt at the offer that Witt made him, it would appear. Witt picked him because he was the most violent and vicious man there, or so it seemed. He offered him fifty pounds. Twenty-five before and twenty-five after."

"For how many of us?"

"All three. Tiptree was not an accident. Gilman was killed the first time he was out of the company of others."

"I wish I had stayed with him. So they merely wished to silence Gilman?"

"It would seem. In Gilman's letter he said that he would expose them if they did not all work on behalf of the bill he was proposing. Then they were to forfeit what he had calculated they made to a charity for escaped slaves. It was a high price he asked. Easily high enough to justify murder in the minds of the three men."

Hollis said, "I myself have wondered if there were other, higher people who wished Gilman dead. From everything I understand, the bill he proposed might have gained the support of your Queen. He had letters of introduction from Mrs. Beecher Stowe, Mr. Ralph Waldo Emerson. Meetings with the dozen most powerful men in this country of either party. America is strong, but England's censure would still mean a great deal to her."

"Interesting," said Lenox.

Hollis smiled a bitter smile. "But there were a thousand men who wished to see Gilman dead. It wouldn't have surprised me at all if he had been killed at the march."

"No?"

"No. Indeed, he knew as much. Not least among the people who wished him ill would be those still doing what Sheridan, Witt, and Jonas grew rich from."

"Importing slaves. You think it still happens?"

"I have no doubt of it at all."

"I must do my best to speak to people about that."

Hollis shook his head. "Do you know, in despondent moments, I think of them sometimes, forced aboard a ship, not knowing what awaits them. Unlike so many of my brothers and sisters in slavery, I have not taken Christ into my heart. I cannot see the point or truth of him. I look to this world for justice. And I ask myself: Who will be the last one, the last passenger, dragged unwillingly aboard such a ship? Who will be the last slave to remember what I have known? And how far in the future will he or she be born?"

A quiet settled over the conversation. Finally, Lenox signaled for the bill. "Would you like to come to my house, Mr. Hollis," he said, "and have a glass of whisky? It settles the stomach."

"Certainly," he said. "I thank you for the invitation."

CHAPTER FORTY-FIVE

How would London remember the months that followed the dawn of 1856?

In Fleet Street it was a time of giddy joy: three Members of Parliament arrested for murder! And from each side of the aisle, meaning that no accusation of political bias could be leveled! The column inches filled themselves. Sketches appeared in all the papers, of every party involved in this spectacular plot.

Yet Lenox observed that as January and then February vanished, the tale took on a strange, confused aspect, which at times he scarcely recognized—casting Sheridan as the witless aristocratic dupe of a scheme hatched by Jonas and Witt, and later more definitely just Witt, so that by the start of February there was merely a general sense that Sheridan had been part of "some mess or other in Jamaica." The other two were more harshly judged by public opinion, yet it was nonetheless for the most part still Winfield Bell who was blamed for the murders of Norman Haase, Abram Tiptree, and Eleazer Gilman.

Forsythe Witt would no doubt remember the start of 1856 as the time of first his capture and then his escape. One evening, apparently not trusting that his testimony was enough, he disappeared from Newgate Prison. Nobody knew how. There was one sighting of him, on a light cruiser to Newfoundland—but the news of it took so long to return to London that Lenox's best guess was that Witt had already found a soft landing place by the time the search for him began. Perhaps even a way back into the slave trade.

Sheridan and Jonas had neither Witt's cunning nor his enterprise. Lenox had ample time to observe them both.

Jonas was a pathetic, self-aggrandizing, blubbering specimen, a monster of some kind or another. The sentimental cross-stitch of Jonas Hall might have been his crest. He would speak in the most maudlin terms about his fatherly love of the slaves at Jonas Hall, for hours if you let him, then change the subject immediately at the mention of the cruelty of their position. Changing it, in general, to his second-favorite subject, which was the injustices he had suffered in the past few months: cut off from the Carlton Club, from his happy rooms, never having raised a hand to anyone, he would say, never having even *laid eyes* on Eleazer Gilman. Always afraid of Witt, only obeying Witt. All this despite the fact that he existed in a state of fair comfort, importing greasy plates of chicken, greedily reading the tabloids, even paying his hairdresser to come in and arrange his delicate strange pillow of hair, his vanity undimmed by the loss of his status.

Yet it was Sheridan who struck Lenox closest to home. Sheridan was bitter, furious, skittish, delusional. His hair had grayed, his face developed deeper lines. But he was nevertheless home to Lenox—as familiar as the scent of tobacco in a gentleman's club. Their lives had been so roughly similar, if one took the view of the great spectrum of humanity, that there was a discomfiting sense that Sheridan's guilt implicated him. At moments Lenox felt he himself ought to stand trial in Sheridan's place.

Absurd, of course. Still, Lenox became desperate to know what his life had rendered him blind to—it was what had made him a detective, perhaps—while Sheridan would do anything to preserve his own myopias.

Cobb would remember the second month of 1856 as the time of his passage back to Washington, case successfully resolved. He took with him four jars of jam from Lenox House and posted his first letter to Lenox from his ship's brief stop in Boston, a long analysis, more than five pages close-written on both sides, of every element of the case.

Lenox studied these pages again and again, scribbling notes to himself, pulling old newspaper clippings for comparison, correcting details of geography, before beginning his own long reply. He hoped (and better yet, knew) that the letter was, as Cobb had signed it, *the beginning of what I hope shall be a long and mutually fruitful correspondence.*

Jane would remember that January and February for the long, empty weeks, Lenox thought, without Deere; Graham perhaps for the resumption of his daily routine, though it was difficult even for someone as close to him as Lenox to say whether such a return was welcome or regrettable, his demeanor remained so even. Edmund? For long days of work, probably, and a few happy hours at home in the country. Slowly, invisibly, but emphatically, he was becoming their father. This struck his younger brother as both enviable and slightly smothering, and he thought that providence had chosen the order of their birth correctly, for few men were happier than Sir Edmund Lenox.

And what about Charles Lenox himself? How was he to remember this time?

On the second Tuesday of January he was at Kitty Ashbrook's salon—Mrs. Ashbrook's, properly speaking—when the man who had paid him such an abrupt visit entered the room.

"Lord Cormorant!" Kitty had said in surprise, and Lenox noticed that she seemed sincerely startled. "We did not expect your return so quickly."

"I shortened my voyage to see you," said Cormorant.

He was a large, confident, fairly handsome

374

gentleman with small eyes, aged perhaps forty or forty-five, and certainly, by how he carried himself, unaccustomed to contradiction.

"Please allow me to introduce you to Mr. Charles Lenox," Kitty said.

"We have met," Cormorant said shortly, and inclined his head.

"Indeed," said Lenox.

It was of course impossible that Miss Ashbrook should show any favor to Lord Cormorant, and for much of that morning and the Thursday that succeeded it, he sat glowering in the corner as Lenox and Kitty talked, their usual lively banter.

She was halting only on the subject of this new wooer. "How do you know Cormorant?" Lenox asked when they had a moment to themselves. "I'm not sure I recognize the title."

"It is quite new," she said, and glanced away. "His father was the first. He was a director of the East India Company. But he studied at Gonville and Caius before that, I believe. The father."

"Ah."

This reference to Cambridge was the first moment, Lenox would later reflect, when he should have known that in the end he would lose his battle. It betrayed Kitty's anxiety that Cormorant came out of trade. His father having gone to Cambridge, before amassing his vast fortune, seemed to vouchsafe that it was not *quite* so.

It took Lenox a very, very long time to realize that Kitty's heart was not his. When the realization did come, it crushed him.

It was a cold morning in the middle of February, with flurries melting as soon as they hit the pavement, the sky a steely white. He had spent a happy breakfast hour poring over a new letter from Cobb, sipping tea and eating eggs as Mrs. Huggins's cats chased each other around his study—immune, apparently, to pieces of toast occasionally striking them in the back, or the irritated commands of their house's owner that they be gone.

When he arrived at Kitty's, it was to find Cormorant in conversation with the maid of the house, Virginia. "It had better be two dozen of the shortbread," he said, and passed her a note, before glancing at Lenox—they had never mentioned their sole encounter previous to these at Eaton Square—and passing into the sitting room.

It was only this trivial moment of intimacy that led Lenox to see how profoundly he had misunderstood the roles he and Cormorant played here.

He had missed it all, he saw in a flash: the whole drama, played out day by day, and he not the hero but the antagonist. He inquired discreetly of Virginia whether his lordship came often—and was told, with a knowing look that near broke his heart, oh, yes, every day almost, including the

Sabbath itself, when he walked Mrs. Ashbrook to the early service; and weren't they all expecting an announcement pretty soon!

It was the maid's ease in telling him this that showed Lenox more finally than anything else that all was settled. He must be, he thought . . . not a joke, perhaps, but no one to take very seriously. The also-ran.

Yet he'd thought he and Kitty had been as close as ever. Certainly they had spoken with as much rushing enthusiasm as they always had in prior days of books, of travel, of the prosaic tales in the news. Every night, as he fell asleep, Lenox had thought of her face and how dear and unique it was to him, how particularly beautiful in its animation. It became the center of his world for a while—the one thing to which his heart answered, not books, not friends, nothing but Kitty Ashbrook's face.

And yet it was Cormorant she would marry.

With Cormorant she exchanged stilted niceties about, for instance, his wine cellar, a subject very close to his heart; or his money, another. Not directly—his money washed itself clean, conversationally, through hobbies, ponies, broughams, a gun collection, a new sailing yacht, a thousand acres in Scotland, each of them a way, like the *very good red* laid down by his father in '23 and now *worth too much to part with,* to mention his wealth without mentioning it.

Lenox hadn't a need in the world. He could afford most anything, and if he couldn't—well, he didn't want a sailing yacht, or a case of red wine worth the same as a sailing yacht.

Yet he discovered what he did need, after all. More than he had conceived even in his innermost soul, he needed love. His mother had been correct. She had sensed that he was or soon would be lonely—and even if her means of remedying that inevitability was inelegant, it had been correct. He wondered—though far off from the problem, dully—if that meant she was also right that he should not be a detective. A thought that had shadowed the whole case, though now lapsed in significance amidst the fog of this rejection.

Ah, how it hurt! The walk home after his conversation with the maid was one of the purest desolation. Never, not in the most cheerless depths of adolescence, had he felt this strange kind of living grief.

He tortured himself, of course, with images of how he had danced with Kitty, conversed with her—of that sublime moment when they had held hands and so nearly kissed.

In the days that followed he walked by her house in a state of alternating panic and self-pity and nausea, debating whether to speak to her.

In the event he returned just once more, that Thursday. He had planned to stay but briefly, yet he found that he couldn't pull himself away from the woman to whom his heart belonged. He simply stared at her much of the time, quite unable to sustain a conversation.

Rather than condoling with him, she seemed more distant than usual. Lenox spent all weekend debating whether to propose—a great fell action, sure to sweep her off her feet he thought—and then debating with himself how to do it, and then going back to whether to do it again, walking the streets, barely eating, seeing no one, no doubt wild-looking, his footsteps taking him unintentionally by Eaton Square.

At last he resolved that he would say his piece. He would ask her—he could not live without asking her.

But the engagement between Miss Ashbrook and Lord Cormorant was announced in the papers on the very next Monday morning.

CHAPTER FORTY-SIX

O ne day in 1686, a coffeehouse in London, popular with sea captains and ship's outfitters seeking the latest maritime news, offered a small insurance policy for a voyage. Eventually, after numerous steps along the way, it became the most significant insurer of slave ships in the world. It kept the name of its coffeehouse days, however: Lloyd's of London.

There was thus a peculiar aptness to the fact that it was Lloyd's that had insured a Plymouth clipper ship called the *Melodia* that sank in the Atlantic that March after an explosion in the engine room, with all passengers aboard. One of these was Wilton Sheridan.

His departure had been the result of some compromise whose lineaments Lenox could only hazily discern—family connections, careful inquiries at court, a promise never to return to London. The American embassy was furious that he had been permitted to leave without a trial. Yet England was England.

It meant that only Samuel Jonas remained to answer for the deaths of Abram Tiptree, Eli Gilman, and Winfield Bell. After a bit of wriggling, the papers were satisfied: a single focus for their righteous anger. As for Lenox, he was unsure where the blame began and ended.

He was also preoccupied. The last weeks of February had been difficult. As he never had before, he woke up in the middle of the night from strange dreams—once one in which he and Kitty were married and living on a tropical island, often one in which he owed a man in an unfamiliar city money, and was looking everywhere to find him, but could not.

After these confused dreams he would stand by his window and stare into the night, his mind groping after something it couldn't articulate, as if by speaking the right word he might retrieve the promise of those blissful weeks when he had been in love.

"I wish you could have met him," he told Lady Jane one day.

The sun was just peeking through the clouds, and they were sitting in her parlor, having coffee and chocolate late in the morning.

"Lord Cormorant? I've no need to."

"He was as dense as a fig pudding."

"One of your own favorite desserts."

"I just don't understand how she could have chosen him."

Lady Jane had been a sympathetic listener to Lenox, whose complaints he knew were unmanly, wrong, the laments of a fellow with no pluck—but couldn't help.

She had rarely spoken to him directly about Kitty Ashbrook, however. Now she did.

"It's my fault," she said.

"Of course it's not."

"I encouraged you." She looked grave. "Yet I confess I understand her position."

"Do you? I wish you would enlighten me."

She rose from the sofa where she was seated and went to the window, which framed her prettily, in her soft pink dress, a few wisps of her upswept brown hair falling across the nape of her neck.

"She will be called Lady Cormorant for the rest of her life," Jane said thoughtfully. "Her place in society is permanently secure."

"And mine is not?"

"You well know that it is. Yet for a woman . . . you have never understood this, Charles. We get but one chance. I've no doubt she'll regret you all her life—what you were to her. Yet she will know as well that she had one chance and made the safe decision."

"Safe! A life of enduring that—"

"Anything at all might happen to you between now and the age of fifty, Charles. You might become fat, or eccentric—more eccentric than you already are for being a detective—or prove cruel."

"A grim forecast."

"When Cormorant is fifty all of that may have

happened to him, too. But his eldest son will still be a lord. She will be the mother of lords and ladies."

"She has not made a decision that guarantees her happiness. Is happiness not the safe decision?"

Lady Jane looked at him as schoolteachers sometimes had, in the distant past, as if the gap in their knowledge were so wide that it was vaguely wondrous.

"Not for a woman," she said.

"She would not have starved with me."

"You might have been shot. Even as you were courting her, in fact, your life was under threat."

"She didn't know that."

"Of course she did. Do you think that the happenings at the Carlton Club are a secret? That your actions are a secret?"

Lenox had, in fact. It was curious to learn that they were not. "I did."

"No. On the contrary, you are one of the most fascinating subjects of the drawing rooms of our London—a dashing adventurer, a bumbling fool. Half the men who cut you are probably jealous of you."

Some part of him glowed, knowing this. He had never even thought of it. But he kept that secret. "Cormorant, though."

"She chose the option with the least risk of unhappiness, and the least chance of real happiness. You ought to pity her the slenderness of those options before you judge her."

"I do not judge her," said Lenox.

"In your heart I think you may."

He looked at the gold box on his desk. "Yes, perhaps. But Jane, over Christmas she sent me a letter, a . . . and in return I loved her. I believe I may still."

"Can you still not understand that she may have loved you in return, Charles? She was not untrue to you—only to herself. And she will know that more fully than you ever could."

It took several days, but this conversation brought some reconciliation to his memories of Kitty Ashbrook. As the first signs of spring appeared, he was renewed; rather than barricading himself in his study, he started to venture out to social events again.

But without the same faith. It had been a consequential passage of time, this. When it began he had believed in love, and he had believed that people were basically decent. Now, a survivor of lost love and an auditor of some of the most terrible stories of slavery he had heard, he was sure of neither.

It must have told in his manner, for more than one person commented that he seemed more reserved now, and his mother, when she visited, observed in a stray moment that she thought he seemed to have passed into adulthood.

Then adulthood could keep itself, he thought. But he had not said it.

On the other hand, he felt a dawning faith in his abilities as a detective. He was more mature because of this time, more methodically careful. He had always been careful—but in bursts, just as long as it was exciting to be careful. It had changed him to overhear his own death discussed. He had missed too much in this case—hadn't interviewed Lady Elaine, just to give one example, or considered the incongruity of the missing labels in Gilman's clothes and the white horse.

Meeting Cobb had changed him, too, in this regard. Observing the American's work at close hand, Lenox had decided it was time for new habits. He dined out less. He spent more time reading, more time learning London's geography and history by heart, more time studying old crimes for echoes between seemingly disparate cases. Most happily, for Lenox, his warm exchange of letters with Cobb continued—transformed, now, into a series of gentle sparring matches over how to investigate a murder, where to start and whom to suspect. It was a subject whose study was shamefully lacking.

After brooding about it for a long time, he spoke at last with his mother about her wish that he leave his career. It turned out to be one of those long misunderstandings resolved in a few seconds: She had never doubted his abilities, she said, only feared for his safety. Was that not a mother's prerogative? Duty, in fact? He understood when she explained it—and after taking it so hard! What a fool. Still, this conversation, also, made him vow to himself to take his career as seriously as he could. If his mother must suffer worry on his behalf, let it be for a cause to which he had not given himself in part but in full.

It was as if the world noticed. He had never been busier than he became that March, cases flying at him so quickly that he had to turn several down.

On the other hand, Sir Richard Mayne was finished with him. Cordial, still, certainly—and perhaps a friend to call on in an hour of real need. But otherwise their relationship was severed. Lenox had elected to stay outside of the Yard, and the meet rejoinder to this was for the Yard to respond in kind.

Lenox tried to make up for it by befriending more constables and keeping his ear to the ground. He discovered the power of pure listening, attentive listening. Nearly everyone on earth wanted to talk about themselves, he began to perceive. Even—perhaps especially—criminals.

Yet it was not any of these subtle alterations that truly marked the end of the period of Lenox's life that he might have called youth. The event that did that was much a starker one. Afterward, he would have traded all he had to return to the time before it.

It came on a day in March of the kind that almost made one believe summer might come again. A few hardy green shoots had emerged from the ground. The air was clear and pure, as gentle as it could be in the smoky city.

Lenox was returning from Parliament. He had dined with his brother there, and now was ambling slowly up Hampden Lane.

Initially, from a distance, he thought the group of men he saw in a doorway was at his door. Had something happened to Jonas? Only after advancing another twenty feet or so did he make out that in fact they were at Lady Jane's house, not his.

His first reaction was to wonder if Deere had returned early, and for a moment he saw, as if in a Gainsborough portrait, Deere and Lady Jane, with the two dogs that the gamekeeper at his ancestral home was keeping careful watch over. He would be so delighted to have them—never a man that loved a dog near his side more than Lord Deere.

It was only when he was fifteen or so feet away that Lenox saw he had misread the situation.

There were four men in military uniform on Jane's step. One, who stood forward of the others, had white hair, a white mustache, and three stripes on his shoulder. He was a general.

Another—very handsome—was Catlett, whose place Deere had taken in India.

Lenox realized that his friend must have been wounded there. Perhaps even quite badly. He started moving more quickly. Only when he had come close enough to see Lady Jane's face, unmoving, utterly white, yet her expression one of a self-control so rigid that to lose it must mean an equally powerful frenzy, did he realize that Lord Deere was not wounded but dead.

CHAPTER FORTY-SEVEN

The Bishop of Kent was speaking—and, like all Bishops of Kent, expected his audience to be rapt and respectful. "Do you know St. Augustine, young man?"

But he had chosen an unfortunate interlocutor to whom to impart this information: Lenox's young cousin Lancelot, who was probably the worst-behaved boy currently serving time at Eton College.

"No, thank goodness," said Lancelot. "Why, where does he live?"

Bishops were made of pretty rugged self-regard, and this one, before whom powerful men of religion cowered, carried on without noticing the reply. "St. Augustine began to convert England to the true religion, Christ's religion, in the year 597 after his birth."

"What, St. Augustine's!" said Lancelot in amazement.

"No!" said the bishop, looking down with annoyance for the first time. "Christ's! How could St. Augustine have converted people nearly six hundred years after his own death?"

"He's a saint, Father, they can do all sorts of things— You mustn't—"

"Don't call me Father."

"Oh, sorry."

The bishop was not to be put off. "Do you know where St. Augustine chose to start his mission?"

The boy frowned. "Oxford, probably. The answer is almost always Oxford."

"Canterbury."

"Oh." Lancelot received this contradiction with complete indifference. "I say, is there a saint who did live for six hundred years?"

"No."

"One of them ought to try."

Now, for the first time, Lancelot had the bishop's undivided attention. "What on earth do you mean, try?"

"Bit lazy, if you ask me, to live for seventy years. If you're a saint, I mean, you ought to stick around and do your bit."

"I can assure you that St. Augustine 'did his bit.'"

"It sounds as if he wandered about Canterbury telling people about Christ from time to time. The curate at school does that."

"You are wholly incorrect. The very pilgrims in Chaucer's *Canterbury Tales* are on their mission in tribute to him."

"Well, fine, that's topping of them. Very decent. I'd have chosen Brighton. But fair play."

Lenox looked at Lady Jane, who was watching the conversation alongside him. "This is the worst party you have ever thrown," he said.

Though she did not laugh, she did smile. "It was short notice," she said, and moved away without waiting for a reply.

For two weeks she had seen almost no one, except, strangely, for Lady Molly Lenox, Edmund's wife and Charles's sister-in-law. That included Lenox himself; he had not seen her until today.

He had written her a long letter, more than ten pages, describing his affection and his many memories of Deere, and entrusted it to Molly. If he had to guess, it probably lay upstairs on a bureau, unopened.

Now it was the day of the funeral, and Lady Jane's strength was worse to him than any display of emotion could have been.

She wore all black, the attire known, rather unpardonably, as widow's weeds. To Lenox the phrase had always conjured images of a lady emerging from a lake, covered in grasses—until at Oxford he had learned the Old English word *waed*, or garment, and the long tradition of wearing black upon the death of a loved one.

Everything was black here. The servants wore black suits, with black armbands. The bishop's robe was black, Lancelot's suit. There was black crêpe over the door knocker.

For a year and a day, Lady Jane would wear black. She could socialize after that period was over, if she wished, and add dark, subtle colors to her dress—lilac, lavender. Her mourning would only truly be finished after two years.

Or never. Lenox knew his friend, and as he watched her move among her guests, paying special care to Deere's young, bewildered brother—suddenly an earl and in a way an orphan for a second time—everything in her actions graceful and easy, dispelling the awkwardness other people felt in consoling her, he saw the abyssal depths of her pain; knew by instinct that she was relying on nothing at all but muscle memory, like a great Athenian runner in the last mile of a race, out of oxygen, far past the last stages of conscious action, legs moving only because that was what legs did. No part of her was alive today; not while her husband lay in a grave.

Lenox had no idea whether this would ever change. He had spent hours discussing it with Edmund. They agreed that the best thing he could do was to be the most reliable friend she had—to cultivate amnesia about the past, to be quiet when she needed quiet, talkative when she needed talk, present when she needed company, absent when she needed solitude.

As the afternoon wore on, there were tears all over the room, many of them shed by men who were not accustomed to crying. But it was such a devastating loss, a man so young, his life before him, loved by all, happy in his young marriage—

gone because a bullet fired during a meaningless skirmish happened to strike him directly in the chest.

Lenox did not want to be among the last people there. He was sure that it would put too much pressure on Lady Jane if he were; they knew each other too well for the dishonesty this kind of day required, upon which it gently rested.

"Lady Jane," he said, at just past three o'clock, "I think I had better take Lancelot back before he brings out his peashooter. He didn't like the bishop."

She smiled. "Just feed him a cream tea. Boys are very easy."

"I am always next door, you know—and frequently bored, and almost never asleep."

"I know, Charles," she said. "Thank you for being such a good friend to James. He loved you."

"He was the best of men."

"Yes," she said. "That's true."

In the weeks that followed, Lady Jane did something strange; she arrogated to her use (as was her absolute right, in the circumstances) all of the people who usually surrounded Lenox.

First it was Mrs. Huggins, who went over one afternoon to fix tea because Lady Jane's maid was ill, and ended up with a bedroom at that house; then it was Graham, who took on the duties of a second butler. Lady Molly remained a constant visitor, soon along with Edmund. Only Charles was not invited.

Even Lancelot spent an afternoon there. They played cards, he said.

"Who won?"

"She did," he said darkly. "I lost a shilling."

"She made you pay?"

"Yes. I said I didn't have it."

"Did you?"

"Yes."

"And she got it out of you?"

"Yes."

"Good," said Lenox with satisfaction, and then reached into his pocket and gave the boy half a shilling. He was at an age when a great deal can swing upon tuppence, after all, and he was returning to the solitudes of school the next day.

Every afternoon, when he had finished his work, Lenox took a slow walk up and down Hampden Lane. His hope was that one of these days Lady Jane would send somebody to call him in. She didn't. He told himself, however, that in a way he was there; in a painless way, through Graham, and Mrs. Huggins, and Lancelot, and his brother. He hoped it was true.

In a way the most unfair thing about Deere, Lenox reflected, was that their memories of him would now be defined mostly by his death. It would become the most important thing about him, that he had died so young.

When in fact it was the least important thing about him, Lenox saw. What had been important was himself: his kindness, his lack of pretension, his curiosity about others.

On an early morning in late April, Edmund stopped by to pick Charles up. They were going to see their mother—to Paddington, to catch the 106 to Markethouse, departing at 9:19.

Edmund watched Lenox dash around his study, packing up a few last papers, letters, notes. "By the way," he said, "did you see they renamed the prize for the chess tournament at the Army and Navy Club after Deere? Rather nice."

"The chess prize?" said Charles, stopping. "Whatever for?"

"He was regimental champion three years running. One of the best in London, they said."

"Deere? No he wasn't. He was . . . I—"

Only at that instant did Lenox realize that Deere had been playing him close for all those dozens and dozens of games—never letting him win, which would have been a condescension, but playing for the friendship of it. So that they might be better friends.

He felt a lump in his throat. He turned away quickly, disguising his sadness in urgency, a stinging in his eyes.

"Shall I wait in the carriage?" Edmund said. "The boys are probably stabbing each other by now. Good thing you're a detective, eh? Ha!"

"Ed, don't make any jokes for the rest of the trip."

Edmund frowned. "My jokes are very popular in Parliament."

"Notably the greatest collection of dullards in England."

"Ah, but not with quite so many murderers now that you've done your bit!"

"Go away."

"Fine. I can see that even the best joke wouldn't make you laugh in this mood. I'll be in the carriage."

Lenox had nearly finished packing his valise. He had clothes at his brother's house—his own childhood house—but there was a diagram of a bank robbery from Cobb that he particularly wanted to study at his leisure. Ah, well, he would have to—no, there it was!

He went outside. His instinct was to go straight into the carriage, but instead he stopped.

Edmund saw him do it. From time to time we are permitted to see the people we love as if they were strangers, and in that April morning Edmund saw Charles, handsome, young, and good, valise in hand, filled with an earnest desire to do what was right. He felt suddenly proud of his younger brother, who was so unlike other men, and yet still perhaps didn't quite sense just how different.

A detective! Well.

He watched as Charles pulled his watch from his pocket. Edmund glanced at his own pocket watch and saw that it was 8:51. They had a good deal of time, and Edmund watched Charles wander over and stand in front of Lady Jane's house, for a long minute, then two, then three.

He pretended that he was organizing his papers. It was all Edmund could do not to lean out of the carriage and shout for him to hurry. But he didn't, and Charles went on waiting, waiting. At last, at the final possible moment when they could go and safely be on time, Charles ran over to the carriage, waving his hand, climbing in even as the horses started off. Edmund helped pull him inside, as did the boys, giggling at the adventure of it.

He hoped that Lady Jane had seen Charles waiting there, faithfully, ready when she was. On the other hand, he knew it didn't matter whether she had or not—that simply the being there, when it was all said and done, an unfailing friend, was enough.

Books are produced in the United States using U.S.-based materials

Books are printed using a revolutionary new process called THINKtech™ that lowers energy usage by 70% and increases overall quality

Books are durable and flexible because of Smyth-sewing

Paper is sourced using environmentally responsible foresting methods and the paper is acid-free

Center Point Large Print
600 Brooks Road / PO Box 1
Thorndike, ME 04986-0001 USA

(207) 568-3717

US & Canada:
1 800 929-9108
www.centerpointlargeprint.com